INHERITED MURDER

Previous Mysteries by Lee Martin

The Day That Dusty Died
Hacker
The Mensa Murders
Deficit Ending
Hal's Own Murder Case
Death Warmed Over
Murder at the Blue Owl
A Conspiracy of Strangers
Too Sane a Murder

INHERITED MURDER

Lee Martin

St. Martin's Press New York

Library of Congress Cataloging-in-Publication Data

Martin, Lee.
Inherited murder / Lee Martin.
p. cm.
ISBN 0-312-11415-X (hardcover)
1. Ralston, Deb (Fictitious character)—Fiction. 2. Policewomen—United States—Fiction. I. Title.
PS3563.A7249I54 1994
813'.54—dc20 94-19654
CIP

First Edition: November 1994

10 9 8 7 6 5 4 3 2 1

My first week in Salt Lake City was spent with Elaine Mowrey, who lived a few blocks from my husband-to-be and virtually across the street from Gilgal. I'd like to dedicate this book to Elaine, patron saint of all the weird people she has gathered around her.

Author's Note

None of the people mentioned in this book, other than obviously historical characters or present government, church, and civic leaders, is real. No murders like those described herein have taken place either in Salt Lake City or anywhere else. This novel is entirely fiction.

But most of the places described in this book, from Gilgal and the Tree to Dee's Restaurant and Russon Brothers Mortuary, are real places; I appreciate the kindness of Grant Fetzer, present owner of Gilgal, in permitting me to set a murder there. I have completely fictionalized all the people who live around Gilgal. I know nothing about the real people, though I have met their dogs.

The Golden Frog Casino, however, does not exist in Wendover or anywhere else. And Georgina's Bed and Breakfast also is fictional; most of the beautiful old houses near Trolley Square are much too small to house any but the smallest of families.

But come and visit Salt Lake City anyway. And when you do, don't miss Gilgal.

INHERITED MURDER

Prologue

Sunday—3:30 P.M.

My shoulders felt as if I had been drinking brandy. In my drinking days, I always felt brandy in my shoulders first, and then in my solar plexus. I don't know why, as no other drinks affected me that way. But that's the way shock affects me, too, and it was shock, not brandy, that I was feeling now, looking at the sprawled body that was the last thing on earth I would have expected in such a quiet place, on what had started out such a peaceful Sunday, on such a pleasant trip for such a positive reason.

It hadn't all been wonderful, of course, even before now. Family trips rarely are; the most unexpected events take place at the most unexpected times, and sometimes the expected events don't happen. For example:

It is not possible to buy jackets in Salt Lake City, Utah, in the middle of June.

Of course, normally nobody needs jackets in Salt Lake City, Utah, in the middle of June. But the weather this year, as everybody helpfully assured me, was far from normal.

Having never been in Utah before, I couldn't comment on that. All I knew was that the Friday afternoon we arrived it was pouring rain, and that night the temperature escaped freezing only by a minor technicality scarcely observable by somebody from Fort Worth, Texas, where it had been in the high nineties when we left. It was thirty-three, not thirty-two, degrees. But it was thirty-three degrees with a howling wind and a misty bone-chilling dampness that seemed to seep through the walls of the house. Georgina Grafton, the hostess of the bed-and-breakfast where we were staying, kept apologizing as if she were the cause of the weather, although she had turned up the thermostat so that the old house near Trolley Square was almost too warm except for the drafts.

In fact, poor Georgina kept apologizing for a lot of things, starting with the conduct of her sister Alexandra. Mentally I agreed that somebody should apologize for Alexandra's conduct, but my own preferred apologist would have been Alexandra.

After we went to our rooms that night, I stood and looked out the casement window set in a small alcove of the bedroom toward what looked like a small private cemetery; mist was rising from it like a whole flock of restless ghosts. Shivering, I closed the curtains and crawled into bed beside Harry.

In the morning our son Hal, because he was the only one of us who did have a jacket with him, took off at ten, that being the earliest we could expect to find stores open, to buy us all jackets or the best available substitutes. As my husband, Harry, and I had signed, and therefore had to countersign, all the traveler's checks, that meant Hal got to use the brand-new Visa card he'd been strictly forbidden to touch except in emergencies, and a desire for Cokes, cashews (for which he had lately developed a passion), and fast food, we had assured him, was not to be construed as an emergency.

He came back, very apologetically, with a collection of sweatshirts. To be sure, they were thick, heavy, hooded sweatshirts, but they were all printed with a variety of pictures and slogans. In consideration of my sensibilities, none of them featured big-mouthed kids yelling "Don't have a cow!" or smarmy ladies saying "Isn't that special." While they actually kept us warm enough sightseeing the rest of the day Saturday, provided we ducked into buildings every time the rain resumed, they weren't exactly what we wanted to wear to church Sunday morning.

But in this unexpected weather we couldn't very well go to church in nothing but summer clothes, and we couldn't very well not go to church when the official purpose of this trip was to deliver Hal to the Latter Day Saints, or LDS, Missionary Training Center. Anyway, Georgina had assured us that the chapel nearest her house had several lovely stained-glass windows. Stained glass is rare in Mormon meetinghouses, and I looked forward to seeing it.

Sunday dawned cloudy and overcast, with occasional squalls of rain and a predicted high temperature of forty-seven degrees. There were no major contretemps; Alexandra, Georgina's sister, behaved decently at breakfast, and coming from her that was a treat. There was a minor problem, though. Harry tried to plug his electric razor into the electrical outlet under the towel rack, as Lori's electric curlers and curling iron were plugged into the one above the sink, and it didn't work. His resulting howl of protest echoed through the house, and Georgina came running to tell him she was sorry, that outlet had never worked, she kept meaning to get it fixed and hadn't gotten around to it; well, actually she kept forgetting because nobody usually needed that outlet, and he should use the downstairs bathroom, the one Georgina's father had used throughout his life. How can anybody react to that kind of hysterically apologetic gabbling? Harry went downstairs to plug in his razor, and peace was restored.

Alexandra left the house before we did, and I didn't know whether she had walked or whether someone had given her a ride. We drove the few blocks we had expected to walk, and we peeled off the sweatshirts in the overheated foyer, walking sedately into the old chapel in our Sunday best trying to look inconspicuous, which is difficult when you have five damp sweatshirts crammed into a bulging plastic bag, one son is a different race from the rest of the family (Hal, whom we adopted when he was six months old, is half Korean, and we can only assume the other half, presumably American, was very, very tall, as Koreans are generally short people and Hal seemed to have topped out at six foot seven), and the other son is whining like mad. But fortunately Mormons are quite used to adoptions, even interracial ones, and to cross and disagreeable small children, so nobody was at all rude to us; in fact, we were made to feel quite welcome.

We carefully did not sit near Alexandra, who had tried several times to pick a fight with Hal. I was sorry not to see Georgina there, as she seemed to be the only one who could control Alexandra, but most likely by Sunday she needed a rest from controlling Alexandra. Then I realized that Alexandra was sitting quite demurely with an older woman who, despite her soft voice and silver curls, had Alexandra totally cowed. I don't mind telling you that was a relief.

The stained-glass windows, which on a sunny day must have been glorious, looked like mud, and Cameron, our four-year-old, wriggled, squirmed, and whined throughout the service. I was aware that he was upset because his schedule was upset, but that didn't alter the fact that he was driving us and everybody near us nuts, and if the weather had been better I might have suggested Harry take him outside. But that was out of the question. And even if this ward had had a nursery, which Georgina had told me she was pretty sure it did not, Mormon children are expected to be able to behave in sacrament meeting by the time they are four. This rarely means they actually do it. Cameron was not the only wriggling, whining four-year-old.

I wasn't about to try to send Cameron to a Primary he didn't know, as we'd just now gotten him to accept Primary at home where he knew people. This, of course, meant we got to take him with us into Sunday school and then I took him on to Relief Society. Lori, Hal's girlfriend, who was living with us for complicated reasons I'll get into later, went with me to Relief Society, the women's group that meets the same time the men go to Priesthood Meeting. At home she would have gone to the Young Women's group, because she was not yet quite eighteen, but she'd be graduating to Relief Society soon enough anyway and I needed her help with Cameron because I was still leaning on a cane as a result of foot surgery in the spring, and I was far from being up to corralling a cross four-year-old at his most rambunctious.

Alexandra, along with her presumably self-appointed caretaker, came to sit beside us in Relief Society, but of course Hal wasn't there so that was all right. I'm sure Hal went to Priesthood. I'm sure Harry, who refused to be baptized when Lori and I were (Hal for seven years had been the only Mormon member of the family), did not go to Priesthood; as it was far too cold and rainy for him to go spend the hour sitting outside on the steps or even in the car, and he certainly didn't want to go back into the chapel with the next ward's sacrament meeting, I suppose he sat in the foyer the whole time. At least that's where he was when we emerged, crawled back into our now uniformly damp sweatshirts (if I hadn't quit ironing clothes ten years ago I'd have remembered how cramming damp things together evens out the dampness), and headed for a nearby restaurant called Dee's for Sunday lunch. Alexandra, I assumed and hoped, had gone home. I couldn't be sure, even though I didn't see her, because she'd spent all day Saturday dogging our steps everywhere we went, so she could conceivably be lurking outside the restaurant even in all this rain, waiting for us to come back out.

By one-thirty, in a break in the cloudiness, we were standing (without Alexandra, so presumably she really had gone home) in the thin, watery sunshine on a sidewalk a few blocks from Georgina's looking uncertainly at the paved walk that angled off between two houses.

"Are you sure this is it?" I asked Harry. "It just looks like a driveway, and there's a chained gate—"

"It's exactly the way Georgina described it," Harry replied, "and the gate is just closed to cars. There's the footpath, exactly as she described it."

"Anyway," Lori said diffidently, "there's the sign. Gilgal."

So this must be the place—what our hostess, Georgina Grafton, had described as the most bizarre spot in the entire state of Utah. The privately owned sculpture garden called Gilgal, open to the public only on Sunday.

As we headed into the pathway between the two houses, I noticed two large dogs snoozing peacefully in front of their doghouses, ignoring the mud so they could lie in the fleeting sunshine, in a fenced pen to the right, behind another fenced pen half-covered with green stalks that soon would be a garden of hollyhocks. To the left, behind the grapevines that festooned the other fence, was a much smaller dog, who became totally hysterical as soon as we passed the corner of his yard. "Oh, hush, pooch," Hal said tolerantly. (At six foot seven, he can afford to be tolerant.)

The dog, who was somewhere between the size of a peanut and the size of a teacup, kept jumping and kept barking. I ignored the dog, not because he was not loud—he was very loud—but because I had just caught sight of a sphinx.

A sphinx carved from a single block of stone slightly larger than a Volkswagen bug. A sphinx with the face of Joseph Smith.

It was a rather good likeness, actually, but seeing the face that I was used to seeing depicted above a dignified dark suit, a high-collared white shirt, and the graceful loose cravat necktie of the early nineteenth century wearing instead a formal Egyptian head-dress and rising from the body of a lion, was startling to say the least. I still had not decided whether I liked it or not, and whether it was appropriate or highly disrespectful, when Hal, who had walked behind me to look at it from another angle, said, "Mom."

His voice sounded very strange, and I turned instantly, felt a jolt of sheer adrenaline somewhere in my gut, and then began to slide inexorably back into my cop mode. Hal was reaching for the key chain on which he had hung the small vial of consecrated oil almost all Mormon men carry with them at all times; obviously he was intending to give the woman a blessing, but I forestalled him. "It's too late, Hal." As indeed it was. Just as I had turned she had let out one deep breath and now her chest was still. Automatically I glanced at my watch and noted the time. In other circumstances I might have tried CPR. But not this time. Considering the condition of what was left of her brain, if it was possible to revive her—which I seriously doubted—it would have been an unbelievably cruel thing to do.

The stonework now facing me was, I suppose, intended to represent an altar of unhewn stone, although it was manifestly obvious that in fact this stone was artistically hewn to appear unhewn.

It was even more manifestly obvious that the body of Georgina's sister Alexandra Howe sprawled facedown at the foot of the altar, still in the flocked lavender organdy dress she had worn to church (which, as inappropriate as it was to her coloring, size, and age, was far less inappropriate than most of what I'd seen her in), with the back of her skull flattened, fragments of her brain lying about on the grass and stone, and the last drops of blood just ceasing to flow from the open wound, was no intention of the artist. Neither, I supposed, was the fist-sized white stone lying beside her head, as it was whitewashed and all the other stones in the garden were naturally colored.

"What, Mom?" Cameron yelled, heading my way as I began to bend over. "What did you see, Hal?"

"Grab him, Harry," I shouted as I checked Alexandra's temple for the pulse I knew I wouldn't find, and Harry—alerted I suppose by Hal's and my tone of voice and the look on my face—did, immediately handing him over to Lori and walking toward me.

"Want down!" Cameron yelled. I did not have to turn and look to know he was struggling and kicking. This is a determined kid. But then so is Lori, and she kept a firm grip on him and resisted the temptation to come and look for herself.

Hal went and took Cameron from Lori's arms and said, "Come on, Lori, we'll walk over to Trolley Square. Nine-one-one, Mom?"

"Yeah," I said, grateful that Trolley Square was so close we could see it from where we had parked the car. Mechanically, I wiped my hand on my clothing and only then realized I had smeared blood not on the sweatshirt, of which I was not overwhelmingly fond, but on my best Sunday dress.

"I could do without this real well," Harry said. "Want the camera?"

"Not my jurisdiction," I said. But I was still staring with sick fascination at Alexandra, whose blood had totally stopped flowing. Then I reached blindly for the camera, and Harry put it into my hands, taking the cane. I can stand on both feet—it's just that it hurts to do so—but I couldn't juggle the cane and the camera both and Harry knew that without its being discussed.

Still staring at the corpse, Harry said, "I wish I'd listened to you the other day."

. . . . .

One

. . . .

BEING ON THE other side of the badge was a distinctly unusual sensation for me, and I wasn't at all sure I liked it.

I gave the camera, its film now depleted, back to Harry, who dropped it into the pocket of his bright red University of Utah sweatshirt. I jotted a few notes in the notebook that is always in my purse, because regardless of my local status, if this one went to trial we were witnesses. After that we just waited, a good distance away from the body, even though I already knew that between the grass and the hard-packed earth that was shedding the rainwater instead of letting it soak in, there weren't going to be any footprints. I couldn't, at the moment, see any possible trace evidence other than the vaguely round chunk of whitewashed stone, which I could tell at a glance would not hold fingerprints.

First to arrive, within about ten minutes of the time Hal et al. departed to find a pay phone, were two uniformed officers, a tall slender woman in, I'd guess, her midforties, with blond hair pinned up at the back of her head, and a man in his early twenties, much shorter than she was, with short, very glossy black hair. Her name tag said MARCELLA, which I took to be a last name, not a first, for obvious reasons; his said GOMEZ. They talked first, briefly, with Harry, who to the great displeasure of the yappy little dog had stationed himself at the front gate to make sure no one else entered Gilgal, and then they came toward me. Marcella checked the body first, to be sure Hal's telephone report was right and it really was a body, and then got on her radio and asked for detectives, Crime Scene, and a unit from the medical examiner's office. "Slow the ambulance down," she added, "we aren't going to need it for a long time yet."

"Ten-nine your last," the dispatcher said. "Sounds like there's a lot of noise in the background."

"It's a dog," she said. "Stand by." She walked somewhat farther away, toward an adjoining backyard where, through an arch of stone with a stone eagle on either side of it, I could see several children playing hide-and-seek. There she repeated, "Get me detectives, Crime Scene, and somebody from the ME's office. Cancel the ambulance for now. This one's a Code Three."

I did not blame the dispatcher for having some trouble understanding. Frankly, I couldn't imagine how, during their brief colloquy, either Harry or the officers had made themselves heard over the yappity little beast, who didn't stop barking until a full five minutes after everybody was back into Gilgal and out of the driveway. The dog began again moments later, and I looked around to see the return of Hal, Lori, and Cameron, all of whom paused just inside the gate, to the great annoyance of the dog, who was totally determined that nobody was going to come and steal his grapevines and hollyhocks. Then a door to the adjacent house opened, and somebody came out and got the dog. I was very grateful.

Obviously I wasn't the only one who was grateful. Officer Marcella took off her hat and wiped rain off her forehead, for all the good that did; the rain was resuming, the children in the adjacent backyard scampered indoors, banging doors noisily, and Marcella hastily put the hat back on just as I pulled up the hood of the damp sweatshirt I was wearing. Looking as if she would rather swear a while, she said, "Gomez, go get something to cover the body to keep the rain off." To me, she added, "Usually they keep the dog in on Sunday afternoon." I must have looked puzzled, because she added, "Half the town knows that."

"I can see why," I agreed. "But even the best of dogs must make occasional trips outside."

"True. Okay, so you're the one who found the body?" She had pulled out her notebook and moved over under a nearby tree, so that she could have some hope of writing without getting the notebook soaked. I followed her under the tree; this wasn't a thunderstorm, and there was no reason to get drenched unnecessarily. There was a shed in the park, but going into it would put us out of sight of the body, and none of us wanted that right now. Well, actually we did, but it didn't seem advisable, even though Gomez, who had walked right past Hal, Lori, and Cameron going every which way without apparently seeing them, had now returned with a heavy plastic tarp—Marine Corps green printed with a leafy camouflage pattern—and laid it neatly over the body to protect trace evidence from the rain. It would work, I thought, as long as the rain stayed light; if it got heavy again, the tarp would make matters worse instead of better because the weight of the water would press it into the ground and flatten anything that might be present. At least it was a plastic tarp, though, and not a blanket, which would have left its own traces while removing traces that might already be there.

"Actually, my son saw it first and then called my attention to it," I explained.

"Why'd he do that?" Gomez asked. He was standing at my elbow, making his own notes in his own small black notebook.

I stared at him. "Why shouldn't he?"

"Well—not trying to be sexist—but seems to me most boys would call for their dad and not their mom if they saw something like that."

"Not if their mom is a police detective and their dad is a helicopter pilot," Harry said dryly. He had abandoned his guard post and walked back into the park and was now standing just behind me, also under the tree. "Admittedly, I've coped with corpses. But not since Vietnam, and that's been close to thirty years ago."

"Oh. Okay," Gomez said. "No offense, ma'am."

"None taken," I agreed. I am perfectly aware that I do not look like a police detective even on duty, with a radio on my belt and a pistol in a shoulder holster; I still have vivid memories of one murderer, totally astonished at being arrested by me, informing me that I looked like somebody's sweet little auntie. Off duty, more than a thousand miles from my pistol, badge, and jurisdiction, wearing a blue Brigham Young University sweatshirt (the store where Hal went wasn't taking sides in the U versus Y feud, and Hal, with a fine sense of discrimination, had gotten his non-Mormon father the U sweatshirt and his Mormon mother the Y sweatshirt) over a floral print Sunday dress, carrying a small beige crocheted handbag, and leaning on a cane, I certainly would not expect anybody to suspect my official status.

"I'm glad we've got a trained observer here," Marcella said, "because I've got a hunch this one is going to be a woolly booger. Still, we'd better talk to your son too, as soon as possible. Gomez, get rid of those kids."

Gomez turned and headed purposefully toward the gate as if he were seeing Hal, Lori, and Cameron for the first time. "That *is* our son," I said hastily. "I mean they're both our sons, and the girl is Hal's girlfriend. Hal is the one who actually saw the body first and called my attention to it."

The reaction I got was neither unfamiliar nor unexpected. Marcella and Gomez looked at me. Looked at Harry. Looked at Hal, and looked up, and up, and up, and then they both turned to look at me again. Then Marcella said, "Oh. Okay. Adopted, right?"

"Right," I said.

"Gomez, you go talk with—Hal, what's his last name? I haven't even gotten your name yet, have I? And the girl, what's her name?"

. . . . .

I provided names, and Gomez walked over toward the kids. "Let's all go over to the shed and get out of the rain," he invited, and—with more delicacy than I would have given him credit for—led them around the far side of the sphinx, around some curious fenced-off mound in the middle of the park which I was later to learn represented the broken idol with clay feet in the Book of Daniel, and into the side of the shed that was farthest out of sight of the covered body.

Marcella meanwhile started asking the usual questions: my name, Harry's name, our Salt Lake City address and phone number, our home address and phone number, what brought us to Salt Lake City and how long did we expect to stay, and so forth. Then she said, "Your son told Dispatch he thought the woman was still alive when you got here."

"Technically," I said.

"Well, I can see that," she agreed. "But she was still breathing?"

"She let out one breath after I turned to look at her, and never took another one. That was it. By the time I could bend over there was no pulse. And as you can see, CPR wouldn't have made sense."

"Obviously not; she was probably brain-dead from the moment the blow hit. And there hasn't been that much bleeding," Marcella said. It was clear that told her the same thing it told me. "Okay, Gomez, what do you want to ask?" Gomez hadn't spent much time questioning Hal; he was back already.

I had, by now, deduced that Gomez was a very new trainee and Marcella was his training officer, and I waited expectantly for Gomez to think of something to ask. When he did, he wasn't very original. "Did you see anybody leave?"

"No," I said. "And that's odd."

He went into deep thought again, perhaps trying to figure out why that was odd, while Marcella said into her radio, "What detective have you got en route?"

. . . . .

"Sosa."

Marcella did not say "Shit!" but from the look on her face I had the distinct impression she was thinking it. "I thought Burton was on call today for Homicide," was what she said.

"Burton is in LDS Hospital getting his appendix out," the dispatcher said with that diabolical glee dispatchers often have when imparting bad news. "You get Sosa."

"Coming from home?"

"Close enough. Coming from church."

"Sosa lives in Rose Park," Marcella told me. That meant nothing to me, and I said so. "Northwest part of town, over the other side of the state fairground," she said. "Call it ten minutes from here, this time of day, on Sunday. A lot longer other times, other days, of course. But it won't take him long today. *Dang,* I sure do wish we weren't getting Sosa." She muttered that last sentence under her breath, to Gomez, who was closer to her than I was, and she probably didn't know I heard her. Gomez shrugged.

But whether she liked it or not, in about thirty seconds we got Sosa. Gomez immediately turned to head back for the shed, and Sosa said, "Not yet, Gomez." This interested me immediately. I thought there must be at least five hundred people on the Salt Lake City Police Department (I found out later there were only three hundred and fifty-two, one hundred and fifty-five fewer than the International Association of Chiefs of Police recommendations; this town was even more seriously underpoliced than Fort Worth was), so why should this detective know a rookie by sight? Had he already known Gomez before Gomez came on the department, or did he immediately learn the name of every new hire? If he could manage that, he was a heck of a lot sharper than I was.

Anyway, Gomez stopped, looked around, and returned.

I couldn't tell yet what Marcella's objection to Sosa was. Presumably—despite such fictional characters as Joyce Porter's Dover—he wouldn't be a homicide detective if he weren't reasonably competent, and he strode in looking like somebody who knew what he was doing.

It was obvious that he was on call rather than on duty. Like me, he was dressed for church, wearing a dark gray suit and a subdued necktie, except that he had a pager on his belt, and I felt instant sympathy. I would not soon forget the day, in the middle of the sacrament prayer, when my pager announced to the entire ward, "Detective Ralston, call headquarters. Detective Ralston, call headquarters." The butt of his pistol was sticking out of his coat pocket. My guess was he'd left it locked in the glove box of his car, as I have been known to do, unsafe though it actually is, and had snatched it hastily when he was called in.

His name was Hispanic, but I didn't think many of his ancestors had come from Spain. Unlike the Pueblo Indian police chief I'd met in New Mexico a few years earlier, he was a big man; he was about six feet tall, bulky in general from the waist up but not from the waist down. Like Big Bad John of the old song, he was "kind of broad at the shoulder and narrow at the hip," so narrow at the hip in fact that his trousers didn't seem to fit quite right, as if he were a little too flat where he sat down (a condition I heartily envied). His face was almost a long rectangle. And when he opened his mouth he had no Hispanic accent at all, or any other accent so far as I could tell. His enunciation was as clear as that of a radio broadcaster, without the pretentious mannerisms most broadcasters seem to have. The other thing that was obvious was that he was in a lousy mood. It wasn't his words, or even his tone of voice, so much as it was his facial expression; all he actually said now was, "What've we got, Marcella?"

Marcella handed over her notebook, which he scanned briefly and handed back. Then she moved out of his way, lifted the tarp, and gestured to the corpse at the foot of the sculptured altar. "That," she said. "We'll go check perimeters." She dropped the blanket to the side and walked toward the back of the garden.

. . . . .

"Good," Sosa said, and bent over as I had done, and as Marcella had done, to touch the temple and check for pulse. He straightened, wiping his hands on a wad of tissue he pulled out of his coat pocket, and dropped the tarp back down over the body. His slight shudder was almost unnoticeable, and his next words were astonishing. "That's blasphemy."

Gomez, who hadn't followed Marcella yet—presumably because Sosa hadn't dismissed him—said, "It looks to me like murder."

"That's the other thing it is. First time you've been here?" Sosa asked, staring at the body again, his voice sounding patient and his facial expression revealing an entirely different mood.

"In this park?" Gomez said. "Yeah."

"You LDS?" Sosa asked without turning.

"No, Catholic, why?"

"Then you wouldn't know what I'm talking about." He said it as a statement of fact, not an accusation. "Don't worry about it. Go help your partner. And get somebody over here to secure the gate." He whirled to look at Harry and me, as Gomez hastily followed Marcella. "But I'll bet you do. Know what I'm talking about, I mean."

"Actually I don't," I replied.

"Don't look at me," Harry said. "I'm a Baptist."

"I do," Hal said.

Sosa looked at him. Looked at the name tag I had questioned whether Hal should be wearing yet, but he had insisted upon so firmly I'd stopped arguing, which said ELDER RALSTON. "Yeah, you would," he agreed. "Just leaving, or just got back?"

"I report to the Missionary Training Center this Friday," Hal said.

"Where are you going after that?"

"Nevada."

"I'm surprised they didn't send you to Korea."

So was I, especially since the bishop had mentioned the possibility at the time Hal had turned in his papers. I was even more surprised that Sosa had realized that Hal was specifically of Korean origin, rather than just of unspecified Oriental origin.

"Okay, tell your mom why I said this is blasphemy."

"Well, because . . ." Hal paused, looking puzzled. "Who are you?"

"I'm Detective Charlie Sosa. And I'm a high priest."

What a high priest means to a Mormon, and what it probably means in other religions, is somewhat different. Any Mormon male the age of Charlie Sosa who behaved himself appropriately would probably be a high priest, but that does not dilute the rank. Hal's respect was obvious as he asked, "How much should I say?"

"You're a priesthood holder," Sosa said. "Use your own judgment."

Not too many people who have known Hal all his life, or even most of it, would tell him to use his own judgment, but even I would have to agree that lately his judgment had improved considerably. "It's just—Mom, don't you know what this is supposed to represent?" His gesture took in the sculpture, not the corpse.

"Well, obviously it's an altar of unhewn stones, but beyond that—"

"After Adam and Eve were . . ." He paused again, looking at Detective Sosa, apparently for signs of disapproval. Then he went on. "Cast out of the Garden of Eden, they built an altar of unhewn stones to make sacrifices on, but they didn't know why except that they were supposed to. But the sacrifices weren't human. Not ever human. You don't have to go to the Temple to know that; it's in the Old Testament and I learned it in seminary."

Most—theoretically all—Mormon teenagers go to seminary their entire four years of high school. If their schools have released time for religious studies, as many states do to accommodate not only Mormons but also Catholics, Jews, and anybody else who has a special program for high-school-age youngsters, a seminary building is conveniently near most high schools; if not, they have early-morning seminary or, in rare cases, correspondence seminary that has group meetings only once a month. As Texas does not have released time, Hal had spent four years banging out of the house at five-thirty A.M. to go to early-morning seminary, usually returning home bubbling over with things he wanted to tell me that I did not want to hear—though come to think of it, I'd learned a lot.

Not noticing my sudden reverie, he went on, "Their offerings were animals and grain and wine and oil. But—whoever killed her—I don't know that they did it on purpose, but where she is, it looks like they did. She's put where—it's like she's a sacrifice. And that's what Brother Sosa meant by blasphemy." He looked at Sosa for confirmation.

"Exactly," Sosa said, and turned back to me. "Since you're not local, I don't suppose you have any idea who she is?"

"Actually we do," I replied. "We're staying in a bed-and-breakfast just a few blocks from here, and she's the owner's sister. Her name is Alexandra Howe. She's twenty-six." I gave the address and added, "The owner is Georgia Grafton."

"Interesting coincidence," he said matter-of-factly, not sounding very interested at all. "Her showing up here just before you did."

"I hope you don't mean that the way it sounded."

"I don't mean it any way," he said. "It's just an interesting coincidence."

"You wouldn't think that if you knew how she followed us around all day yesterday," I answered. "Anyway, I don't know that she arrived just before we did."

"She hasn't been here long," he said.

"I don't know that, either."

He looked at me with annoyance. "Would you care to explain that statement? I thought you were a cop."

"I am a cop," I said, beginning to wonder just how long he'd been in Homicide. This didn't jibe well with what I'd noticed a while ago, his knowing a rookie's name, his being alert and observant enough to spot Hal's exact racial background. "I know how long she's been dead, because I saw her die at exactly one-forty-seven by my watch. I know she didn't live long after she was hit, because there's incredibly little bleeding for that massive a head wound. What I don't know was how long she was here before she was hit. Last time we saw her was after church, just after twelve o'clock, and we went to lunch after that. I don't know where she went. But it's perfectly possible she came here to wait for us, in which case she could easily have been here an hour or so before she was struck."

He looked momentarily dismayed and then muttered, "I think I'm losing my mind. If I don't get some sleep—never mind. Sorry. You said she followed you around all day yesterday, and might have come here to wait for you. In that case, if you had agreed to meet here, wouldn't she have known when you were arriving?"

"We didn't agree to meet here," I said. "I told you she followed us around all day yesterday. I didn't say we wanted her to. She's very curious about us, and on top of that she's been trying to pick a fight with my son."

"Which son?" He was looking rather incredulously at Hal's size and at Cameron's size.

"Hal."

Sosa looked back at the tarp-covered mound, his eyes seeming to measure the body under the tarp, and then at Hal. "*She*'s been trying to pick a fight with *him?*"

"That's what I said. When she wasn't trying to play with Cameron as if she were the same age he is, and trying to figure all of us out. At least that's what I think she was doing. And that's why I think, since she knew we were coming here after lunch, she might have come here to wait for us so she could go on following us."

. . . . .

"Why's that? It seems like a very strange thing for a grown woman to do. All of it. Following people around, picking fights with people twice her size—"

"She's got—she had—multiple personality disorder," I said. "And at least one of the personalities had this thing for following people around to figure out what they were doing. Another personality seemed to be highly belligerent toward teenage boys."

"Hadn't we better let a psychiatrist diagnose that?" he asked.

"A psychiatrist *did* diagnose that," I retorted. "Her sister told me. But I assure you that nobody, seeing her alive, would have any trouble diagnosing it."

"Mr. Sosa," Harry said softly, "there's something you better know."

"What's that?"

"All Officer Marcella asked, and all she wrote down, and therefore all you know, is that Deb is a police officer. Let me expand on that a little. Deb is a detective in the Major Case Squad. She's also worked in Homicide and in the Sex Crimes Unit. They still refer homicides to her—but only when they're extra-complicated. You're not talking to a crossing guard."

Sosa looked totally nonplussed, and then recovered. "I apologize," he said. "Of course I didn't think you were a crossing guard. We've got one woman in Homicide here and I wish we had more. It's just—I don't know you."

Obviously he didn't. And equally obviously, I wasn't going to have the kind of situation I had four years ago, when Hal and Lori decided to spend an unauthorized spring break in New Mexico and I wound up helping a very small-town police chief clear a nasty murder series. Salt Lake City, Utah, unlike Las Vegas, New Mexico, had (I assumed at that moment) quite an adequate police department of its own, and unmistakably I was being warned off. This wasn't my case.

. . . . .

"Let's start over," he said then. "I didn't mean to insult you. I never mean to insult a fellow officer, but from what they tell me I'm always doing it." (That, I thought, explained Marcella's reaction.) "I guess I'm short on tact. A lot of my fellow officers aren't too crazy about me because of it, and sometimes I'm not too crazy about myself. But I've got a murder to work, and I need your help. You might as well call me Charlie; most people do."

"In that case," I said, "you might as well call me Deb. Most people do. And my husband is Harry. You met Hal and Lori; the baby is Cameron."

He nodded to everybody, with an expression indicating that this was more introduction than he wanted. "We're shorthanded," he added, which was exactly what I had just concluded they were not. That was when he told me the size of the department, and added, "Allowing for shift changes and days off and so forth, we've only got about thirty people to put on the street at any given time, and this is a good-sized city. We only have seven people in Homicide counting the sergeant, and one of them is on vacation and one is on compassionate leave—his mother just died—and one landed in the hospital early this morning to have his appendix out. And Friday morning I found the body of a potential federally protected witness floating in the Jordan River. You know what I mean?"

I knew exactly what he meant. He meant he had FBI agents up the ying-yang right now, and didn't need any more problems. Why anybody had decided he should be on call today was beyond me, except for the obvious fact that if half the squad was gone everybody else had to do double duty.

"We didn't find this body to annoy you," I pointed out all the same. "I'd really much rather we hadn't found it at all."

"Obviously," he said, and turned abruptly as someone else came in the Gilgal gate, walking neatly past the uniformed officer now stationed there. I assumed it was somebody Sosa knew and was ambivalent about, because I noticed a brief relaxation in his shoulders followed at once by increased tension. "Hi," he said, and waited as the woman, black case in hand, approached us.

"This is Kate Rolley," he said, and then amended his introduction slightly. "*Dr.* Kate Rolley. From the state medical examiner's office. Kate, Mrs. Ralston found the body."

"Hal found the body," I corrected.

"I'm Hal," Hal put in helpfully.

"Elder Hal Ralston found the body and at once directed his mother's attention to it because his mother is a homicide detective in Fort Worth, Texas," said Charlie (since he wanted me to call him that, I would do so), and I decided against correcting him again to explain that I am not officially a homicide detective. I had the impression that the edges of his patience were fraying quickly.

Dr. Rolley said hi to me and immediately knelt beside the body, opened her black kit, and put on rubber gloves. Then she glanced up. "Has it been photographed yet?"

"No," Charlie said.

"Actually I took some snaps," I said, "but your crime-scene people haven't been here." (Ultimately, my pictures were never even developed, because Harry left the film in his sweatshirt pocket and I washed the shirt.)

"I wish they'd hurry," she said. "I need to get a thermometer in fast, if I'm going to determine a time of death."

"I can tell you the time of death, Dr. Rolley," I volunteered. "I was here when she actually died."

"Oh, that helps a lot," she said. The words could have been sarcastic or sincere, but the tone was clearly sincere, and she glanced around at me eagerly and added, "Do call me Kate."

Nice people in Salt Lake City, I thought, and told her the time of death, which of course I had written down, and she immediately wrote it down too. Charlie, I noticed, did the same this time; he hadn't written it down the first time I told him. Then he did the rest of what I would have done a little earlier: he compared his watch to mine, decided they agreed, and then compared his watch to Kate's. "On the nose," she told him. Nobody was going to do anything else until the body was photographed.

A couple of crime-scene technicians came next, and the four—detective, doctor, and crime-scene techs—walked around together, checking the overall scene, checking perimeters for signs of any escape route. My instinct, of course, was to follow them, but I knew quite well I would not be welcome. No matter what I was at home, here I was a civilian.

The sun had come out again and the kids in the neighboring house were outside, this time all lined directly behind the arch separating the two backyards, staring into this one. I saw Charlie stop and ask them a couple of questions, which the oldest of the kids answered, but I wasn't close enough to hear the conversation.

Finally Charlie and Kate returned to me and the technicians removed the tarp and began taking photographs. Kate asked me to go over, once again, exactly what I had seen after Hal called to me and I turned, and then she said, "I don't see how it could have been much over a minute between the time she was struck and the time you saw her, and yet you didn't see anybody. That's weird . . . maybe she's got some condition which slowed the blood flow, but I can't think what it could be. Well, I'll see what else I can find when I get inside."

Charlie walked over to get in the technicians' way, probably not deliberately, but one of the technicians, with an eloquent gesture toward heaven, suspended his work and got out of Charlie's way. Charlie pointed to the whitewashed stone. "Have you ever seen that before? Or anything like it?"

"Not that I can think of," I said. (But memory stirred in me. Somewhere, recently, I had seen something like it. But I couldn't remember where, or in what connection.)

Charlie was watching me, almost, I felt, following my thoughts.

Now he said, "We'll leave the crime-scene people to finish up here. I'd appreciate it if you and your family could follow me in to the police station, where we can get a little more information and maybe some formal statements, but before we do that, why don't you lead me to the guest house—bed-and-breakfast, you said?—and let me break the news? Or would Mrs. Grafton be home, do you think?"

I assumed that Georgina would be home, and told him so. In solemn procession, we drove the few blocks to Georgina's, and Harry said, "If it's okay with Charlie, why don't you go in with him and let the rest of us stay in the car? I'd just as soon not go bursting in on her right now, lock, stock, and baggage."

That was not the way the quotation went—it's lock, stock, and barrel—and the fact that Harry, who's far more interested in guns than I am, had it wrong told me that he was highly wound up by now. It was okay with me if he and everybody else stayed in the car. It was also, it developed, okay with Charlie. I had expected it would be.

Never mind the rest of it. Breaking the news is never fun, and it was pretty obvious that nobody was going to get any information out of Georgina very soon. I asked if she'd like me to stay with her for a while, and she sobbed, "No, no, I've got to call my other sister—Cynthia—she'll come over—"

Feeling like a rat, I went and got back in the car with Harry, noticing that Cameron was whining quite a lot, and we followed Charlie into the police station.

He started the formal statements with Hal, but limited that statement to Hal's spotting the body and immediately calling my attention to it, and made it clear in the statement that Hal had seen nothing I didn't see. It was unlikely, he assured Hal, that he'd need to be called in from his mission to testify, as I had seen everything he had seen.

He then talked with Lori only long enough to determine that she had seen nothing at all. He then went on to Harry, but as Harry couldn't possibly have seen anything I didn't, he kept that statement brief also. By the time he turned to me, Cameron had moved from whining into outright howling. "I'm sorry," I said, jiggling him on my knee because by now he was too cross even for Lori to hold him. "It's just that his time schedule is all mixed up, and he got to bed late last night, and on top of that he's missed his nap two days in a row—"

"Harry," Charlie said, "would you mind very much taking the rest of your family back to the place you're staying, so that child can get his nap, and let me bring your wife home later?"

Harry's face said he did mind. We were supposed to be on vacation, and our time together is limited enough at best. But murder is murder, and he answered, "No, that makes sense."

After my family had left, Charlie asked, "Do you mind if I turn on a tape recorder?"

"Not at all."

"I didn't figure you would. But I had to ask." He got it out, put it on top of his desk, opened a fresh tape cassette, and inserted it. "This is Detective Charlie Sosa, Salt Lake City Police Department. The date is . . ." He went on through the normal date, time, and place litany, and then continued, "I'm talking with Detective Deb Ralston of the Fort Worth Police Department in connection with the death of Alexandra Howe, white female twenty-six years old. Detective Ralston, do you know this tape recorder is turned on?"

"Yes, I do."

"Have you consented to this statement being taped?"

"Yes, I have."

"Okay. Tell me about it."

One tries to ask open-ended questions at a time like this, but this wasn't just open-ended, this was funnel-mouth open. "Where do you want me to start?" I asked helplessly.

"Anywhere. Start at the beginning."

. . . . .

How many times I have told people to start at the beginning—but the fact is one never really knows where the beginning is. "What would you call the beginning?" I demanded.

"I don't know, what would *you* call the beginning? Tell me how you happen to be in Salt Lake City. Tell me how you happen to know Alexandra Howe. Don't worry about whether something's relevant; I'll decide later what's relevant."

"Well—when my son Hal, that's Harold Ralston Junior—"

"Whose statement I got on paper about half an hour ago?"

"That's right. All right, my son Hal got his mission call, and we hadn't been on a family vacation in years, and . . ."

. . . . .

Two

. . . .

HAL'S MISSIONARY FAREWELL, a special church service attended by the entire ward, or congregation, as well as by as many guests as could be packed into a crowded sanctuary, had been almost three weeks ago, on the first Sunday in June. When I say crowded sanctuary I speak quite literally: they had to put so many rows of chairs behind the pews that eventually they opened the folding doors to the gymnasium and put several more rows of chairs in the gym. I couldn't help wondering whether there were really that many people who wanted to see Hal's farewell, or whether the huge crowd was there because nobody could really quite believe that scatterbrained Hal Ralston was really going on a mission, and they all had to come see for themselves.

That afternoon we had a reception at home (Lori and I had spent what felt like weeks preparing the munchies, which vanished in hours), which was even better attended than the farewell, largely by Hal's friends, Mormon and otherwise, though fortunately, considering the size of our living room, they didn't all come at once, as they did at church. The Mormon friends were wildly congratulating him, wishing him a successful mission, and slipping money into his pocket every chance they got—the missionary is supposed to support himself the two years of his mission on money he has saved and on money his family provides, but in practice friends help too—and the "otherwise," mostly teenagers, were screaming with laughter at the idea of Hal taking off to be a missionary. Hal to my surprise remained imperturbable.

The week before, in the stake president's office, the stake president and our bishop had formally set Hal apart, giving him a special hands-on-head blessing dedicating the next two years of his life to his missionary service, and after that he was officially a missionary, which among other things meant he wasn't allowed even to touch Lori until after he got home and was formally released from his service. ("That's right," Charlie said approvingly.) In fact, Lori immediately began addressing him as "Elder," which I understood and Hal understood, but which seemed to drive Harry slightly up the wall because to him "Elder" is not a word used to address a nineteen-year-old.

Hal also was not supposed to watch television except the news, or listen to music that wasn't spiritually uplifting, or read anything that wasn't connected with his mission. He hardly had time to think about the situation the rest of that week. It was full of such things as driving over to the Temple in Dallas to receive his endowment, a sacred ceremony held only in the Temple, which Lori and I could not attend because we had not been members long enough and Harry could not attend because he was not a member at all. Hal returned from that bubbling over with things he was very excited about but could not tell us, and after that we were scurrying around finishing getting all his clothes ready, realizing as we did so that the chances of these clothes lasting him the two years they were supposed to last were absolutely zilch. Of course I could not possibly take off work—leaving for three weeks in the middle of the summer for the trip itself was the most anybody would allow me—so my evenings were especially hectic as I sewed on buttons, did laundry in addition to the laundry Lori did during the day, and dashed out to the cleaners to pick up suits and to Sears, Penney's, and K Mart to replace shirts and socks that had unaccountably vanished in the last two weeks, and to purchase other last-minute supplies

Hal kept suddenly realizing he needed. Apparently he was under the assumption that the stores in Nevada, where he would go after leaving the Missionary Training Center, do not stock toothpaste, shaving cream, or razor blades.

Hal meanwhile was packing and unpacking everything, making lists and losing them, and putting all his rock tapes and Elric books into boxes and then getting them back out and offering them to Lori for the duration. She accepted the rock tapes but not the Elric books, about which she feels approximately the same way I do, and the Elric books wound up in storage for the next two years along with Hal's drum set, weight bench, and other impedimenta. The Terry Pratchett and Piers Anthony books were another matter; I have given up attempting to pretend that I read them only when Hal leaves them lying around, and so he considerately put them all in my bedroom, from which I removed them to one of the maze of small rooms Harry has transformed our former garage into. There they would still be available for reading but would not sit on my floor for two years, as Hal evidently intended.

Hal seized possession of the camera and took pictures of everything he wanted to be able to look at for the next two years, from the family, including cats and dog, to the mesquite tree in the front yard and the Archie Black Owl etching on the living room wall. Those, of course, had to be rushed to a one-hour photo processing lab so he could put the pictures in his suitcase.

But Sunday, after the reception was over and things settled down and Hal had time to realize he was really going to be gone for two whole years, he also had time to realize he wasn't allowed to kiss Lori good-bye. Which posed a little bit of a problem, because unlike most missionaries he didn't have a girlfriend somewhere else in town; Lori had a bedroom right across the hall from him. And unlike most missionary parents we weren't taking Hal to the airport Monday morning and putting him on a plane to Salt Lake City, there to be met by some official church gofer—excuse me, messenger—and escorted to the Missionary Training Center at Provo. No, Monday morning we packed ourselves and large amounts of gear into the dark brown van we'd borrowed from my son-in-law Olead Baker and took off for a long-delayed family vacation. And as I've indicated, due to extreme complications in her life, Lori was now a member of our family.

As Hal and Lori helped to load the car, they took great care to remain at arm's length from each other, to the extent that I finally had to call the bishop (who is a police officer the rest of the week) and let him explain to Hal that he wasn't misbehaving if he accidentally ran into Lori when she was carrying a sleeping bag and he was carrying an ice chest. When we finally departed, Hal was buckled a little morosely into the left rear seat, Lori was buckled into the right rear seat, and Cameron was sitting between them, on his own little car seat that buckled onto the regular seat belt and lifted him up so that he could see out the windows too.

The dog, also buckled into a seat belt—a special doggy one we'd purchased from the vet, and have you ever tried to get a pit bull to sit still for such indignities as that? (At that Charlie shook his head and said, "I can't imagine being dumb enough to have a pit bull at all," to which I did not reply)—was in the middle half-seat with the ice chest at his feet, so that everybody except Cameron had a window. Usually Pat, unlike most dogs, hates to ride, but now that he had a window all his own, with the wind blowing right on his muzzle (Harry disapproves of air conditioning in vehicles and refuses to use it even if it is present) instead of his being pushed down into the floorboards as he usually was when he went to the vet, and with all his people present even if he wasn't quite close enough to kiss either Cameron or Lori, he was in doggy heaven.

My husband, Harry, claims that it was my idea to take the pit bull with us on our trip. It should be perfectly obvious that the decision was his.

("Oh?" Charlie said with uplifted eyebrows.)

. . . . .

The problem was that we couldn't quite afford to sleep in motels throughout the trip (well, actually we could, but Harry didn't want to spend the money), and Harry decided that a nice family camping trip would be good for us all. But I am a cop, and very few cops are exaggerating when they check "yes" on standardized psychological tests to that question about "Somebody wants to kill me." Also, experience makes us cautious in situations other people take for granted; we've seen too many people get hurt or killed when they were doing no more than going to the grocery store, much less sleeping outside. I usually carry a pistol just about everywhere except to bed, and I have one within reach even there. But the varied—often highly varied—gun laws of the states and the national parks we intended to visit suggested to me that this time the pistol would be best left at home, locked in my desk at work.

But I would feel somewhat insecure sleeping in a tent or—more likely, considering there were five of us to use a very small tent—in a sleeping bag outdoors on the ground, if I had no armament of any kind, especially since, as I have mentioned, one of the purposes of the trip was to leave our six-foot-seven son, Hal, in Provo, Utah, at the Missionary Training Center. Going home it would only be me (five foot two and unarmed, without nearly as much training in unarmed combat as I ought to have, and leaning on a cane to boot), Harry (an ex-Marine with what I consider a survivalist fetish, but with a bad limp left over from a helicopter accident), Hal's girlfriend, Lori (still not fully recovered either physically or emotionally from the hit-and-run accident that had led indirectly to her moving in with us), and our son Cameron (four years old).

Harry first suggested, not entirely facetiously, that we could take along his machete, or he could buy a sword cane or a bowie knife or a switchblade or a set of brass knuckles, and I reminded him, not at all facetiously, that such things probably would be illegal in most of the places we would be going; in fact, several of them are illegal everywhere. He then said the pepper spray Lori and I always carry on our key chains should be adequate, and I agreed and hoped that would put an end to the discussion, which it did not. He then pointed out—only he insists I did—that if we had Pat with us we'd be perfectly safe. Even the most determined thug is unlikely to mess with a pit bull who is curling one corner of his mouth to show his teeth, meanwhile saying "Rrrr-rrr-rrrrrr."

("That's the only use for a pit bull that I know of," Charlie agreed, and I reproachfully told him Pat is a very sweet dog, at which he laughed.)

We finally agreed, not without misgivings, to take the dog along. We had arranged for a friendly neighbor to come in and water the houseplants, bring in the newspapers and mail, mow the lawn, and feed and pet the cats and change the litter boxes as necessary, and of course with the cat door the cats can get in and out all they wish. We did take the precaution of using phone books, heavy trash cans, and the like as doorstops, so that no cat could inadvertently shut a door and shut herself into a room for the rest of our trip.

The borrowed van would easily hold all of us, all of our gear including the camping equipment, the pit bull, and the mastodon-sized suitcase we'd bought for Hal's mission, and since we kept the dog on a short chain attached to the trailer hitch at night he was no real problem as we camped our meandering way from Fort Worth, Texas, to Salt Lake City, Utah; even though your average pit bull can tow a jeep a short distance, Pat wasn't up to pulling the van. (That is, he was no real problem until he started to cough as we got farther into the mountains. I figured that was probably the altitude, and he'd get used to it.)

Anyway, it was Hal and Lori, not Harry and I, who had decided where everybody would sit, beyond the obvious given that Harry and I were in the front seats, generally with Harry driving because he is of the old school that believes that if a man is in the car he is the driver, even if his wife is a cop and a better, because less absent-minded, driver than he is.

We did most of the sight-seeing part of the trip while Hal was still with us, taking an extremely meandering route that took us through many places including Carlsbad Caverns (where we left Pat in a local pet-boarding facility while we explored; Harry wanted to push me through the caverns in a rented wheelchair but I declined on the grounds that the cane was adequate), the Painted Desert, the Grand Canyon, and then backtracked and detoured to drive up through Colorado into Grand Teton National Park (where Pat started coughing), and Yellowstone National Park, (Charlie said, "And if you were going to the moon you'd go by way of Mars and Venus, right?") before we drove up into Idaho to visit Craters of the Moon (where Pat added barfing to the coughing), and then down to Promontory Point and the Golden Spike National Monument, where the continental United States was first completely connected east to west by rail.

It started raining while we were at Golden Spike inspecting the brightly painted replicas of the old locomotives, and it rained all the way into Salt Lake City. By the time we reached Georgina's we had cleaned out the van after Pat about fifteen times. We were nearly out of paper towels, and with the windows shut to keep out the rain we were traveling in a constant aura of dog barf and Lysol spray, which I particularly dislike because too many people try to use it to mask the smell of long-dead human corpses. It cannot mask that smell, nothing at all can ("You are so right," Charlie agreed), and the misuse of it for that purpose has only made the smell of Lysol highly detestable to me.

We arrived at Georgina's Bed and Breakfast, a lovely old three-story (four-story, counting the basement) brick house near Trolley Square in Salt Lake City, on Friday afternoon before we were due to have Hal in Provo the following Friday. The first problem came when Georgina looked at Pat, who was huddled on the front porch with the rest of us and coughing again, and said, faintly, "Oh dear."

"What's wrong?" I asked, and then turned abruptly, startled, as a tall, gawky woman with graying brown hair danced from the front door onto the porch and then into the rainy-wet yard, attired in what looked like about seventeen layers of different-colored chiffon draped over a tie-dyed multicolored (mainly blue) tunic, which in turn hung over tie-dyed multicolored (mainly blue) tights, thick yellow socks, and backless sandals with thick leather straps—either Birkenstocks or a good imitation thereof. She twirled around, singing a discordant assortment of "La-la-la-las." She swooped back onto the porch and began dripping around Harry and Hal, carefully avoiding the dog.

("And that's your first sight of the victim?" Charlie asked, and I nodded.)

"Sandy, stop that!" Georgina said sharply.

"You're s'posed to call me—" The petulant voice sounded more like that of a child than an adult, despite the evidence of age, and the woman—Sandy—went on dancing, flinging a pink layer of chiffon onto Harry and a violet layer onto Hal.

"Alexandra, go in the house at once and put on some decent clothes," Georgina said, somewhat less sharply. "You may not be Salome today."

"Mama was Salome."

"Mama was a dancer. You're not. Go in the house now." Sandy, or Alexandra as the case might be, went sullenly back up the front steps, slamming the door behind her, and Georgina, after taking the chiffon back from Harry and Hal and draping it over her left forearm, returned her attention to Pat. "Well, it's just—when you said a dog, I thought, maybe a poodle. Or a cocker spaniel. I didn't anticipate—what *is* it?"

I explained that he was half pit bull and half Doberman, with the pit bull half predominant, and Georgina said, "Well, I'm sure you can see that he won't work out in the house"—I heartily agreed, especially since he had now completed the coughing spell with another barf, fortunately onto the ground this time—"and I don't have a fenced backyard—"

"I need to take him to a vet anyway," I said, "and maybe the vet can recommend a boarding clinic."

Georgina suggested Pet Stop, which she described as a complex of boarding and grooming facilities, pet and pet-supply store, and veterinary clinic on the other side of the downtown area, and after we finished unloading the van Lori and I left Harry and Hal to deal with Cameron and unpacking while we headed for the boarding facility. The owner took one look at Pat, who was still coughing, and said firmly, "No. I'm sorry, but I can't accept this dog."

"Why not?" I asked.

"Because he's sick, and we can't run the risk of passing whatever he has to the healthy animals."

"I think he just hasn't adjusted to the altitude," I said. "We live in Fort Worth, and that's not far above sea level."

"I've seen a lot of lowland dogs here," the owner said. "They generally do just fine, and even if they don't, they don't cough and vomit like that. That dog is sick."

I really didn't believe her. Pat, in my experience, is never sick, and he had started all this at about five thousand feet. Hoping I could find another place to take him, I passed the house that stood between the store and the veterinary clinic and took him on in, hoping they wouldn't tell me I had to make an appointment and come back later. As I explained to the receptionist what we were doing there, a large black cat that had been sleeping on the desk leaped lightly to the floor directly in front of Pat, and Pat, who hadn't seen a cat since he left home and was probably missing them, nosed the cat eagerly, clearly asking it to run so he could chase it. I did not echo the sentiment; the entire reception area had been carved out of what had apparently once been the small front room of a house. The waiting room was minuscule, and I was holding on to Pat's leash so firmly that I nearly backed into an ornate fireplace complete with mantel. Fortunately the cat declined; it simply lay down on the floor in front of the door and began to take a bath. Pat looked at me, frustrated, and I told him, "The cat doesn't want to play."

Cats are like that, Pat obviously thought. ("This does not fit my impression of a pit bull," Charlie admitted.) He sat down on the floor with a loudly disgusted thump and resumed coughing until he got in to see the vet, who diagnosed acute bronchitis and tonsillitis. "But I didn't even know dogs had tonsils," I protested.

"They do," the vet assured me, "and this is very contagious. I'm sorry, but I cannot allow this dog to be boarded anywhere at present. I'll get you ten days' worth of medicine for him, and then you'll have to take him home."

"Home," I said carefully, "is Fort Worth, Texas. And we're going to be in Salt Lake City a week."

"That sounds like a problem," the vet admitted, "but an animal with a contagious disease can't be admitted into a boarding facility. Surely you understand that. You'll have to find a private home, preferably one without a dog, to keep him. If he's not over this by the time he's taken all the medicine, or if he seems to pick it up again, you'll probably have to see your own vet about getting his tonsils out. But I'm sure you understand why I can't allow—"

Actually I could understand. My hunch was that Pat had caught the disease in a boarding facility in Carlsbad, New Mexico; the facility was one of several that advertised on enormous billboards, as people often travel with pets, which obviously they can neither leave in their cars nor take with them through the cavern, and I hadn't seen a veterinarian in attendance. I didn't want to be the one to pass anybody's bad deed along to someone else. So we departed, leaving the vet and his assistant disinfecting everything including the floor, and took with us a packet of pills to give Pat twice a day for the next ten days. I hoped Georgina had room in her refrigerator for a large chunk of cheese, because the only semi-easy way to get a pill down Pat is to hide it securely in a square of cheese, which he then gulps down too fast to notice the pill. Lori sat in the car and told Pat he was a good dog while I went into the pet store next door and bought Pat a heavy tie-down hook and a strong, and much longer, chain. Then I swung by the first grocery store I found, and Lori went in and bought the largest possible box of Velveeta while I sat in the car and told Pat he was a good dog.

I then went back to Georgina, leaving Pat alone in the car temporarily while Lori trailed behind me, and explained. Georgina said resignedly, "Well, put him somewhere in the front yard where he won't get tangled up with the Russian olive."

"Is that what I keep smelling?" I asked.

She nodded. "This time of the year they're almost cloyingly sweet. I get sick of it, myself. Anyhow, about the dog. If you put him sort of to the right of the house he can get up on the porch when he wants to get out of the rain but he won't be close enough to bother the postman—and come to think of it, as many burglaries as there are in the neighborhood, I ought to be thankful for a nice loud dog. He is loud, isn't he?"

"He's definitely loud," Harry agreed wryly, and then told me, "I would go attend to the tie-down hook, but—" He nodded toward Cameron, who had gone to sleep in his lap.

"I'll take care of it," Hal said with a quick glance at Alexandra, who was standing at the dining room table peeling potatoes. He seemed very nervous; unaccountably so, I thought for a second before Alexandra began to sound off.

"You do that," she yelled, her hazel eyes narrowing, glinting, and her voice this time carrying the uncertain harshness of a boy whose voice is in the process of changing. "I knew you'd run away. You're scared of me, aren't you?" She headed around the table toward him, still holding the paring knife, and Hal precipitated himself out the front door with Alexandra following him, and Georgina following her, before I could do more than take a step toward any of them. (Charlie sat up straighter, obviously paying close attention now.)

Lori yelled a loud and protesting "Hey!" as Georgina dashed out the kitchen door, through the dining room, through the living room, and out the door.

"Alexandra, you come back here!" she was shouting as she ran.

As I headed for the door myself, I heard Alexandra jeer, "You're just hiding behind the dog because you know I don't like dogs!"

"I'm taking care of the dog," Hal yelled back, "and I don't know what's the matter with you! How am I s'posed to know whether you like dogs or not? I don't even care! I told you I don't fight girls!"

"Alexandra, we do not ever run while carrying a knife!" Georgina shouted. "And besides, he's a missionary! How do we treat missionaries?"

"No, he isn't," Alexandra yelled back. "He's not a missionary! He's a boy!"

"Alexandra, come here right now!" Georgina roared, and this time presumably Alexandra obeyed, because Georgina came back in the house with one hand firmly around Alexandra's right wrist. I noticed that the paring knife was still in Alexandra's right hand, and shuddered slightly. "Now, you go back to your room and stay there until supper is ready," she said, deftly taking possession of the paring knife and putting it on the table.

Alexandra stomped up the stairs, and Georgina dropped into one of the living room chairs, which included faded red and gold brocade and mahogany Louis Quinze and faded electric-blue brocade and walnut Queen Anne chairs, all of which could have done with reupholstering ten years ago. Not knowing what to say in so bizarre a situation, I took the cheese out of Lori's hand and picked up the paring knife to cut off a chunk, in which I carefully hid the pill. When I got outside, Pat was sitting smugly on the porch out of the downpour while Hal, out in it, was screwing the tie-down hook into the ground with the chain already fastened to it. I gave Pat the cheese and then, while he was occupied with that, I went and unfastened the chain—this involved untangling it from around Hal (Charlie, not used to Hal, looked vaguely dazed at this description)—and looped it through the railings of the front porch for the moment.

Pat finished the cheese, and I heard the slight *thunk* as the pill dropped to the floor of the porch. Pat looked up at me expectantly.

He can't always manage to do this, but he's very proud of himself when he succeeds. If he can spit out the pill while consuming the cheese, he then gets more cheese.

Feeling like swearing, I took the soggy pill back inside, cut off another chunk of cheese, cut a hole in it, stuck the pill in the hole, and then jammed the cheese I had cut out of the hole back in so that the pill was totally sealed inside. I stood and watched as Pat, with sincere relish and the obvious pride of a dog who has put something over on his person, gobbled the cheese and, this time, the pill as well.

By now Hal was through screwing the hook into the ground; the hook seemed long and strong enough to hold even as wet as the ground was right now, and I untangled the chain from the porch railing and gave it to him. I stood on the porch watching him reattach the chain to the hook.

Then he went indoors and headed straight for the hot shower he definitely needed by now. Harry was gone—evidently upstairs to our bedroom—and Lori was now holding Cameron, who was still asleep. "Where's Georgina?" I asked, and Lori nodded toward the kitchen.

"Has anybody told you where our rooms are?" I asked.

"Second floor," Lori said. "The family's are on the third floor. I haven't gone to look yet, but Harry said y'all have the front right and I have the front left and Hal and Cameron have the back left. Hal said he put all the suitcases and stuff up there. There's supposed to be a couple coming later in the week, probably tomorrow, for their honeymoon that'll have the back right."

I did not envy anybody who tried to have their honeymoon in a house otherwise occupied by our family and an apparently demented woman, but I couldn't do anything about that. Leaving Lori to cope with Cameron—she holds him whenever she can, particularly since hugging Hal is no longer allowable—I went upstairs to see our bedroom for the first time. Harry was in it unpacking, which he theoretically had done already, except that he must have been holding Cameron most of the time Lori and I were gone. "I really don't think we ought to stay here," I said.

"We've already paid for it," he reminded me.

"Yeah, but—"

"And we can't afford a motel."

"Really we can," I pointed out. "We didn't want to spend the money, but we do have it." That was perfectly true; when he returned to work for his old employer, in a much better position, he had received a thousand-dollar-a-month raise, and our son-in-law Olead Baker was absolutely refusing to let us repay the money he had given us while Harry was out of work.

"So you want to go to a motel when we'd need at least three rooms and would have to figure out what to do with a sick dog."

"Harry, that woman was chasing Hal with a knife."

"That woman is demented, but—"

"I noticed that, and—"

"She doesn't do anything but yell. She was chasing Hal, but I doubt she even remembered she had a knife in her hand."

"I remember one case—"

"I know the case you're talking about," Harry said. "You've told me about it five hundred times. A woman was paring potatoes and her husband jumped on her and beat her up and she tried to ward off the blows and accidentally stabbed him in the heart, and if you believe that I've got some seafront property in Arizona I want to sell you. There's no similarity except Alexandra was paring potatoes. She wasn't that close to Hal . . ."

"I just don't like—"

"We're staying," Harry said with considerable finality.

Even then I probably could have argued him out of it, but it would have taken quite a lot of arguing and for the moment I didn't feel up to it. Maybe he was right. Maybe I was overreacting on the basis of my own background. ("Today he said he wished he'd listened to me," I told Charlie, who nodded.)

But I was too full of adrenaline to sit still. Heading back downstairs, I went into the kitchen to ask whether I could do anything to help, and Georgina answered, "No, that's all right."

"Well, since your sister seems to have bailed out . . ."

"I didn't really expect any help from her," Georgina said, sounding extremely weary and depressed. "I just hoped giving her the potatoes to peel would keep her out of trouble. As you can see, it didn't. I suppose you're wondering what's the matter with her."

"The question crossed my mind," I admitted. "I'm sorry to ask, but is she dangerous?"

("What did she say to that?" Charlie asked. I did not point out that Alexandra was the victim, not the killer, so the question was moot. Obviously he knew it. I'd have asked the same question; so often the cause of a murder is found in the personality of the victim.)

"Not so far as I know," Georgina said. "As I already mentioned to your husband, she yells a lot, but that's all. She used to be pretty cantankerous when she was a kid—even violent at times—but she's twenty-six now. I know it must have startled you when she took off after your son like that, but all she'd have done even if I hadn't brought her back in is yell. She has MPD. Do you know what that is?"

"Multiple personality disorder," I said. "Yes, I know what it is. Is she under a psychiatrist's care?"

"Oh, yes," Georgina said, "for all the good that does."

. . . . .

("I'll want to talk with her psychiatrist," Charlie said. "Do you know his name? Or her name?"

"I'm getting to that," I said. If Captain Millner can put up with my narrative style, so can Charlie Sosa.)

"MPD is terribly hard to treat," Georgina went on, "and Sa—Alexandra—is very volatile. It's not that she has so many different personalities; she just has a few. The problem is that she goes through them so fast. At home she can be three or four different people in an hour. What's really weird is that she holds down a job, and most of the time she doesn't switch while she's at work."

"Then she has some control over it," I said.

"Apparently. But it doesn't seem to be conscious control." Georgina sighed under her breath. "I suppose you wonder why we're trying to remember to call her Alexandra." *You suppose a lot of things, but this time you suppose correctly,* I thought without answering, and Georgina went on, "She has a twin sister, Cynthia. Nothing's wrong with her except depression, and being around Sandy much is enough to depress anybody, but when they were little, before San—Alexandra—developed her problems, our parents called them Sandy and Cindy. Now Hart Bivins—the psychiatrist; he's also an old friend—says it might help Alexandra to develop a sense of her self as distinguished from other selves if we remember always to call her Alexandra. I don't see that it's doing any good, frankly, but we pay Hart enough for the advice, I guess we'd better take it."

"At least it's worth trying," I agreed. "It must be difficult for you, trying to cope with her and run this place at the same time."

"It was easier when Dad was alive," she said, "but the only alternative is to put her in a hospital, and I can't afford to."

"I can understand that," I said, feeling like a garden of platitudes, and decided to change the subject. "Do let me help you with something; you look so overloaded, and I'm not used to just sitting around while other people work."

. . . . .

Glancing at my cane, she said, "Then it looks like maybe you'd better get used to it. Sorry, I know that sounded rude, but—"

"I had foot surgery in the spring," I explained, "and really I'm almost well now."

("I wondered about that," Charlie said.)

"It's nothing permanent," I added. "I just sort of lose my balance sometimes. But I'm fine when I'm not trying to walk."

She was determined that I should not help. I was determined I was going to help; at least it would give me something to do with my hands. In the end, I wound up sitting on a high stool making a large salad while Georgina did everything else.

Alexandra came back down for supper, and I think at that moment even I would have realized at once that she had MPD, because she was now completely different. She totally ignored Hal; she sat behind Cameron and tried to engage him in conversation as if she were the same age as he. Her eyes were wide; her voice was that of a five-year-old, and she ate rapidly, hunched over her food and glancing quickly around at everyone who spoke. After supper she said, "May I be excused?" Without waiting for an answer, she laid her napkin beside her plate, left her chair, and scurried back up to her third-floor room.

The altitude, and the hectivation of the day, had me exhausted, and after supper I went and unpacked what I expected to need the next day. Then I turned on the small television in our room—Georgina had advertised cable, but as I expected it was only minimal service—and checked the weather.

Low tonight, thirty-three degrees. High tomorrow, forty-seven degrees. Rain off and on all day Saturday, Sunday, and Monday. This is Utah, I thought unbelievingly. Everybody told me this is a desert. And in June? It should be hot and dry.

I went on and finished unpacking, hunting for what I knew quite well I had not packed. Of course we hadn't brought jackets.

Why should we? For Utah? In June?

Three

. . . . . .

By Saturday morning I had almost convinced myself that Harry was right that we should stay. Despite the lurid headlines one frequently sees about MENTAL PATIENT GOES ON RAMPAGE and so forth, your average mental patient in my experience at least is far more likely to be a victim than a danger to others. (Charlie nodded at that.) Yes, Alexandra had done a lot of shouting and yelling last night, but she'd also tried to dance and sing. Harry was undoubtedly right that she'd totally forgotten the paring knife was in her hand when she went after Hal. And what did she do to Hal? Really, no more than yell.

Surely Georgina, who seemed quite alert and was likely conscious of potential legal troubles, wouldn't have begun a guest house if she had any reason to anticipate serious problems from Alexandra. Surely I had no cause to feel as jumpy as I felt.

Or so I kept telling myself. Hal had no such compunctions. When I knocked on his bedroom door to be sure he was up, which he was, he jumped so violently that he hit his head on the shelf of the closet where he'd hung his shirts. When I asked him to go out and buy the jackets (which, as I have mentioned, turned out to be sweatshirts) he went gladly, but he shied like a half-blind horse at the staircase leading up to the third floor, where Georgina and Alexandra had their rooms. He did stop on the front porch to talk to Pat, but when he heard the front door open he was off to the van in half a second, not even pausing long enough to notice that it was only me taking the dog his food, water, and medicine.

Pat promptly succeeded in spitting out the pill again. In no mood to further spoil an already spoiled pooch and a half-spoiled morning, I simply opened his mouth and dropped the pill down his throat. Do not try this with a pit bull you do not know; their jaw power is proverbial. ("I wouldn't dream of it," Charlie assured me.) I went back in to bathe and dress Cameron; he at least was in a good mood, as he usually is in the morning. I knew Lori would be glad to do it, but she was still asleep, and anyway, it was pleasant to associate with someone in a good mood just for a momentary change.

Not that Harry was in any way crabby. He just wasn't quite there. Having neither ham radios nor computerized bulletin boards nor people around various other campfires to talk with last night, he had wound up sitting up until the wee small hours of the morning watching the late late late show (in Georgina's parlor, of course, not in the bedroom where I was sleeping), and now was moving as if he had left his brain in Fort Worth.

Finally realizing I would have to wake Lori if I expected her to get up, I did so, and she crawled out of bed with every evidence of extreme drowsiness, which was doubtless an accurate impression, or of course she'd have awakened when I was dressing Cameron, a noisy undertaking at best. She is still on antidepressants since her mother's suicide (Charlie lifted his eyebrows at that—actually one eyebrow; he does the Spock bit to perfection—but said nothing), and they tend to make a person drowsy in the morning. The night's commotion had resulted in her taking hers three hours late—but Cameron, as I said, is very loud while being dressed. I pointed her in the direction of the bathroom, suggesting she arouse herself up by washing her face with cold water. As it happened, the moment her feet landed on the icy hardwood floor she snapped wide-awake, but that didn't mean she was in any way in motion or dressed.

I went back to see if Harry was dressing, which he was not, and suggested that a bed-and-breakfast, being at least a semipublic place, might not be the best place for him to appear at a meal in his pajamas, no matter how much a concession to modesty the pajamas might be in place of the Skivvies he normally wore to bed. He yawned widely, agreed, and headed toward the bathroom, which Lori, also still in pajamas, had just vacated.

I was beginning to feel just a little bit like screaming. Our first day in Salt Lake City, all the sight-seeing we'd planned to do, and my family individually and collectively was acting as if it were still the middle of the night.

Then I told myself I was too uptight. I really shouldn't be this way; I should go with the flow more. After all, we were on vacation. And although ten o'clock Salt Lake time—which was when I had sent Hal after jackets or sweatshirts—was eleven o'clock Fort Worth time and we're normally all up and moving by then, we'd spent most of the last week and a half sleeping on the ground—all right, in sleeping bags, but even with a ground cloth I had certainly felt as if I were sleeping directly on hard cold dirt—and we were all tired. I would calm down. Definitely I would calm down. I would quit hassling the family.

With that resolve, I went to see whether Lori was dressed, which she was in the process of becoming, and whether Hal was back with the jackets, which he was not, and whether Harry was dressed, which this time he was. By now Cameron was running up and down the stairs in great delight, as we do not have stairs at home and he rarely gets to play on them. I tried to corral him, but Georgina said, "Don't worry, everybody's up anyway. Unless you're afraid he'll fall."

All right, I was. But he was, after all, four years old and I was being silly.

We did all manage to assemble ourselves at the breakfast table eventually—about ten-thirty—and our lateness was just as well, as Georgina too appeared to be running late. Alexandra, I was pleased to note, was dressed in denim jeans and a red T-shirt, briskly setting the table and remembering to ask all of us whether we wanted milk, orange juice, water, or coffee. She did not seem disposed to argue with or attack anybody, including Hal, who had returned with the sweatshirts and was not delighted to see Alexandra, no matter how sensibly she was dressed and conducting herself.

But he apparently decided he would behave himself at the breakfast table if it killed him; besides that, he was hungry. Hal is *always* hungry. The rest of us are hungry at more or less conventional times, but our bodies were still running on Central time. Some or all of us might still be sleepy, but it was past breakfast time and actually nearly lunchtime for all of us, and we dived in. We had pancakes with maple syrup (fortunately Georgina, apparently anticipating that not all of her guests would like the calories in regular syrup, also had the light kind, which is the only kind I like), small link sausages, and scrambled eggs with some sort of small cubical crunchy fried potatoes mixed in with them. Alexandra ate neatly, made some small conversation, and remained calm.

Sometime during breakfast Hal noticed an array of sports trophies in a glass case in the dining room, along with numerous photographs of individual girls and whole teams of girls with softballs and bats, basketballs, and volleyballs, and asked about them. I suspected that was more to make conversation than because he was really interested, but Alexandra replied, "Oh, yes, all us girls learned to play softball and all that other stuff when we were just little things. We used to take part in pitching contests and that sort of thing, and we nearly always won. I won more than anybody else. I'm a real good pitcher, aren't I, Georgina?"

"Indeed you are," Georgina agreed. "You always were the best of us all."

"Daddy taught us. Daddy taught me 'specially," she said in a little-girl voice. "Daddy liked me best, didn't he, Georgina?"

"I always thought so," Georgina said enigmatically.

Alexandra's face had changed subtly, I noticed as she said to Georgina, in a little-girl voice, "Why did Daddy have to die?"

"He was old, Alexandra," Georgina said, making her voice superficially soothing despite a frazzled undertone Alexandra probably wouldn't be able to hear. "Old people die."

"Mommy wasn't old, and she died."

"That was different."

"I want my *daddy,"* Alexandra wailed, throwing down her fork and leaving a trail of syrup and butter across the immaculate white tablecloth Georgina had put over the dark walnut table. "You let them take my daddy away, and I want my daddy back."

"I can't do anything about that," Georgina said. "They took Daddy away because he died, and I can't change that. And if you don't want to leave the table, you must behave now."

"Is he with the ghosts?"

"There aren't any ghosts," Georgina said.

"There's the Holy Ghost, so there!"

"That means spirit, not dead person." Georgina was remaining a lot calmer than I would have been under similar circumstances.

"My mommy's ghost talks to me."

"She can't, Alexandra, she's dead and there is no such thing as a ghost."

"There are ghosts in the cemetery," Alexandra insisted.

"No, there aren't."

"There are too. I look out my window and see them all the time."

"Alexandra, you're being silly. Hush now and eat your breakfast. I don't want to hear any more about ghosts."

Alexandra finished the meal in total silence, eating rapidly, her eyes darting from one of us to another as each person spoke. Georgina, giving no indication of even noticing, went on talking to us, telling us different places she thought we might find interesting.

Unfortunately, Alexandra was listening too.

That didn't matter to us right then, and I didn't notice, as I went to rebathe and re-dress Cameron, a procedure always necessary after pancakes, that Alexandra had vanished. Of course if I had noticed, I probably would have been relieved.

What Alexandra had overheard began to matter as we toured Trolley Square, only a few blocks from Georgina's. Georgina had told us it was built in the old trolley barns, and Harry, after examining it, announced that it is Salt Lake City's answer to Ghirardelli Square in San Francisco, where he has been and I have not. We found it touristy and expensive but fun withal—Harry especially was entranced by the display box into which he inserted a quarter and got to watch trains run and lights flash—except for the fact that everywhere we looked there was Alexandra, looking like a pixie in childlike pink flowered shorts and top with lace at the hem, pink and white snow boots, and a dark blue jacket and hood with a pom-pom on it, dodging in and out trying to look at us without our seeing her. *Does this woman have an unlimited wardrobe for every one of her personas,* I wondered but did not ask. Hal jumped every time he saw her, and soon he began jumping even when he *didn't* see her, every time he caught a quick movement out of the corner of his eye.

Lori tried to take his hand and he pulled away from her, muttering, "Can't."

Even under this stress he was remembering that he was presently a missionary. I was proud of him but heartily sick of Alexandra. No matter how often, and how fervently, I assured myself that the woman was mentally ill and not responsible for her actions, I couldn't help thinking that rarely before in my life had I met such a total nuisance. ("But people don't usually get murdered just for being a nuisance," Charlie pointed out, with which I had to agree.)

When we got in the car and drove downtown, to park in ZCMI Mall and walk over to Temple Square, we thought we were rid of her. We watched videos, stared at dioramas, admired statues. But we had forgotten about the buses and the trolley that runs from Trolley Square to all hotels and downtown locations every fifteen minutes or so. And for all practical purposes Alexandra knew our itinerary.

After a while there it was again, that pixie head in the blue hood popping out from shrubbery, peeping around corners, following us through dioramas.

For a wonder, she didn't follow us as we went up the long ramp to the Christus statue. ("That's interesting," Charlie said. "Wonder why not?") We sat for nearly half an hour in the peace of that quiet room, looking at the calm of the statue against its backdrop of the stars and planets and nebulae of the universe, until Cameron began to squirm and reluctantly we went back down the ramp—to find Alexandra waiting for us, sitting composedly in a chair in the Visitors' Center.

She followed us over to Crossroads Mall, where, in view of what he called our dwindling money supply, though it wasn't actually dwindling that badly, Harry felt constrained to decide we should lunch at McDonald's. I felt constrained to offer Alexandra a hamburger too, for which everybody else in the family glared at me, but Alexandra politely refused. She went and waited outside in the corridor and ate candy, a five-year-old waiting until her friend's dinner was finished so her friend could come out and play again.

After we sat down with our hamburgers, Hal commented, "Mom, if that woman keeps pestering people like that, sooner or later somebody's going to kill her. And I really truly mean that."

. . . . .

"I'm surprised somebody hasn't already," Harry agreed, and took a large bite of cheeseburger.

"We have to remember she's not doing it on purpose," I said, trying to sound somewhat more tolerant than I felt.

"The hell she isn't," Hal said violently, and then put his hand over his mouth. "Oops."

"I think oops," Harry said dryly. "For what purpose did we make this trip? Or is that appropriate missionary language?"

"I said 'oops,' " Hal pointed out indignantly.

("And, of course, Hal was right," Charlie pointed out. "But I suppose the real question is not how annoying she was, but what she found out and how serious it was." I agreed to that. A nosy person is usually just a pest, but sometimes—quite inadvertently—that kind of pest can turn into a real danger to somebody. And that's when murder happens. At least that's one of the whens.)

I'd listened to Hal and Harry snipe at each other quite long enough, and decided it was time to change the subject. I tried baseball. That usually works. It worked this time, and soon Harry and Hal were discussing the pennant race, which was yet months off, trying to decide who would win the World Series before they even knew who would get into the World Series, and for the moment at least both Hal's inadvertent profanity and Alexandra's tenacity were forgotten.

We finished our lunch and went back out into the mall, where Alexandra promptly resumed following us. I decided it would be a little less unnerving if she actually walked with us, so I invited her to join us. "Georgina says I can't annoy the guests," she said, "so I guess not." And she went right on following us.

Crossing a few more streets, we went to first to the Joseph Smith Memorial Building to see a video about the pioneers, then to Beehive House, where Brigham Young had lived with one of his wives and some ten or twelve of his children. Many more of his wives had lived in Lion House next door, but that wasn't available for touring. He had, the tour guide told us, given a separate house and farm to every one of his wives who had children; the childless wives in Lion House had helped him to administer the Church, the territory, and later the state.

She went on to tell us that Brigham Young had been a firm believer in the abilities and rights of women: he'd said repeatedly that there was no reason whatever why a woman shouldn't be just as competent a doctor, lawyer, or merchant as a man. He'd sent several women back East to medical school when the idea of women doctors was still totally horrifying to most of the United States, and women in Utah before statehood had had the vote. Of course, they'd lost it when Utah became a state, and didn't get it back again for quite some time.

She told us also that if Brigham Young had had his way, Utah, Idaho, and parts of several other states would have all been the state of Deseret, an ancient Egyptian word meaning "the Land of the Honeybee." Not that there were any honeybees in Utah until the settlers brought them here, but rather, the honeybee, a diligent worker, had been adopted as a symbol of the intention of the newly settled area.

All this was quite interesting, and I'd probably have found it even more so if I hadn't constantly been watching with my peripheral vision to see where Alexandra was going to pop up next. Right now she seemed to think she was five years old and she seemed to want to play with Cameron and otherwise be treated as a child, but Georgina had warned me of her volatility and I had already seen it for myself. I was worried about what she might do if she changed personalities, and from what Georgina had told me I hadn't seen all her personalities yet. (Charlie made a note on his desk pad. My guess was he was reminding himself to find out about the rest of Alexandra's personalities.)

Alexandra, momentarily ignoring all of us, grabbed one of the find-it sheets handed out to children and then crowded into the front of the group in every room, eagerly marking to show she had found Sister Young's black silk dress, President Young's grandfather clock, the best dinner china, and all the other items on the sheet. She followed us through the entire tour, which ended in the little store Brigham Young had kept for his wives and children to get their dry goods, food staples, and the like without having to go to public markets. She snatched the free sample of horehound candy and sucked on it eagerly (I found it nasty-tasting, and was very puzzled at the story of the one naughty Young daughter who, every time she went to the store to get cloth or thread, would add a pound of horehound candy to her list thinking she was getting away with it).

Out in the garden, Alexandra suddenly switched modes. Up until now she had been, so far as I could tell, the child Alexandra, playing tag with people she was curious about. Now, suddenly, the belligerent Alexandra was back. She swaggered up to Hal and demanded, "Why are you running away from me?"

"I'm not running away from you," Hal mumbled, manifestly doing exactly that. To be precise, he moved halfway behind Lori, apparently assuming that since Alexandra so far had left Lori alone she could be trusted to continue to do so.

Which she did; in fact, to judge from her actions, she wasn't even aware Lori was there. "You're scared of me! You're scared I'll beat you up!" The woman, her voice again that of an adolescent boy, danced around like a boxer, her scrawny fists clenched.

I glanced around for Harry, but he was still in the store, Cameron having taken an inexplicable liking to the horehound candy. Obviously, it was time for me to step in. "Alexandra," I said, in my sternest voice, "you go home right now."

I should have done it hours earlier. She went. Not, I was to discover later, home, but at least she went away and left us alone.

The rest of our day was somewhat quieter. We went to see Brigham Young's grave, on a grassy knoll that, before the city had grown up, would have been visible from Beehive House. Several of his wives, including Eliza Snow, author of some of the church's most beloved hymns, were buried there also, and it was a quiet, peaceful spot.

We had contracted to eat supper Saturday night with Georgina, and she'd told us she planned to serve at six. We made it back with ten minutes to spare, only enough time to wash up.

At least we would have had time to wash up by six. There was an unfamiliar car parked in the driveway. Assuming it was the honeymooners who were expected today, I thought nothing of it, nor did Harry, who simply parked at the curb. Although it was early evening, daylight savings time (for which I frequently curse the name of Benjamin Franklin), and very near the summer solstice, the clouds had continued to darken until it seemed late evening, a cold wet evening in winter, and the yellow porch light was welcome.

Pat was whining and jumping on his chain, and we realized why when we took two more steps toward the house, because by then we could hear the shouting.

". . . my house too, and . . ."

"It is *not* your house," Georgina shouted. "My father—"

"I put up the money to buy out Cindy, and you were glad enough to take—" The male voice was hoarse with anger.

"It was a *loan,* and I . . ."

"Needed it. I know. You needed it if you were going to have your bed-and-breakfast. Well, Georgia girl, you put it in joint tenancy when you took the money."

"I know, but—"

"Look, I'm not trying to rain on your parade. You're welcome to keep the bed-and-breakfast; I'll live up on the third floor with you, and I'll keep my day job just like I always have and just come home at night. I won't be in the guests' way. It's not as if we were strangers," the male voice went on, slightly more calmly. "Or have you forgotten you're my—"

. . . . .

"I haven't forgotten anything," Georgina said, her voice sounding indescribably weary. "Cully, you don't understand—"

"You're damn right about that," the male voice—Cully—said. "I don't understand how a woman could turn away from her husband for—"

"I'm not turning away from you! Cully, I told you you don't understand. You've just got to be patient. It isn't *safe* right now."

"*What* isn't safe? Look, if you'd just get rid of Sandy . . ."

"What do you suggest I do with her?" Georgina asked. "She's my responsibility."

Harry touched my arm and gestured toward the car. I nodded, and had turned to head back to it, making shooing-chicken motions at the children and barely hearing the male voice ask, "When does she get to be somebody else's responsibility?" when the front door opened and Georgina and the man, who was about six feet tall, a hundred and eighty pounds, with blue eyes that might normally have looked friendly, and curly dark blond hair, came out on the front porch.

"Oh, hello, Deb, Harry," Georgina said, her voice pitched so high it was on the verge of hysteria. "I was beginning to worry you wouldn't make it to supper. This is Cully Grafton, and he's just leaving. Do come on up on the porch and get out of this awful rain! I'm beginning to wonder if we're going to have any summer at all this year!"

We were caught. We couldn't retreat now without making things worse. So, reluctantly at least on my part, we went up on the porch, where the dog was ecstatic to have all his people back. (Cully and Georgina weren't his people and didn't count, but they were out of the reach of his chain.)

"I'm Georgina's husband," Cully said, "and Georgina is mistaken. I'm *not* just leaving." Georgina looked at him. "I thought I'd at least stay for supper," he said blandly.

"Well, if you insist . . ." Georgina said. I supposed she was trying

. . . . .

to surrender gracefully; her enthusiasm was underwhelming. "Oh, Deb, have you seen Alexandra? She left this morning and hasn't come back yet."

"We saw her at Trolley Square, and downtown," I said, without going into detail.

"Well, that's okay then, she likes to spend Saturday just roaming around. It's just, usually she's back for supper, and—oh, there she is! Alexandra, did you *walk?*"

Alexandra, walking up the driveway in a drenched jacket and cap and ignoring Georgina's question, stopped short at the sight of Cully. "You don't live here anymore," she said.

"Thanks to you," Cully agreed, his eyes visibly narrowing in the porch light.

"I don't like you!" I couldn't tell which Alexandra we were hearing now, the frightened child or the belligerent boy. "I told Georgina to make you go away!"

"Oh, did you now," Cully said. "Well, I've got news for you. Your sister's grown up. She's allowed to have a husband if she wants to. And she wants to."

"Oh no she doesn't!"

"Suppose we let her speak for herself," Cully suggested. He swung around toward Georgina. "How about it?"

"Cully, I can't handle this right now," Georgina said. "Oh, let's go eat, maybe then we can all think better. Alexandra, go get into some dry clothes at once and come back down to dinner."

"Remember I want tea," Cully said.

"I'll make you tea." That caused another ten-minute delay, during which Cully, Georgina, and Alexandra, when she returned in flowered flannelette pajamas, continued sniping at one another, and I continued to lose what was left of my appetite. Lori and Hal both looked totally wretched, Harry acted as alert as if this were a military training exercise, and only Cameron seemed his usual self. But eventually even he began crying. No wonder—even by Utah time, which his body was not set for, it was well past his bedtime and he hadn't even had supper yet.

Supper temporarily revived my appetite. The main dish was a delicious casserole of lean ground beef, chopped onions, and brown rice rolled into balls that Georgina called porcupines, cooked in a spicy tomato sauce, and I resolved to get the recipe. With it she served homemade bread, baked potatoes with regular and no-fat sour cream, butter, light margarine, and bacon bits, and a vegetable compote, along with a relish tray of green and black olives, celery and carrot sticks, and something else crunchy and white that I didn't recognize. I'd have asked her except that she seemed totally distracted, trying to keep Cully and Alexandra from attacking each other.

On the surface, that didn't seem necessary. Cully apparently had decided to regard himself as our host, and was exerting his charm to the utmost. He offered me tea. I refused it. He poured it anyway. Georgina said, "Cully, she's a Mormon."

Cully apologized, took the tea to the kitchen and poured it out, and brought me a fresh glass, which he refilled with the fruit punch that was on the table along with the tea. "Anybody besides me want tea?" he asked.

Harry, who actually would rather have had the tea than the fruit punch, refused, presumably because he didn't like Cully, and we all drank fruit punch.

It seemed to me the place was swirling with undercurrents I couldn't identify. If I had correctly figured out the sequence—and I thought I had, because the argument we'd walked in on had been pretty explicit and the discussion at the table continued so—Cully and Georgina had been married several years ago. They'd lived in this house, comparatively amicably despite Alexandra's resentment, until Georgina's father died, at which time Georgina had insisted with no real explanation that Cully move out for a while. It didn't make sense to Cully and frankly, it didn't make sense to me.

. . . . .

Nor did the quarreling, coupled with Cully's elephantine attempts at geniality, add to the pleasure and comfort of the meal. I think we were all glad to get away from the table. But the quarreling continued on into the living room, where Cully demanded, "Where'd you hide my whiskey?"

"I haven't done anything to your whiskey," Georgina said. "It's wherever you left it."

Cully opened the door of an old-fashioned floor radio that had been transformed into a liquor cabinet, found a half-gallon bottle of Canadian Club, and poured—and drank—what looked to me like an iced tea glass full. It must have been close to twenty ounces, and there wasn't even any ice in the glass. Mentally I cringed; even in the days when I did drink, that much would have had me out like a light. "Anybody want some?" he asked, waving the bottle around.

Nobody answered, and he gestured toward Harry. "You look like a man to me. How about a shot?"

Not having changed religion when the rest of the family did, Harry has not totally stopped drinking. But he's choosy about his drinking buddies. He replied, "Your idea of a shot and mine don't jibe. I'll pass, thanks."

Cully poured himself a second glass, and then, ignoring Harry's refusal, poured him a full glass and set it down beside him, where Harry ostentatiously ignored it.

By now Alexandra was sitting down on the floor behind the couch, curled up like a pretzel in training, with her right thumb stuck in her mouth. With her left hand, she began twirling a lock of hair.

Cully was getting louder again, and Georgina sat down on the couch and put her hands over her ears. "Cully, please go away! You didn't used to drink like this!" she shouted.

"I didn't used to drink like this because my own sweet—dear—little wife didn't try to show me the door every time I came in sight. Damn it, you're still my wife and I'm still your husband, and you don't make a hill of beans of sense telling me it's not safe for me to be here. Not safe for who? That crazy bitch behind the couch? Then send her away. Not safe for me? What's going to happen to me? Not safe for you? You keep on trying to get rid of me and you'll think not safe. The hell I'll go away," Cully yelled. "I'll knock your block off if you try to give me marching orders."

Harry stood. "Mr. Grafton," he said, "far be it from me to interfere between husband and wife, but I really can't sit here and listen to you threaten—"

"Then I suggest you go upstairs where you don't have to listen," Cully said, choosing his words and enunciating them with the extra care of a man who was by now completely drunk. "I intend to get to the bottom of this. If I can't live in my own house, I damn well intend to find out why."

"Alexandra, go upstairs," Georgina said. "Harry, Deb, it's all right, he won't . . ."

Alexandra didn't budge. She went right on sucking her thumb and twirling her hair. I didn't know what Georgina was going to say Cully wouldn't do, but whatever it was I suspect she was mistaken, because right then he swung at her. She backed out of the way quickly enough, nearly falling off the couch in the process, and Hal stood too. At six foot seven, he towered over Cully Grafton. "I think you'd better leave now," Harry said.

Harry knows how to make it clear he means business, and Hal doesn't need anything but his size to intimidate anybody. Between the two of them, they convinced Cully Grafton he'd do well to depart.

That did not, we all knew, mean that he would not decide to return an hour later. Drunks are unpredictable, and Cully, despite a surface charm, obviously turned into a mean drunk.

"I'm sorry," Georgina said, flinging herself back down on the couch and bursting into tears.

. . . . .

Harry, who hates it when anybody cries around him and he can't do anything to comfort the person, turned abruptly and drank out of the glass Cully had poured for him. He did not drink all of it; nobody I knew would, and I realized belatedly that I should have thought of something better to do than let Cully get out on the road in that condition. ("You sure should have," Charlie agreed.)

"Lori," Harry said, "why don't you go up and take your imipramine?"

"I already took it," she said in a rather colorless voice. "I had it in my purse. Hal, let's go get Cameron ready for bed."

"I think I'd better stay here a while longer," Hal said grimly. "He might come back. You go on."

Lori took a deep breath. "Alexandra, do you want to come help me?"

Alexandra uncurled herself from behind the couch and said, "Yeah" in a very cheerful voice. She trotted after Lori like a five-year-old.

"Maybe I shouldn't have tried this at all," Georgina said, her voice muffled behind the Kleenex she had grabbed. "Maybe it was a losing game to start with. You certainly ought not to have to pay to stay in a madhouse. Anyway, a B and B has to have repeat business to survive, and it's a sure thing nobody's going to want to come back. Not with Alexandra acting like she's acting—she was a lot better for so long, she's gone downhill so far since Daddy died—and Cully coming over and getting drunk. He didn't use to be like that; I wouldn't have married him if he had been—I knew he wasn't in the Church but he seemed so nice, and he really was until all this happened. If I could just make him understand, I don't want him to stay gone forever, just till I can get Alexandra under control again."

"How long has your father been dead?" I asked, thinking to myself that if I were married to somebody who acted the way Cully was acting I'd want him gone permanently.

. . . . .

"Six weeks. Just six weeks. I keep thinking Alexandra'll get better again, but it's like he was the only one holding her together—and I don't want to put her in an institution, I don't know what I'd pay for it with. I wish to goodness somebody would *really* do something about the health-care mess in this country—"

"I think everybody wishes that," Harry said, obviously relieved that she had finally stopped crying and was onto a subject everybody discusses all the time.

I looked around for Hal and didn't see him. Then I heard unmistakable sounds from the kitchen.

Hal was doing the dishes.

Wonders never cease.

(Charlie didn't reply to that. Instead he said, "So Cully Grafton sees—saw—Alexandra as standing between him and his wife and home?" I nodded, and Charlie said, "I think I better locate Cully Grafton and have a nice long talk with him."

"I'd do it if I were you," I agreed, at which Charlie looked at me rather sharply.)

. . . . .

Four

. . . . .

"ANYTHING ELSE YOU can think of?" Charlie asked finally, after I had walked him on through Sunday morning.

Visualizing the scene, I nodded. "Where was her purse?" Charlie said nothing; he continued to look at me, as I said slowly, feeling my way, "She had a purse at church. I remember. It was white, an envelope bag with a shoulder strap"—I wound up having to draw him a picture of an envelope bag before he could figure out what I meant; I still say men and women don't speak the same language—"and it looked like leather with brass fittings. It was pretty new, I think, because it wasn't scuffed any. She had it at church, but it wasn't by the body, and if it was in the park anywhere I didn't see it."

"Neither did I," Charlie agreed. "So you think the killer took it?"

That would be the most obvious explanation, but I wasn't sure it was the right explanation. *Did* the killer take it? Or did she take it home and leave it there and go back out? But if she did that, why didn't she change clothes at the same time? That frilly organdy dress certainly wasn't well suited for stalking purposes, and if she went back to the park looking for us, then stalking was what she was doing. And anyway, if she did that where were her keys, because I hadn't seen any beside the body, and Georgina kept the house locked and insisted that Alexandra take her keys everywhere she went; she'd issued keys to Harry, me, Hal, and Lori as well, so that we could get in if we stayed out later than she stayed up. I remembered Alexandra's keys yesterday at the mall, clipped onto the zipper of her jacket and clanking everywhere she went. I mentioned that to Charlie, and he nodded again.

"Well, we'll see if it's at the house," Charlie said, and stood. "I should say 'they'—the purse and the keys both—but my guess is the keys will be with the purse. If they're not at the house, I'll check the park again before we get too hasty. I suppose you're about ready to go."

I was well past ready to go, and had been since I'd gotten there, but saying that to him would have been unkind and unnecessary. He hadn't wanted another murder on his plate right now, any more than I wanted one when I was supposed to be on vacation.

Indications of personal ownership were all over the unmarked sedan we got into: a dry-cleaning bag on the floor of the backseat, various personal property—driving gloves, a box of ammo (the police here had gone into automatics, I noticed, as they were doing most places and I was still resisting because the only automatic I ever owned jammed on the third shot of every second clip no matter how many new clips I bought it), a set of scriptures in a brown zipped leather bag, and a small pocket hymnal—strewn on the front seat and sticking out of the open glove box, and I must have looked puzzled, because Charlie said, "You don't have take-home cars in Fort Worth?"

I shook my head. "Not unless you're pretty high up the totem pole, anyway. Or unless you're in an on-call status, and then you just have it temporarily."

"We do here. Everybody does."

"Even the uniform officers?"

"Even the uniform officers," he confirmed. "The city decided instead of investing in more officers they'd invest in more cars. That way if somebody's off duty—on his way to the grocery store, say—

and something goes down he can handle it right then. Or if somebody has to get called from home, he doesn't have to run into the station first and get a car. Effectively, everybody's on duty all the time if he—or she—is driving. The idea is it gives a small department the effect of being a much larger one."

"Must use up a lot of overtime," I said.

"Some," he admitted, "but it's probably not as expensive as hiring that many new officers."

"So how does the system work?" I asked.

He shrugged. "Pretty well, actually, though it would work a lot better if we had that hundred and fifty-five more officers the city's not likely to approve. But people do like having the cars. Of course you're not supposed to take a city car out of the metro area without permission, but all the same it keeps most people from having to buy a second family car, and that's a big savings in family budgets. Me, I don't have a car of my own. Just a motorcycle. I don't go out of the city much in the winter anyway, and if I need to I rent a car. Spring, summer, fall, what the hey? It's just me. I can go on a bike. Bear Lake, Wendover, wherever. Even up in the mountains camping. Just throw a one-man tent and a few supplies into the saddlebags and take off. Now—" His face clouded a little.

"Now what?" I asked. This was going to be a short conversation—we had already pulled up in front of Georgina's—but he looked troubled enough that I thought I ought to be sympathetic.

"Now my son thinks he's going to come and live with me," Charlie said abruptly. "And I don't know what I'm going to do about it. If he stays of course I'll get a car, I can afford one easily enough, that's not the problem."

"He's been with his mother?" I decided not to ask what the problem was. Somehow I had a hunch I was just about to hear.

"He's been with his grandmother," Charlie said. "I was in the Army when he was born. His mother died when he was two, walking across a street to buy a carton of milk and some lettuce and tomatoes from a convenience store, and hit by a drunk driver. She had John with her in a stroller—he was to the age he was fussing about being in a stroller, but she didn't figure she could cope with him and the groceries both at once, so she put him in the stroller and put her purse and the groceries in this little basket at the back of the stroller. At least that was what the storekeeper said. She shoved the stroller out of the way when she saw the car coming. She had time to get John out of the way, but not herself. I was overseas then. She'd been living with her mother, on the reservation. It looked—best—for the boy to stay with his grandmother. He already knew her. He didn't really know me. And I couldn't take him where I was stationed; I wasn't high enough rank to have my family with me unless I paid their way, and on an E-Three's salary you don't take your family to Frankfurt. I probably could have gotten a compassionate discharge to take care of him, but I'd still have had to work somewhere and he'd have still been left with a baby-sitter too much of the time. And I thought—see, I was in the Indian Placement Program. You know what that was?" He'd draped his arms across the steering wheel and was looking directly at me in the pale afternoon rainlight.

I shook my head.

"Then you haven't been in the Church long."

"No, not very. But I think you guessed that already."

"Well, the schools used to be pretty lousy on the reservations. Some still are, for that matter, but most are better now. So a lot of kids were—and still are, for that matter—sent to boarding schools, which tend to break up the family horribly, and depending on who ran the boarding school you were indoctrinated into whatever they wanted you to think. Most of them were religious schools, except for the few the government ran, which tried for the most part to eradicate any sense of your own people. Anyhow, the LDS Church didn't have boarding schools. Instead, for twenty or so years, they—the Church—would take Indian children—mostly Navajo, but some other tribes too—off the reservation, with their parents' consent, and send them to live with some nice Anglo Mormon family, mostly in Utah or Idaho, where they could get a better education and learn to function in the white man's world. It was better than the boarding schools, of course, because you were still in a family even if it wasn't your own family and you were living in the real world instead of the artificial universe of a boarding school, but—well, I got a better education than I'd have had on the reservation, there's no doubt about that. And I love my foster parents. But my real mom and dad died when I was nine years old. Nobody knew what killed them, then; my Little Father, that's my mother's oldest brother, my old uncle, insisted they'd been witched, but looking back on it I wouldn't be surprised if it was that hantavirus you hear so much about now. From what little I know, the symptoms fit it, and no telling how long a virus like that could be on the reservation without anybody noticing or caring. The fact that the medicine men, the singers, connected the deaths with the weather makes sense, and suggests their traditions already knew this cycle existed."

"It doesn't make sense to me," I said. "The weather increased the piñon crop, I read, but the scientists say the mice that carry the virus don't eat piñon nuts."

"True. But suppose you're a predator, and if you have a chance to choose you'll eat a nice, fat rodent that *does* eat piñon nuts, but if you can't get one, then you'll eat any rodent you can get hold of. This year there's a good crop of piñon nuts, so there's a large population of the piñon-eating rodents. So you eat them, and you leave the other rodents alone. So the other rodent population increases also, and that's the rodent population that carries hantavirus."

"Maybe," I said, not fully convinced, although his suggestion actually did sound reasonable. I suppose my problem was that if that was true, I couldn't see why the scientists hadn't thought of it.

"Anyway, back to the Indian Placement Program. The way the

program worked, most of the kids would go home in the summer, so they'd stay in touch with both worlds, but after that, I didn't, except one year I went and spent a few weeks with my uncle and that didn't work because I was too far out of touch already, and he stayed mad at me all the time because I couldn't follow the traditional ways. Couldn't, because I couldn't remember what they were, but he saw it as wouldn't. And so, I lost track of my roots. I don't speak Navajo anymore, and let me tell you, linguists say it's the hardest language in the world to learn. It's got noun and pronoun numbers and inflections and verb tenses that don't even exist in English or in any other language linguists have found except Apache, and Navajo and Apache are closer related than Spanish and Portuguese. I'm not going to sit down now and learn it from scratch. So—I'm not really Navajo anymore in the sense of being connected to the nation. But I'm sure as hell not white."

"So you left your son with your mother-in-law, hoping he'd grow up—whole."

"Yeah," Charlie said. "I'm neither fish nor fowl. Maria, my wife, she was Mormon too, we were married in the Arizona Temple, but she was part of the nation. Her mother's traditional Navajo. In the Navajo a child belongs to its mother's clan. I don't even *know* my clan. My uncle should have taught me all that, but he didn't. My son belongs to Maria's clan, which is Maria's mother's clan."

"What does that mean, your mother-in-law being traditional Navajo?"

"It means a lot of things. As I said, a kid belongs to his mother's clan. So my wife belonged to her mother's clan, and my son belongs to that clan. Obviously I could find out what clan I belong to, but—it doesn't seem to mean anything to me, because I don't know what it means to be one clan or another clan, except I feel like it ought to. My uncle—I shouldn't really say he didn't teach me because I think he tried to, but he was telling me in Navajo and by then I couldn't even speak Navajo and he wouldn't translate it into English because he thought I was stubborn, just refusing to admit I understood him. I remember when I was a little kid, before we were into the Church, my father was always busy with clan stuff, but I wasn't in his clan. Not that I was left out completely, Navajos are sociable people during any kind of ceremonials—like to live alone in small family groups, but the more people you have at a sing the better it's supposed to work. My Little Father always told me he'd teach me about the clan when I was older, but by the time I was older, I wasn't really Navajo. So that's one thing it means—my son is in touch with his clan, although I'm not, and he's closer to Maria's older brother than he is to me. Maria's brother doesn't like me, by the way. Another thing it means is that I've never laid eyes on her, my mother-in-law, I mean. Traditional Navajo, a woman's mother and her husband never meet. So if I was going to the reservation to visit John, I'd have to meet with him outside in the bower while my mother-in-law was inside the hogan, or I'd have to go sit in the car while she walked over to somebody else's hogan and then I could go in to talk with John. John's grown up more fragmented than me, rather than less. He hates his mother for dying. He hates me for leaving him on the reservation. He hates his grandmother and uncle for keeping him on the reservation. He hates the Church and his clan, quite impartially, for not making him happy and he hates the world for not running the way he wants it to. He told me he hates the schools on the reservation. So I said he was plenty old enough not to need a baby-sitter while I was working, so he was welcome to come and stay with me and go to school. I told him I'd love to have him do it. I moved out of the one-bedroom apartment I'd had since I got back to Salt Lake City and got a two-bedroom and got him furniture and so forth. So he came here and stayed two weeks and said he hated the high school here because there weren't enough Navajos in it. He hated the high school on the reservation because there were too many Navajos in it. But he went back to the reservation anyway. And then, late May, I got a letter from my mother-in-law with John's report card in it. He'd failed everything, and she couldn't handle him anymore and she was sending him to me. That was two weeks ago. He didn't show. Until I got home from fishing that woman out of the river and he was sitting on my back steps, me soaking wet and going into hypothermia, and John sitting there on my back steps looking like he'd just bitten a green persimmon."

"Sounds like just what you needed right then."

"Well, yeah, except at least then I knew where he was. So I took him down the next day and enrolled him in summer school."

"Is he going?"

Charlie shrugged. "It starts tomorrow. He damn well better go. But—his grandmother said he was running with some pretty rough kids there and getting into more trouble than she knew what to do with. A kid who'll run with rough kids one place'll run with rough kids another place. And there are plenty of rough kids in Salt Lake City, and plenty of trouble to get into."

"I didn't picture—"

"Most people don't," he interrupted. "You think you're coming to Salt Lake City, the home of the saints, and everything's hunky-dory. Well, let me tell you something. There are two hundred and fifteen separate youth gangs in the Salt Lake Valley right now—that we know of. Year or so ago the captain of the West High football team shot a man after a concert at the Triad Center. Captain of the football team, had a girlfriend and a baby, already had been promised a full scholarship to a major university. He threw it all away. Shot a man dead because he was wearing a red shirt."

I didn't have to ask what wearing a red shirt had to do with it. The Bloods wear red shirts. Whether or not the dead man was a Blood, he had identified himself to other gang members as a Blood. I winced involuntarily, thinking of a fifty-square-block house-to-house sweep we'd conducted in Fort Worth about a year earlier picking up every gang member we found and a lot of non–gang members on every charge we could think from armed robbery and aggravated assault to unpaid traffic tickets, thinking of the hundreds of illegal (for various reasons) weapons from RGs to Uzis we'd seized on that raid, as Charlie added, "And John—if I can keep him here—will be going to West High this fall. So there's plenty of trouble he can get into here," and then asked, "Why am I telling you this?"

"Because you know you'll never have to see me again after next week?"

"Maybe," he said. "Or maybe so I can put off going into that house to face that woman again. But it's not going to get any easier."

He swung open the car door and headed for the house, obviously assuming I could open my own car door. Which I could, but his stride was so much longer than mine that he'd already knocked on the door, and Lori had opened it, before I reached Pat and paused for the obligatory scratch behind the ears.

Georgina was in the kitchen chopping vegetables. I wanted to point out that we didn't expect her to feed us tonight, that we could go out, but when I said something under my breath to Harry he said, "I already told her that. She said she'd rather keep busy."

It was not my case. Charlie had made that plain. So I stayed in the living room with such of my family as was about; judging from the noise I was hearing, Hal was watching television upstairs despite the fact that he was not supposed to be, and Cameron I assumed was still sleeping. Lori, having done her duty by opening the door, was back in a chair looking slightly pale—for the rest of her life, in cold wet weather, she'd be feeling every mended bone from where a car had hit her and knocked her a hundred and twenty feet not quite a year ago. But she wasn't complaining; I was sure she'd taken ibuprofen, and now she was working on her recently acquired crochet skills (unlike most new craftswomen, she'd begun with a sweater for herself rather than for her boyfriend) and Harry was on the couch reading a *Soldier of Fortune* he must have stopped somewhere and bought today, because the last copy of it I had seen was at home, and was last month's. I sat down beside him. "How'd it go?" he asked.

"It went," I said. What else was there to say? I hadn't the faintest idea what good anything I had said might have been, and besides that, I was eavesdropping like mad on the conversation going on in the kitchen.

Georgina had already asked when she could have the body for burial, and Charlie had told her he didn't know yet, maybe Monday afternoon, maybe sometime Tuesday. Then he asked her if Alexandra had come home after church, before leaving again.

"I don't know," Georgina said, sniffling a little. "I was taking a nap."

"Problem is, we didn't find her purse and keys," Charlie said. "If they're here, then we can take that as a signal she did come home. If they're not . . ." He left that sentence unfinished.

"You want me to go look for them?"

"If you like," Charlie said. "Or I could look myself. That might be easier for you."

"Go ahead," she said. "I—yes, that would be easier, I think. I can show you her room, or—"

"Would Mrs. Ralston know where her room is?"

"It's just at the top of the stairs. I guess she knows."

"Would you mind if I took her with me?"

Well, I thought, *maybe I was more in this case than I thought I was.* At any rate, I shortly found myself rather laboriously ascending two flights of stairs, holding on to the rail rather than using my cane. I had not actually been on the third floor before, having had no reason to be there and even less inclination to climb the necessary stairs, but there were only two bedrooms there, one on each side of the stair landing. One was very neat. One was not. In the floor of the one that was not were the clothes Alexandra had worn yesterday while stalking us, as well as several other days' worth of clothes. "This one," I said.

Charlie walked in, looked around, and said very quietly, presumably so that Georgina wouldn't hear him, "How in the hell is anybody supposed to find anything in here?"

Which, even if he hadn't told me, would have let me know he hadn't lived with a teenager since he got through being one himself. "You start at one end," I said, "and work to the other." I checked the bed first, under the tumbled covers, behind the bed between it and the wall, under the bed (which involved pulling out, and putting back, quite a number of things ranging from highly overdue library CDs and cassette tapes, which on second thought I kept out and stacked on the dresser so Georgina could return them, to used sanitary pads, which to be perfectly frank I nudged about with the end of a coat hanger).

Then I remade the bed, roughly but efficiently, and started picking up the clothes one at a time and tossing them on the now-flat surface. I was interested to notice that Alexandra apparently had had two identical lavender dresses, as there was one lying on the floor, soaking wet from the jacket that had been flung on top of it. If I were Georgina, I'd do a couple of loads of laundry today even if it was Sunday. A lot of these clothes were wet, which was no wonder considering how long it had been raining, and if left lying around they might mildew, though come to think of it, in a climate like Salt Lake was supposed to have, mildew might not be the problem it is in Fort Worth.

I shook out each item of clothing carefully, feeling the pockets for keys. Meanwhile Charlie was methodically opening drawers and examining their contents, pulling out books from the shelves of romance paperbacks to see what might be stashed behind them, checking closet shelves.

Twenty minutes later we had agreed that although we might easily have missed a single key, we probably wouldn't have missed that key chain Alexandra used, which was a collection of about sixteen interlocked key chains each with its own usually large ornament—vials of water with glitter in them, horses' heads, fuzzy dice, and so forth—together with about four keys, and we certainly wouldn't have missed a white envelope bag with brass fittings. Ergo, it wasn't there, which meant there was an even or more than even chance that the killer had the bag.

Belatedly—very belatedly—I wondered where her jacket was. I'd found the jacket she was wearing on Saturday, but it was still dripping wet and couldn't have been worn since. I didn't know if she'd had another jacket in church, because by the time I'd gotten in she was already seated and would have had the jacket off, but we'd talked with her in the foyer as she was leaving and—I couldn't remember. I just couldn't remember.

"Lori," I said when we got downstairs, "did Alexandra have a jacket with her when we were leaving church?"

Lori gave me that look adolescents reserve for their elders who have clearly flipped out. "Of course," she said. "It was white, sort of a wool melton. It was clean, but it looked pretty old. It had a gray plaid neck scarf pinned to it."

"A smooth-looking wool weave," I translated for Charlie. "And it's not much in fashion right now. My guess would be, maybe ten or so years old."

"Alexandra had had it for about six months," said Georgina, who had come into the living room wiping her hands on her apron. "She fell in love with it one day at DI and just had to have it. I told her I'd buy her a new coat, she didn't need that old thing, but she said that was the coat she wanted. I suppose I shouldn't complain, it was only seven dollars and I'd expected to spend at least seventy."

. . . . .

"What's DI?" I asked.

"Deseret Industries," Charlie said. "Utah's answer to Goodwill. I didn't see anything like that coat upstairs."

"I didn't either," I agreed.

And that was a little bit odd. It made perfectly good sense for the killer to take the purse, the keys. But why not leave the coat with the body?

"I'm through here now," Charlie told Georgina. "If I need to come back later I'll let you know. And either I or somebody from the medical examiner's office will call you as soon as the body can be released."

"What about her car?" Georgina asked. "Maybe her keys are in there."

Charlie and I were both staring at her, and if my expression was anything like his we were both open-mouthed. "Her car?" I finally got out. "Alexandra had a driver's license?"

"Of course," Georgina said, sounding surprised that I hadn't known. "It wasn't a new one, of course, but she did have to be able to get to and from work, and the bus system in this town just doesn't run after six P.M. and it's so hard to get around on foot in the winter—and her psychiatrist said it would be good for her—"

Maybe it was good for her, I thought cynically, *but what about the other drivers on the highway? Would I really want to be driving on the same street with somebody who had suddenly, mentally and emotionally, become a five-year-old?*

Charlie, unlike me, had to be on official behavior. He had his notebook out again, and was getting a description of the car. A white Escort, eight years old, four-door. The license number.

"I never saw it," I said feebly. "I saw your car, out in front, but I didn't realize—"

"She always parked in the garage," Georgina said, sounding a little surprised. "She's—she was really a much better driver than I've ever been. I don't know, maybe it goes along with being a good pitcher. I couldn't get a car out of that little garage without taking the door frame off, but she didn't have any trouble at all. And she was really proud of that car, she kept it washed and waxed all the time, so I said I'd let her use the garage and I'd just park under a tree in front. That was why I was surprised she walked Saturday. And Sunday—she always rides—rode—to church with Aunt LaRae, but if she's going anywhere after that she takes her car."

"Then suppose we go and look at the garage," Charlie suggested. "You do have copies of her keys?"

"Oh, of course," Georgina said. "Sometimes I had to drive her home, when she—sort of forgot things."

We—we being Georgina, Charlie, Harry, and I—went and looked in the backyard garage, which must have been built forty or more years ago and was actually too narrow for most modern cars, which probably explained Georgina's difficulty: Her car, though as old as Alexandra's, was a Chrysler, and Chryslers, unlike Escorts, are not notoriously narrow or short cars. The driveway in front of the garage was paved and flat, and a basketball hoop hung above the garage door.

A white Escort, eight years old, all four doors locked, was parked neatly inside the dirt-floored garage, with the pull-down garage door pulled down and padlocked and the side door that opened onto the footpath to the house also closed and locked. The sparkle of the wax job told me it couldn't have been driven since the rain started Friday night.

There was no purse, and no bundle of keys, in or near the car or anywhere else in the garage, which was actually very neat. Charlie got out and walked around outside, checking the tufty grass that grew along the wall, pointing his flashlight in various directions in the hopes of getting a reflected flash of light that might signal a key ring, a white purse with brass fittings. But there was nothing there.

"You mind if I look?" Harry asked hopefully.

. . . . .

"It's okay with me if it's okay with the lady," Charlie said.

With Georgina's permission, Harry prowled carefully among the cans of dried vegetables, wheat, and so forth that filled the shelves at the back of the garage. His luck was as good as Charlie's. No keys, no purse. Only a lot of cobwebs and dust and a few spiders.

We all trooped back inside, where Charlie said, "I'll keep in touch, and you let me know if you hear anything."

Georgina nodded, wiped her hands on her apron again for about the tenth time, and turned to head back into the kitchen.

I followed her. "Would it be easier for you if we left now?" I asked. "I mean, all you have to cope with, you don't need us—"

"Please stay," she said, sounding as if she might burst into tears. "Please stay. If you go I won't have anything to do, and that's so much worse. I did put off that honeymoon couple, so I wouldn't have to settle somebody else in, but you're already here, and—please stay. But now, if you'll just go and sit down, everything's almost ready. . . ."

Which I took to mean she needed time to herself. I did not insist on staying in the kitchen and helping her. I went into the living room and sat down. Cameron, finally rested enough to be allowed into polite society, scampered down the stairs in an extreme state of undress to join me. "What are you doing?" I demanded, rushing to intercept him as Lori giggled and Hal, who had abandoned the television, laughed out loud.

"I'm a pleasant bird," Cameron announced.

"Well, you can be a pleasant bird with clothes on!" I said, shepherding him back up the stairs.

"But animals should definitely not wear clothes!" That is an approximation of the title of one of his favorite library books, which features on its cover a hedgehog or porcupine trying to wear a sweater, with its spines sticking through the cloth.

"When people pretend to be animals they definitely *should* wear clothes," I informed him.

"But I sweated a lot and when I woke up my pants were wet!"

"I sweated a lot" has become his euphemism for wetting the bed. This allows him to change clothes, and get his bed changed, without admitting to what he now sees as a serious faux pas. Sunday or not, we were definitely going to have to do at least one load of clothes, and when I volunteered to get the wet things out of Alexandra's room and do them at the same time Georgina seemed grateful, perhaps because the laundry room was on the second floor, so doing laundry would keep me out of her way in the kitchen.

When Cameron and I came back down for supper, Cameron had decided he would rather walk around the world in four fur feet, like an animal in another of his favorite books, and had given up on being a naked pleasant bird, particularly when I pointed out to him that pleasant birds couldn't have dinner at the table but had to eat birdseed on the front porch and Pat might chase them away and eat the birdseed himself.

Cameron went out with me to help feed, medicate, and pet the dog, who thanked him with large slurpy kisses that made me hope most devoutly that whatever Pat had was not people contagious. Obviously I would have to keep the two apart until Pat got well, which was not going to set well with either dog or boy. I took Cameron in and washed him again before we ate.

On the day of her sister's death, Georgina succeeded in producing a delicious eggplant lasagna with about four kinds of cheese in it, garlic toast, and a salad with more kinds of greens in it than I had ever seen, followed by an almond cheesecake.

I did not understand this woman.

Almost at the end of the meal, she asked diffidently, "Is it true that you're a policeman?"

"I'm not an anything *man,*" I said, as I always answer this question. "But I am a police officer."

"And a detective, not just somebody that hands out parking tickets?"

. . . . .

"Mom's the best detective in Fort Worth," Hal said proudly, a statement I found profoundly embarrassing.

"Well, the reason I asked"—she was toying awkwardly with her silverware—"is that there are some of my friends, and some of Alexandra's friends, who wouldn't talk with the police no matter what, but if you try to talk with them . . ."

I didn't want to. I was on vacation. But how do you say no to this kind of appeal?

Very easily, I suspected, if I allowed Harry to catch my eye. Which I carefully did not do as I answered, "I'll be willing to talk with them, but you'll have to understand that if they tell me anything important I'll have to tell the police, and then the person will still have to talk to the police anyway."

Harry didn't say anything until we were alone, much later that night, and then he said, "Even on vacation you can't keep your nose out of crime, can you? Deb, *when* are you going to learn to put something else and somebody else first?"

"I don't know," I mumbled. "But Harry, she sounded so desperate. . . ."

"Well, I'd like to spend a little time with you myself," he pointed out. "I thought that was one of the purposes of this vacation." After a long silence, he said, "This is an unofficial investigation, right?"

"Obviously. I don't have any jurisdiction here."

"Then if I went along with you to help out . . ."

I turned and looked at him for the first time since this discussion started, and found him grinning openly. "Let Hal and Lori sightsee," he said. "Cameron can chaperone—Lord knows they couldn't get into any trouble while coping with him. I always did wonder what kind of a detective I would have made."

. . . . .

Five

. . . . .

IT SEEMED, THOUGH in retrospect I can't figure out why unless it had to do with Hal's height, to make the most sense for Hal, Lori, and Cameron to take off in Olead's van immediately after breakfast (eggs scrambled with cottage cheese and diced ham, potatoes O'-Brien, and fresh hot buttermilk biscuits, and why in the world wasn't this woman running a restaurant instead of a bed-and-breakfast?), while Harry and I borrowed Alexandra's car. There wouldn't be any trouble with that; Georgina had enough native caution that she had insisted the car be registered in her name rather than Alexandra's, so she gave us written permission to drive it, a list of people to talk with, and of course the keys.

I wondered how late at night she'd sat up to think of this list she provided us. It was thorough, including not only names, addresses, and telephone numbers, but also descriptions of the specific situation in which she and/or Alexandra would encounter these people and her own estimate of how good a relationship Alexandra had with them. She'd done it, she told me, on the computer she'd bought to keep all her business records for the bed-and-breakfast, so it might have been just an expansion of part of a personal address or telephone book.

The first place we went was to the small geological firm where Alexandra had worked. It was even smaller than I had guessed from what Georgina told us, and I had a hunch it wasn't doing well.

Although I am aware that many upscale small companies operate out of old, architecturally interesting buildings, this building was just plain old and about as uninteresting a building as I had seen in a long time—plain red brick with peeling yellow paint and a front porch lacking even the pillars and balustrades that were found on many of the old houses in this area.

In my ignorance, I had supposed before arriving here that given the Mormon tradition of plural marriages (ended over a hundred years ago, except in some very strange sects long since disowned by the Church) and the still-extant Mormon tradition of very large families, most of the older houses in Salt Lake City would be quite large. I had been wrong—although there were some enormous and gaudy Victorian gingerbread edifices—most of the oldest houses I had seen were red brick and exceedingly small. If a family with more than one child had ever lived in this one they must have stacked up the children at night like cordwood.

I glanced around at Harry, who had dressed the way he must have thought he would dress had he really been a detective. Although he was unarmed, and I was more grateful than ever that I had not brought any weaponry on this trip because legal or no he might have decided to appropriate it, I could detect certain influences of Dirty Harry. He had on a plaid shirt, which, unfortunately for the effect he was trying to produce, was scarcely visible under the red University of Utah sweatshirt (yes, it was still raining), a pair of khaki trousers, sports socks, and Hush Puppies.

He was also trying to walk like Clint Eastwood. As Clint Eastwood hasn't, at least to my knowledge, spent several months in the hospital pursuant to crashing a helicopter, and does not have a resultant limp, that wasn't working too well either.

I was just dressed as me, in dark blue slacks with pockets (I detest clothes without pockets), a blue embroidered T-shirt, and the blue Brigham Young University sweatshirt Hal had bought me, along with white socks and pink and white sneakers, which were already wet and uncomfortable.

We went up the walk together and paused on the front porch, thankful to be back out of the rain. The sign on the front door said RING BELL AND COME IN. So I rang the bell and we entered. Clearly the area around the front desk had been decorated by Alexandra. It included china puppies and kittens and pictures of puppies and kittens (but Georgina didn't have any dogs or cats; why?), a couple of photographs of Alexandra at the pitcher's mound and one of her holding a trophy, and various "cute" things such as wicker baskets of plastic flowers. But to my surprise, it also included an IBM 486 computer, a Hewlett-Packard LaserJet III printer, an off-brand color printer, and a fax machine. Alexandra at work must have been at least reasonably competent, to be trusted with this sort of equipment.

I could hear somebody clattering down the stairs at the back of the building. "What is it?" he called before he was in sight.

"Mr. Mullins?" I said. "I'm Deb Ralston, and this is my husband, Harry. Georgina Grafton asked us to drop by and talk with you."

"If she wants me to rehire that dingbat sister of hers, tell her nothing doing."

Harry and I glanced at each other. Georgina had not told us Alexandra was now out of work; in fact, she had been adamant that this was where Alexandra worked, and we'd had to promise to get there about the time Alexandra should be arriving in case Mr. Mullins hadn't heard. Harry said, "Alexandra's dead."

This gave Ted Mullins, who had finally arrived in the front room, pause. "She's what?"

"She's dead," I repeated, watching him closely for reaction, of which there wasn't much. He was a rather small man, fiftyish, with slightly long gray-brown hair, brown eyes with gold-rimmed glasses, very nattily dressed—especially for a geologist—in brown wing-tip shoes, ornate argyle-design dress-thin socks, brown slacks, a beigeish turtleneck, and an elaborate brown knit vest that looked cashmere.

"You a cop?" he demanded.

"I'm with the Fort Worth Police Department, and—"

"In Salt Lake City? Come on!"

"As my wife was trying to say," Harry said, in a carefully polite voice with slightly jagged edges to it, "she's a detective with the Fort Worth Police Department. Alexandra Howe's death, of course, is being investigated by the Salt Lake City Police Department. But Georgina Grafton asked us if we would be willing to ask a few unofficial questions to go along with the official investigation."

"And you're saying Sandy's dead?" Unlike Georgina, he had not adopted the psychiatrist's recommendation that only the name Alexandra be used. "What happened to her?"

"Somebody bashed her in the head with a rock at Gilgal, somewhere around two o'clock Sunday afternoon," I said baldly.

"Well, lady, Sunday was my parents' anniversary, and at two o'clock Sunday afternoon I was having dinner with my father and mother, three brothers and their wives, and two sisters and their husbands, and about nine hundred nieces and nephews. So deal me out."

"I just wanted to ask—"

"I fired her Friday. Told her I didn't want her back on the premises again. That goes for you too." He turned and began to stride determinedly back toward the room he had come from.

"Mr. Mullins!" I called after him.

He paused, turned back to face me from what originally must have been the dining room when this was a private home. Now it contained a ceiling full of strong fluorescent lights, a floor crowded with several drawing tables, most of them with charts pinned to them, and a row of map files against the outside wall partially blocking the windows. "What now?"

"There must have been a reason why you fired her. I'm sure she's been a trial for you all along, and it was generous of you to give her a chance." This was probably laying it on with a trowel, but sometimes that's what it takes to get answers. It was working; he had begun to smirk. "So what was the last straw?"

"The last straw? You want to know what the last straw was? You want to know why I fired her?" The smirk vanished more quickly than it had arrived. He marched back into the front room and reached into the trash can. What he brought out had at one time, I could barely make out, been some sort of very complicated multi-colored chart. Now it was a row of paper dolls holding hands. "*That*'s why I fired her! Now hit the road, okay, because I've got work to do." He gestured at the collection of gewgaws around the desk. "Why don't you take that stuff with you? Get all her stuff, I don't want it around here and I don't want Georgina over here bawling while she gets it. Here's a box." Thrusting a cardboard carton he'd grabbed from under the desk into my hand, he headed to the back again, and this time he did not turn and come back. From the direction he had gone, and the sounds we heard and the smells that began drifting through the house-cum-office, I surmised that he had gone to make coffee. Most likely he lived as well as worked in this building.

"Now what?" Harry demanded very softly.

"Now we gather up everything that's obviously Alexandra's, and then we leave," I said. "Even if we *were* official he's entirely within his rights to refuse to talk with us. As we're not official . . ."

"Do we look inside the desk?" Harry asked.

I had to think that one over. Normally, as sorely tempted as I was, it simply would not be legal. But this time we had a request from the person who controlled the property that we remove Alexandra's "stuff," and surely some of her personal possessions might be in the desk. So that could be taken as a mandate.

Collecting the things on top of and around the desk took only a couple of minutes, and I didn't much worry about whether any of it was breakable, as I was pretty sure Georgina would give most of it to Goodwill—excuse me, DI—anyway. Then we began digging through drawers. Harry took the right pedestal; I took the left pedestal and the lap drawer, as I am somewhat smaller and more flexible than he is and could jam myself into the corner far more easily.

We found pens and pencils and rubber bands and thumbtacks and paper clips and tape and address labels, which we left, and we found makeup and a package of sanitary pads and a toothbrush and toothpaste, which we put into the box. In the lap drawer I found a silver CTR ring. I had to explain to Harry that the embossed CTR meant "Choose the Right," from a song that begins "Choose the right, when the choice is placed before you," and children are given these rings when they are about ten. The original rings, some sort of silver-looking metal, are presented by the Church; parents will often buy their children more durable rings; and even nicer CTR rings, silver or even gold, are frequent gifts between semi-engaged young men and women. Many people continue to wear them throughout life; you'd think Harry would have noticed that since we went to Deseret Books on Saturday both Hal and Lori were now wearing gold CTR rings on the third finger of their left hands. I put the CTR ring, which looked privately purchased, not Church issue, into the carton. That Georgina would probably keep, unless she decided Alexandra should be buried wearing it.

We found several boxes of crayons, which I hesitated over, until I also found another chart—this one apparently computer-generated, measuring the underlying land structure somewhere by bouncing seismic activity off rocks below the surface structure—which had large drawings of flowers all over it. I took the crayons.

I left the chart, which I suspected Mullins was going to have cats over when he saw, on top of the desk.

There really wasn't anything else there that seemed personal. No letters, no appointment books, no nothing. Nothing that seemed in any imaginable way to relate to her murder. Harry called, "I think we got all her stuff. Anything else, you can trash. We're going now."

"Yeah," Mullins called back.

The next person on our list was Cully Grafton. Harry and I agreed we didn't see much use in talking with Cully Grafton, but we'd promised Georgina we'd follow the list exactly. Grafton drove one of those trucks that pulls up to work locations honking its horn madly, so everybody will rush out and buy goodies, and Georgina had thoughtfully included his entire route on the print-out she gave us. We caught up with him at an automotive repair shop. "I'm not sure what he's going to say to us," Harry pointed out, "in view of the fact that last time I saw him I threatened to knock his block off."

"He was trying to knock Georgina's block off," I replied, "and anyway, he was probably too drunk to remember."

Whether he was too drunk to remember or not, he acted a little more cordial today, though we had to wait ten minutes before we could talk with him, while he dealt out ham sandwiches and potato chips, Cokes and fruit drinks, and accepted money and made change. Finally he slammed the louvered metal doors closed and said, "Sorry. But business is business. Now. What can I do for you?"

It developed that he did remember who we were. He did know Alexandra was dead; he said Georgina had called and told him, and he'd at least tried to sound sympathetic. "But don't ask me to say I'm sorry," he added, "because I'm not. She was a sly little slut, always prowling around listening in corners, and she couldn't stand for anybody but her to have any attention. She didn't want Georgina and me to marry, and from the moment we were married she did everything she could to break us up. Well, she succeeded, at least for the time being. I don't know how long it's going to take me to talk Georgina into letting me move back home, but damn it, I'm not going to let that little slut reach out from the grave to keep me and Georgina apart."

"Where were you Sunday afternoon?" I inquired.

"Sleeping it off," he answered flatly. "And no, I didn't have any witnesses watching me do it. Believe it or not, the only woman I want in my bed is my wife. But that's all I was doing. Sleeping it off. I wanted Alexandra hospitalized. Not murdered. Just hospitalized. That's all."

I could well believe he had been sleeping it off. The way he had looked Saturday night, I was frankly surprised to see him awake and functional Monday morning. But there was no proof that was what he had been doing.

And proving it, or disproving it, was Salt Lake City's problem, not Harry's and mine. We went on to the next name on the list, one Ellen Stromberg. Georgina's note said, "Don't get to Ellen before eleven because she probably won't be up. She's Alexandra's friend, and I don't really know her."

At eleven-fifteen, Ellen Stromberg was semi-up. She was awake and on at least her first, probably her second, cup of coffee; she had on a thick pink quilted housecoat over a nylon nightgown, and her feet were thrust into quilted pink slippers with matted plush linings. She had not combed her lush brown shoulder-length hair and it was evident that she had not washed her face since sometime yesterday, as the smeared remains of old makeup were still on her eyes and cheeks. A copy of the *Salt Lake Tribune* was open on the table in front of her, from which I surmised that we were too late to get her first reaction to Alexandra's death.

Harry explained who we were and what we were doing there. Disconcertingly, Ellen Stromberg yawned. "Yeah," she said, "I mean, I'm sorry as hell about Sandy Lu getting, you know, Sandy Lu dying—"

Involuntarily I interrupted, "Sandy Lu?"

"Yeah," Ms. Stromberg said, "her name was Alexandra Louise and she liked us to call her Sandy Lu. Like I said, I'm sorry as hell about what happened, but I don't know what Georgina wants me to tell you. Georgina doesn't like me. She says I get Sandy Lu in trouble. I keep telling her Sandy Lu can think of enough trouble to get in herself. But if she was killed yesterday, I can't help. I mean, I didn't see her yesterday."

"When did you see her last?" I asked.

Ellen had to think about it, before she finally said, "Saturday night a week ago. We went out to this new club that's opened up in town, and man, it was swinging! Live band and everything! But I still don't know what Georgina wants me to tell you."

"I think she just mainly wants you to tell us what Alex—I mean Sandy—acted like around you," I said. "You—uh—did you know—?"

Before I finished the question, which I was trying to phrase in such a way as to determine whether Ellen knew about Alexandra's MPD without my mentioning it, Ellen said, "You mean about her being like a bunch of different people? Man, wasn't that something? I wish I could do that—just turn into somebody else! It must be a lot of fun. Sometimes she'd do it at parties. It would be funny—I mean, Sandy Lu, when she's Sandy Lu that is, is just this real party girl, I mean she loves to get out and drink and dance and everything, but then all of a sudden it'd be like there was this little kid sitting there and she didn't know what was going on—I mean it would be so funny, she'd look real puzzled and start sucking her thumb—and sometimes especially when she got drunk she'd play like she was a teenage boy and she'd start wanting to fight with everybody. . . ."

"Sounds like the life of the party," Harry said. "Must be a lot of fun to get a five-year-old drunk."

Totally missing the sarcasm in his voice, Ellen said, "Oh, she *was* the life of the party! And she was so *cute* when she acted like she was five years old—I do wish I could do that! Everybody loved to have her around! Too bad her family lost all their money, just think what kind of parties she could throw if they still had it! Man, I'd love to go to some of those parties!"

"Did their family used to be pretty well off?" I asked.

"Oh yeah!" Ellen said, wide-eyed. "I mean, you know that great big house Georgina has, man, that's bigger than the governor's mansion! You've seen the governor's mansion, haven't you? Just right up there on South Temple, with a fence around it? You know, it burned Christmas a year ago and they're fixing it? It's just about four blocks from here, on the corner of 600 East and South Temple, and Georgina's house is lots bigger."

I had some vague memory of having seen a large fenced dwelling with fire marks on it at the spot Ellen was trying to describe. I did not have any memory at all of its being smaller than Georgina's house; in fact, I was absolutely certain that Georgina's house was considerably smaller. But I wasn't about to argue. I just listened, as Ellen went on, "They were so rich it was just unreal! They had everything: two new Cadillacs every year, Mrs. Howe had *three* mink coats, they had all these Mexicans working for them, never had to do anything themselves, not even clean their own rooms. My mom told me all about them. And now Georgina's taking in boarders. Would you believe it? I wonder where all that money went? Something like that's a shame, isn't it?"

I agreed it was a shame, and did not explain the difference between running a bed-and-breakfast and taking in boarders, not that there is anything shameful about taking in boarders, and ultimately Georgina might discover that was more dependable than what she was trying now. Later, in the car, Harry said, "Well, wherever their money went, I hope it went to something more sensible than the kind of parties that gal is talking about. Deb, I don't think she ever did figure out that Alexandra wasn't just *pretending* to be other people."

I agreed, and consulted my list as to the next person we were going to. One LaRae White, and Georgina's note said, "She's our grandaunt and she's eighty-two and pretty frail, so you might want to find out if she knows before you ask her anything."

LaRae White was the woman who had sat beside Alexandra in church. She was indeed rather old, though I wouldn't have guessed her as more than about seventy-five, but she was awake and dressed, and she had her newspaper open on her couch. Her eyes were red, but she recognized me from Relief Society and burst out, "That poor child! That poor child! What happened, do you know?" Then, belatedly, she asked, "Did Georgina send you? Would she like me to help her plan the funeral? The bishop does know, doesn't he? And the Relief Society president? What can I do? Oh, I'm not even thinking, please sit down, here's a place for you, Brother—" She came to a dead halt. She couldn't remember our names.

"Ralston," Harry said, and I hoped she couldn't recognize the acute discomfort in his voice. He isn't a member of the Church, and the Brother This and Sister That addresses, which come so naturally to the rest of us, grate sharply on his nerves despite the fact that a lot of Baptists do it too.

"Brother Ralston," she said, "my dear husband, God rest him, always liked this chair, so I'm sure you'll like it too. Sister Ralston, you sit here, now, what can I do?"

Sitting gingerly on the edge of the overstuffed chair—I felt as if I would disappear entirely if I tried to lean back—I said, "I don't know how much you know about what happened—"

"Very little," she said. "Just what the paper said—that Alexandra was found dead at Gilgal, isn't that terrible, that nice peaceful place, and that your son found her, that's the nice big boy who's just leaving on his mission, isn't he? Adopted, I suppose? Weren't you lucky to get him, a fine boy like that? It makes me so sad when I watch on television, all those choice spirits in children nobody wants, those minds and bodies just wasting away in orphanages when they could accomplish so much and bring so much joy to so many families if these silly laws that make adoption so difficult and expensive would just be changed. But such a terrible way to start his mission, I suppose he never saw anything like that before. . . ."

Actually he had, but I wasn't going to say so. It became obvious I had to interrupt to get a word in edgewise, and Harry's Southern manners are such that he is just about congenitally incapable of interrupting any woman other than me. "It was quite a shock," I agreed.

"And your little boy, I hope he didn't see it?"

"No."

"Your daughter must have kept him away from it."

"Actually she's"—I intercepted a glance from Harry and changed what I had been about to say, namely that she was Hal's girlfriend—"our foster daughter. No, we haven't adopted her, she's old enough she doesn't really want to be adopted, but she'll go on living with us. And yes, she kept Cameron, that's the baby, away from the scene. But as to what happened—" I had decided to follow Sister White's lead and talk as fast as I could, in hopes she would be too polite to interrupt me.

It didn't work. She burst in, "Oh, yes, do tell me what happened! I really need to know, but of course I didn't know whether to call Georgina and ask—"

"Somebody hit her in the head with a rock," Harry said from the brown recliner Sister White had practically shoved him into. "She was still alive when we got there and died just seconds later. Yes, the bishop was notified; he was over at the house for about an hour Sunday night, and so was the Relief Society president. Of course the police are investigating, but Georgina asked us to talk to a few people to see what we could find out."

"But why?" Sister White asked, sounding honestly bewildered and addressing Harry, not me. "I mean, not why was she killed, of course you don't know that, but why does she want you to ask people questions?"

"My wife is a police detective," Harry said, "and Georgina just felt some people would be more comfortable talking to us instead of—or as well as—the local police."

She was gazing at me again, her eyes very wide. "Oh, my dear, how *fascinating!* I always thought I would like to be a police officer, or maybe a lawyer, but of course women just didn't *do* such things when I was a girl, not most women anyway, there were always a few who did, at least a few who were lawyers, of course there weren't any women police then, but I never knew anybody, so it was just like nobody did. So! What would you like to ask me?" She composed herself on the sofa, eyes wide, hands crossed neatly in her lap, as if prepared for a two-hour interrogation.

"Just tell me what you can about Alexandra," I said, "and about the family. I'm sure you know about Alexandra's problem, and we know different people saw her in different ways. How did you see her? What kind of people were her family? Georgina said you are her grandaunt. . . ."

Sister White leaned forward slightly. "Well, let's start with the family. We were quite well off originally, we had been for many generations, I don't know if Georgina told you the family was here by about 1880 and at one time we owned the house Georgina lives in now and the ones on each side of it. Plural marriages, you see, and the first Brother Howe in the valley wanted each of his wives to have her own house but he wanted them all to live close together."

"Wait a minute," I said. "Wasn't there heavy federal opposition to plural marriage by the 1880s? I thought I had heard there was a heavy crackdown, and that was when the Mexico colony was established."

"Oh, yes, a lot of opposition," Sister White confirmed, "but they were mainly after the church leaders, and the first Brother Howe—his name was Elias too, just like my nephew—never was even a bishop. All the federals knew was that there were three houses on this street, all belonging to people named Howe, and I think, you know, that *somehow* they got the idea the women were sisters-in-law and the other two husbands were off working in the coal mines." She tittered. "Can't imagine how they would have gotten that idea. They got along so well, you know, loved each other like sisters. Oh, dear, they were very well off, and the family owned a jewelry store, I don't know if it was the first in the valley but it was certainly one of the nicest. But one of the houses burned, let's see, about 1890—so tragic, it was a terribly cold winter night and Sister Isobel Howe and her five children were all asleep upstairs, and she had the three children of Sister Dorcas Howe with her because Sister Susannah Howe had just had her first baby, and they were all in one room because it was so cold, and she must have put too much green wood in the fireplace, and the chimney caught fire and spread to the whole house. Sister Dorcas Howe, the one whose three children were with Sister Isobel Howe, was staying with Sister Susannah, the one who'd just had a baby, so there Brother Howe was with one of his wives and eight of his children dead, and then the wife who'd just had the baby died of milk leg, and so there he was with just one wife and the baby of another wife."

She paused briefly as if to get her breath, and Harry opened his mouth. I thought for a moment he was going to say something, but then he subsided, and I said, "You certainly are up on all this."

"Oh, yes," she said, "I'm the family genealogist, and I've just been putting together a nice family history—not that anybody will ever want it. But maybe it can go in the DUP Museum."

The Daughters of the Utah Pioneers Museum was one of the places we hadn't gotten to yet, and I was beginning to wonder if we were ever going to get there. Sister White now went on as if there had been no interruption from her or anyone else. "Poor Elias was so sorrowful he never married again, well, of course he wouldn't because that was the year the Church forbade any more plural marriages, and they never had any more children. The remaining Sister Howe, that was Dorcas of course, raised her sister-wife's baby as her own, and if anybody asked her if she was bitter because her own children were dead she would say she would have them again in the spirit world because they were born in the covenant, and if she didn't take proper care of the other poor mite she'd have to explain to her sister-wife why she didn't. But I think she loved him dearly, and he grew up to be such a comfort to her. He was my father and the grandfather of Elias Howe, who was father to Georgina and Alexandra and Cynthia. Elias's father was my brother, you see, but he died so young, with only the one child. So sad, such a big family and the name dies here, though there, that's silly of me, isn't it, of course there are plenty of other people named Howe! But our family's coming to an end, I suppose. I only had daughters, but even if I'd had sons they'd have been Whites, not Howes. Really I thought Elias would never marry, just rattling around in that big old house by himself he was, working at the jewelry store and playing baseball when he could, and then he must have been past fifty when he went off to New York on a buying trip for the store, and came back with a twenty-year-old bride. Married Miranda in New York, he did. You just could have knocked me over with a feather—he never said a word to anybody, and they were married in the city hall, can you believe it? Sealed later in the Temple, so the girls were born in the covenant, but still! I think part of the reason was

Miranda's maiden name was Smith, and Smiths from New York, well, you always wonder if they might be, you know, *distant* kin of the prophet. Not that it's an uncommon name at all, so that doesn't say anything. Well, of course she was a Church member, even Elias wouldn't think of marrying outside the Church, but I don't think she really had a *testimony,* but I suppose he thought she'd get one when she got here. And then they had Georgina and then waited six years before Alexandra and Cynthia were born. Never a boy—I think Miranda lost one or two between Georgina and the twins and they might have been meant to be boys, but who knows, maybe it was meant to be this way? Of course Alexandra had no children, and Cynthia and Georgina don't either, and Georgina's the only one of them who's even married now, and I'm afraid I don't think much of her husband, do you?"

I agreed that I did not, and she went on, "And of course even if Georgina does have children, or if Cynthia remarries and has children, they won't carry the Howe name either. And of course the jewelry store's gone, Elias inherited it; my own dear husband was in the insurance business and we were so glad Elias was able to keep the store going, but really, you know, I always felt he had more affinity with baseball diamonds than with the kind that come in rings!" She tittered. "So that went, oh, dear, well, it must have been right after Miranda died." With that she suddenly ran down.

"When did that happen?" I asked.

"Oh, dear, it must be all of twenty-five years ago now. Well, maybe not quite that." She counted on her fingers, lips moving silently. "Well, Cindy and Sandy were five, and they're—Sandy was—twenty-six now, so it would have been twenty-one years ago now."

"What did Elias do after that?" Harry asked.

"He went to work for somebody else, still in a jewelry store. He was a certified gemologist, you know, and gems were really all he knew—that and sports, but he couldn't make a profession out of that. Not to say people don't, and didn't even then, but he never was that good."

"Do you know when Alexandra developed her . . . affliction?" I asked, as tactfully as possible in view of Sister White's advanced age.

"When her mother died," Sister White said. "We always believed, you know, that she saw it."

"Saw it?" Harry asked.

"Miranda was murdered, you know," Sister White said. "I thought sure you knew that. We always thought Sandy saw it. But she never could—or never would—explain. If anybody asked her she would just start screaming and then curl up in a little ball and start sucking her thumb. It was so sad, she was such a sweet child before that happened, she and Cindy weren't quite identical twins, you know, but they were so much alike, so lively and always such happy children, and ever since then, she's just been so difficult; of course I could always control her, and Elias could until he died, but really nobody else could, and poor Georgina hasn't a clue as to how to handle her. I offered to have her come here and stay with me, but Georgina insisted it was her duty, and really it wasn't, you know, especially after she married. I really *don't* approve of her husband, but all the same a husband's first duty is to his wife and a wife's first duty is to her husband, and Sandy really got so *very* spiteful, quite determined to break up the marriage, and I said send her over here to me. But Georgina said I couldn't have handled her for long. But I could, you know. I was the only one who could, after Elias died."

"And that was how long ago?"

"Six weeks. Just six weeks ago today my dear nephew was buried."

"You said Miranda was murdered. How was she murdered?" I asked.

"Oh, I wouldn't know about that," Sister White said. It was manifestly obvious that she did know. It was also manifestly obvious that she had no intention of telling us, and that the discussion had abruptly ended. I tried one more question, about why Elias had lost the jewelry store, but Sister White didn't know about that either, and I desisted.

"So ten to one that was the trauma that triggered the MPD," I said in the car.

"I thought MPD was almost always triggered by sexual abuse," Harry said, glancing nervously at me. Sexual abuse was a sore subject with us these days. My shrink, who was *not* either my psychiatrist friend or my psychologist friend, but a semistranger I had hired at their recommendation, had been a little nervous about letting me go this far away while I was still at what she described as an early stage of healing. Personally I was sick of healing. I couldn't see that I was healing at all. When I went to the shrink's office all I did was cry, and all that did was make my sinuses hurt.

But I had not developed MPD, despite ten years of sexual abuse, and so far as I know neither had my sister. At least every time I ever saw her she was herself.

"I've read a little about it," I said, "and they say that although sexual abuse is the most common trigger, any kind of very severe trauma can serve as a trigger. Physical abuse, a severe psychological shock. The real woman the book *Three Faces of Eve* was written about thinks that what triggered hers was seeing the body of a tramp in a drainage ditch she'd been warned to stay away from very shortly after one of her baby cousins died and was buried in baby clothes that had been hers."

Harry shrugged. "I'll take your word for it. You about ready to eat?"

"Let's check in with Georgina first and let her know what's going on."

We didn't tell her what kind of answers we'd been getting, and she didn't ask us. My hunch was that she knew and didn't want to know. We did tell her everybody so far had cooperated, and she said, in a rather thin voice, "I thought they all would. Now, if it's all right with you, and please tell me if it's not, I want to set it up for Alexandra's psychiatrist and Cynthia—that's Alexandra's twin sister—to come for dinner tonight, so you can talk to them. I wouldn't charge you for that dinner, of course, it's you helping me. They might be able to tell you things—I don't know, maybe I'm wrong, but I just have the feeling the police won't be able to get the right answers on this. But you're different. You *knew* her, and they—the police—don't. That Detective Sosa, he even looked like an *Indian*. What do *Indians* know about people like us?"

I started to point out to her—but didn't, because it would have been pointless—that Charlie Sosa had grown up in the Salt Lake Valley, was a BYU graduate, and knew the culture of this area far better than I did, which meant that his chances of clearing the case, whether he had ever seen Alexandra alive or not, were far better than mine. I did express my feelings in the car, to Harry, rather freely, and he answered, "People are people. I never did think you had to be taught to hate or fear. What puzzled me was her asking us who she could invite to dinner. It's her house."

She had offered us lunch—not much, she said, because she wasn't expecting us, maybe grilled cheese sandwiches and potato chips—and Harry declined for both of us, on the grounds that he'd seen a hamburger place called the Training Table that he wanted to try out. "Oh, you'll like it," she said, "it's very good, but mind you watch the steps going out. I took an awful fall there once, and with your foot problem. . . . Well, if you're sure the dinner is all right—I'll go call Cindy first."

She was on the phone by the time we left.

The hamburgers at the Training Table were wonderful, and so were the fries, a serving of which was enough to feed Hal and Harry both and still have some left over. As we didn't have Hal with us and had in our ignorance ordered two servings of fries, we had a lot left over. I obediently did not fall going down from the raised floor, though I was rather grateful for the cane, and we went out the door and walked toward the car—and found all four tires slit.

"You're a homicide detective," I pointed out to Charlie Sosa. "What are they sending you out on a tire-slashing for?"

"Because you found Alexandra Howe's body," he answered baldly, "so for the time being anything to do with you is interesting."

We were all sitting in his car while an ident tech tried to find a few dry spots on the fenders to dust for prints. Having been an ident tech myself, I would have refused to try, but I wasn't in charge of this case. "It was childish," I said aloud.

"What?" Charlie said.

"It was childish. Slitting the tires. It was childish, like—like hitting somebody in the head with a rock. So what I'm wondering is, were the tires slit because the car is Alexandra's and somebody doesn't know Alexandra is dead, or were the tires slit because we were using the car to ask questions about who killed Alexandra and maybe getting closer than somebody wanted us to get, and that somebody thought slitting the tires would stop us?"

I had another sudden glimpse of why Officer Marcella, on Sunday, had been rather dismayed to know she was getting Charlie Sosa. He swelled up like a pouter pigeon and said, "You were doing what?"

"Asking a few questions," Harry said. "Georgina asked us to. Look, man, you already said you're shorthanded. We weren't trying to poach in your territory. Deb told Georgina if anybody told us anything that looked like any use at all she'd turn it right over to you. But Georgina gave us a list of friends and relatives and asked us to talk to them. We did. That's all."

Of course he asked what everybody said. Of course we told him, and of course he considered that none of it was of any interest whatever, which I could have predicted to start with.

We wound up having the car towed to a service station, after a fast call to our insurance agent, who said our comprehensive would cover the new tires because we were using the car as a substitute for our own at the time of damage. Charlie, a little mollified by our cooperation but still far from cheerful, dropped us back by Georgina's, where I decided to ask Georgina a little about what Sister White had told us.

"Yes, my father was a jeweler," she readily agreed, "and I agree with Aunt LaRae that I don't think he liked the job much. Losing the store—yes, that must have been about the time Mother died, but I really don't know what happened. It was something—I just don't know. He'd bought something somebody ordered, and he didn't get it insured, and then it vanished, and it was so valuable he wound up losing the store because of it. That's all I know, but I was just ten when it happened. I remember him crying, sitting at the table talking to Aunt LaRae and crying, saying, 'First Miranda and now this, and the way Sandy is doing, I just don't know how I can go on.' But I was only ten years old then. I don't remember much. Anyway, what could any of this have to do with Sa—with Alexandra's death?"

"I don't know," I said. "It's just, so many people have brought it up, I thought I'd ask. How—I'm sorry to ask, but how did your mother die?"

"She was in the front yard," Georgina said. "That's all I remember. She was in the front yard. It was about twilight, and she was in the front yard, and Cindy was in the house watching television, and Sandy was in the front yard beside Mother, lying on the ground curled up sucking her thumb. Daddy and I had been to the grocery store. We got home and Mother was lying in the front yard—I'm sorry, I don't want to think about it!" She turned and ran up the stairs, taking them two at a time.

. . . . .

I sat down beside Harry. After a while he started snoring, so I put my sweatshirt back on and went out to take the dog for a walk. Even on the leash, which I felt was essential considering neither the dog nor I knew this neighborhood, Pat seemed to enjoy the walk immensely.

We turned to the left after we went down the front steps, and I walked past the red brick house that was almost identical to the one Georgina owned and we were now staying in. Who had it now, I wondered, and then wondered whether it mattered. We went around two blocks; Georgina had told me one block in Salt Lake City was equal to an eighth of a mile, so all four sides of two blocks would make a mile, which was a nice little walk considering the condition of my foot.

As we approached the house again, I noticed beside it the vacant lot I'd identified Friday night as a private cemetery. I hadn't really paid it any attention before, but after the story Sister White had told us I did pay it some attention—enough to notice a wild growth of iris that hadn't been thinned in years, a background of evergreen trees, and in the middle of a well-mowed green lawn three plots each surrounded by a black-enameled wrought-iron fence. The plot to my right as I stood facing it was quite large for a grave, but I realized why when I read the names—not name—on it: ISOBEL HOWE, BELOVED WIFE OF ELIAS HOWE, 1860–1892; JOSEPH HOWE, BELOVED SON OF ELIAS HOWE, 1880–1892; OLIVER HOWE, BELOVED SON OF ELIAS HOWE, 1882–1892; BRIGHAM HOWE, BELOVED SON OF ELIAS HOWE, 1883–1982; SARIAH HOWE, BELOVED DAUGHTER OF ELIAS HOWE, 1887–1892; EMMA HOWE, BELOVED DAUGHTER OF ELIAS HOWE, 1889–1892. . . . The names seemed to go on forever, though of course really there were only nine, a woman and her five children and her husband's three children by another wife, all burned to death trying to stay warm on a cold windy night more than a hundred years ago, buried in a common grave on the spot where they had died, with burned brick from the house used to wall the graves and the lot that had become a family cemetery. The smaller one on the left had a single name on it: SUSANNAH HOWE, BELOVED WIFE OF ELIAS HOWE. This was the one who'd died of milk leg, which, if I recalled correctly, was usually the result of keeping a woman in bed too long after childbirth so that her circulation failed.

The one in the middle was Elias Howe, 1845–1929.

He'd spent thirty-seven years of his life looking out the window at the graves of two of his wives and eight of his children.

Georgina, and her sisters, had spent their entire lives looking out at the graves of their kin.

What effect would that have on someone as sensitive as Alexandra was?

I went back to the house, noted that the van still wasn't back, petted Pat a little more and left him on the front porch, and went in the house and up to my room, where I cried myself to sleep without having the slightest idea why I was crying.

I woke in darkness that was the result of heavy clouds rather than clock time, when Cameron climbed into bed with me and whispered (all my children have always thought that it doesn't count as waking Mom if you whisper her awake), "We went up in the mountains, and it was nice."

"Was it?" I said drowsily, sitting up.

"Yeah. But now I want a *b-i-i-i-g hug*."

He got his big hug, and then I went back downstairs.

· · · · ·

Six

I'D FORGOTTEN THAT Georgina had invited her dead sister's psychiatrist and her surviving sister to dine with us, and that dinner was to be served at five. Georgina hadn't forgotten. And even today, the day after her sister's death with the body lying in Russon Brothers Mortuary after having been released by the medical examiner, she had outdone herself. Roast beef with glazed potatoes and carrots and onions, with brown gravy on the side. Homegrown horseradish in a cream sauce of her own devising. Homemade hot rolls. A large tossed salad with a tart homemade dressing. And peach cobbler with vanilla ice cream, not homemade but a very good commercial variety. She must have been cooking all day, except for an hour-long trip to the mortuary she'd made sometime in the early afternoon.

Cameron enjoyed his dinner very much.

I can't truthfully say that any of the rest of us did, especially with Georgina frequently glancing nervously at the clock; the body would lie in state from seven P.M. till ten P.M. and she had to be there, which meant dinner had to be finished by six forty-five. But since the general idea of this carefully contrived dinner was for people to talk, rushing everybody didn't fit her agenda either.

Harry and I with the rest of the family, all suitably cleaned up and dried off, went downstairs about four-thirty and seated ourselves in the living room. I for one felt ridiculously like someone in a play, and I was as nervous as if I expected to forget my lines. We all gravitated to the same places each person had sat the day before, as if they had somehow become our assigned seating. Hal turned the television on and then back off again, glancing guiltily at me, although he knows I don't consider it my job to cause him to conform to mission standards, before the rest of us had time to hear more than one word of whatever was on television. He then moseyed, or meandered, with a put-on carelessness that wouldn't have fooled a fly, back to where he had been, and sat down again.

You would never believe we are normally a very noisy family. Not a one of us could think of a word to say. Georgina, with an apron on over a dark blue church dress, had firmly refused all help in the kitchen, but every time the doorbell rang she rushed out to answer it before any of us had time to get out of our chairs. I wouldn't have been half so nervous if she had just given me something to do. But this enforced inactivity with Georgina bustling around as she was made me very uncomfortable—so uncomfortable, in fact, that I decided I was never going to stay in a bed-and-breakfast again. It was too much like being a guest in someone's home, except that all the rules were different. When I am a guest, I expect to help. In a motel, I don't expect to sit down to dinner with the owner. It was all too confusing for me.

LaRae White stuck her head in briefly about five minutes after we came downstairs, to announce that she was going over to the mortuary in case somebody arrived to visit early. "That's nice of you," Georgina said, "but I don't think they have—her—ready yet."

"Well, I'll go over there anyway," Sister White said. "Now, don't you work too hard, Georgina; it won't do any good at all for you to work yourself to death, and that's what you always try to do. I know you, you've been that way all your life."

. . . . .

"I'm not working too hard, honestly, Aunt LaRae," Georgina said, sounding desperate. "I'm just—it takes my mind off things to stay busy. But really I've got to get back to the kitchen now."

Sister White departed, looking as if she would have preferred to remain but was too polite to say so if she wasn't invited. We sat silent for another couple of minutes before Lori, no longer able to stand the silence, began to tell us rather feverishly about their trip to the mountains. She carefully emphasized what a careful driver Hal was on the narrow, winding mountain roads, and how he had observed every speed limit sign.

I gave that report the credence it deserved. I have ridden with Hal. However, I expected he probably was more careful on the mountain roads than he usually is at home; like me, he's used to driving in flatlands, and mountain roads scare him. Only Harry, who had barreled around Germany during his Marine career, felt totally comfortable with curves and switchbacks with thousand-foot drop-offs. I drive them at fifteen miles an hour, which is why he won't let me drive them if he's in the car. He drives them at fifty, while I sit on the passenger's side with my hand over my mouth and my heart in my teeth.

Hart Bivins arrived first of the invited guests, about a quarter to five, hanging his rain-wet beige jacket on the old-fashioned hall tree by the front door and turning inquiringly toward us, and extending a hearty hand to each of us in turn as Georgina introduced us. He even shook hands with Cameron, who looked rather bemused by the gesture. Usually nobody but the bishop did that.

I disliked Hart Bivins virtually on sight and didn't know why. *I do not like thee, Doctor Fell. The reason why I cannot tell; but this I know and know full well: I do not like thee, Doctor Fell,* I mused silently. Maybe it was something like that, a gut antipathy toward a man in a profession I really don't trust despite having several friends in it and a dear son-in-law headed for it. Or maybe it was the fact that he was trying a little too effusively to be friendly, warm, cordial, and genial, and the whole thing didn't quite come off, at least for me. He was a rather tall man, with graying hair, blue eyes, a pug nose, and a surprisingly deep tan for this time of year; I guessed he must have spent a lot of his winter on the ski slopes. His yellow polo shirt, khaki pants, and Weejuns with white socks, just right for the official season but totally wrong for the weather, struck the precise note of casual elegance to jar completely with Georgina's old-fashioned living room and dining room, with their polished hardwood floors and old brocade, mahogany, and walnut furniture. But maybe I was the only one who noticed that.

Cynthia followed him less than two minutes later, throwing Georgina, who had been called away from the kitchen twice in that short a time, into a distressing array of dithering.

I wasn't sure I liked Cynthia—still called Cindy by her family, who seemed not to notice the incongruity of using Alexandra's full name but continuing to call Cynthia by her nickname—either. Georgina must have gotten all the family's likableness. But maybe that was an unfair thought. I had no way of knowing what Alexandra would have been like if she hadn't been so emotionally damaged by her mother's murder or whatever it was that caused her splitting, and I couldn't be seeing Cindy at her best the day after her twin's murder.

There was a strong similarity between Cindy and Alexandra but there were even stronger differences. Cindy seemed taller than Alexandra, although I was pretty sure she really wasn't. Her coloring was identical, but her wildly disarranged graying brown hair, which looked as if she'd started out to tease it and then hadn't known what to do next, was startlingly different; Alexandra's hair at least had always been in order. Cindy was wearing brown slacks, a brown print blouse, white socks with red stripes on the cuffs, and high-top sneakers. Although Georgina had told me Cindy was divorced, she still wore her wedding and engagement rings, and she was wearing a dark brown leather fanny pack with the pack turned to her left instead of carrying a purse. She dropped her car keys into the pack only after she came in the door, removed her brown sports jacket, and hung it on the hall tree. I heard the keys jingle as she sat down in a faded electric-blue Queen Anne chair, which clashed wildly with the two faded red brocade Louis Quinze chairs, and stared at us, only nodding at Georgina's rather nervous introductions. Cynthia's last name, which I had not been told before, was Harvey.

We remained in the living room, where Georgina served iced V-8 with a celery stick in each glass as an aperitif. Georgina then rushed about distractedly, putting the roast on the table and shouting, "Cindy, have you got your garden in yet?"

"Too wet," Cindy said laconically. Those were the first words I had heard her say. Her voice was slightly like Alexandra's, but not distinctively so.

I wasn't sure Georgina heard her, as by then she had rushed back into the kitchen. She returned to the dining room carrying a divided vegetable bowl, and said to me, "Cindy's the only real gardener in the family. Aren't you, Cindy?" Then she dashed back into the kitchen, leaving Cindy to nod agreement to an empty space in the room.

I itched to help Georgina, but of course she didn't want me to, she wanted me to sit in here and talk with her other guests, not that I could see that doing much good. Cindy asked me the dog's name and then tossed her coat back on and vanished out the front door with her glass, and Hart—he'd asked us to call him Hart—took three small sips and then, as soon as Georgina was out of sight again, he stood up, walked over to the old floor-standing radio Cully (or someone, at any rate) had transformed into a liquor cabinet, and opened the door. Removing a bottle of Smirnoff's, he poured a modest ounce or so into the V-8 and held up the bottle invitingly, glancing around the room. Evidently he knew more about Cully's liquor cabinet than Cully himself knew; equally evidently, he didn't want Georgina to know he was helping himself and her guests. Harry hesitated, then held out his glass and accepted a little of the vodka.

Hal looked disapproving but otherwise kept his opinions to himself. He had better, I'd told him months ago. Harry had a perfect right to have an ounce of vodka if he wanted one, and I once had to point out to Hal that Harry isn't bound by the rules of a Church he hasn't joined, no matter who else in the family has. The bishop had backed me up in this, and Hal had promised not to nag.

Hart proceeded to exert himself to be charming. I am no good at small talk and never have been. Cameron, sensing the unease in the room, climbed into my lap and stayed there, sucking his thumb, which he almost never does unless he's very upset, and Hal and Lori sat like two lumps, almost but not quite close enough to touch each other. Hart and Harry carried the conversation, such as it was, and of course it eventually moved over into the area of sports and Hal leaped into it. With that, Lori visibly began to relax and Cameron, who had dozed off, awoke with a start and looked around.

Then Georgina came out, wiping her hands on her apron. Noticing what she was doing, she hastily took off the apron and wadded it up in her hands and tossed it back into the kitchen before saying, "Let's go to the table." Then, realizing Cindy's defection, she said, "Oh dear."

"I'll go get her," I said, and went out the front door, balancing Cameron on my left hip as women have probably carried babies and small children as long as women and babies have existed, favoring my hurt foot only slightly.

Cindy was out on the front porch feeding dog biscuits from the fanny pack to Pat, who was gobbling them as fast as she would offer them. "Georgina says dinner's ready," I told her.

She gave Pat one more dog biscuit and scratched behind his ears, zipped her pouch, and said smugly, "Dogs always like me."

Pat would like an ax murderer if the ax murderer would give

him enough dog biscuits. I knew that for a fact: an ax murderer, well, a hatchet murderer, had once fed him dog biscuits. Not that the murderer had been a threat to me, but still it said a lot about the discernment of the dog. But I didn't tell Cynthia that; I just followed her up into the living room, shutting the door quickly about six inches away from Pat's nose.

"Dogs don't like Sandy. But they always like me."

I suppose that was when I began to wonder whether Alexandra's problem had been the result of something that started earlier than her mother's death, perhaps a birth trauma or some prebirth malnourishment or injury. Because Cindy, who presumably was normal, sounded almost as odd as Alexandra.

Dinner was very subdued, as everybody carefully avoided the topic that Georgina had gathered us together to discuss and continued to talk sports (a lot) and politics (a little) with considerable concentration on Hillary Clinton's health package and whether it would ever actually be implemented. "I'd rather have Hillary than Bill for president," Harry commented at one point.

"Oh?" Hart said, with lifted eyebrows. "How so?"

"He's nothing but an overgrown frat rat," Harry said. Having worked his own way through college, he had little patience for people who—from his point of view, which is not necessarily accurate, as in this case it was not—had it given to them with extras. "Just look at him! Remember that photo of him walking to church near the White House in a baseball cap?"

As Harry is no fashion plate himself—he still lounges around the house in an old Marine Corps T-shirt despite the fact that it has been well over twenty years since he was a Marine—I am always amused to hear him discussing the president's attire. But he feels very strongly that presidents should dress presidentially, and he'd been totally scandalized ever since the news one day showed Mrs. Clinton, impeccably and presidentially dressed on her way to a meeting, pausing to kiss good-bye a husband who was wearing sweatpants, a sweatshirt with a longer T-shirt tail hanging out underneath it, grubby sneakers, and a baseball cap.

The talk continued in that vein for several more minutes, with me staying strictly out of it. It was only after Georgina had taken away the roast beef and vegetables and brought us all plates of cobbler that Hart Bivins, who didn't eat much of the dessert—I assumed he wanted to keep his boyish figure—folded his napkin and said, "Shall we move into the topic at hand?"

I could have taken the conversational lead anytime I wanted to, but I hadn't. Now, illogically, I was annoyed that Hart had. "What do you consider to be the topic at hand?" I asked.

"Georgina told me that we would attempt to discover who would want to kill Alexandra, and why," he said.

Cindy wriggled, and I glanced at her. Her lips were set in a tight line. Then she burst out, "You might want to discuss that. I don't. She was my sister!"

But obviously you don't intend to go to the funeral home tonight, I thought, looking again at her clothing. *Why?* But that probably wasn't a fair thought. Some people are made extremely nervous by funerals and bodies, and simply will not go to a viewing no matter how near to them the deceased was.

"She was my sister too," Georgina said, "and—"

"But she was my *twin!*"

"Which is all the more reason why you should want to know who killed her," Hart said.

"You don't understand about twins," Cindy yelled. "We still called each other every day to find out what we were wearing, so we'd be sure to dress alike!"

"Georgina, I told you not to allow that anymore," Hart said sharply.

"Be reasonable," Georgina said wearily. "How am I supposed to know what they're talking about on the telephone? How do you expect me to enforce it when I only see one of them?"

"I see your point," Hart admitted, and then abruptly changed the subject. "Georgina, will you begin? Try to characterize Alexandra as well as you can, leaving out her personality disorder. Don't worry about repeating information we all know; that's fine. Right now we're trying to fit all this into context for Deb and Harry."

"Where to begin," Georgina said, although I expected she'd been thinking about this all day. "All right, my father told me the doctors told him that Alexandra and Cindy started out to be identical twins, but for some reason having to do with the placenta Cindy got more of the prenatal nourishment. So Alexandra was born about two pounds smaller than Cindy, and had to stay in the hospital in an incubator about a month and a half after Cindy came home. Eventually she caught up in size, but she was sickly all through childhood, and people tended to give over to her—"

"They sure did," Cindy burst out. "I remember one time—"

"Let Georgina talk now," Hart said quietly. "You'll get your turn later."

"Well, she was pretty spoiled by the time she was two," Georgina said, "and she stayed that way until she was five. After that . . ." She shook her head. "What can I say that isn't connected with her psychiatric problem? If you try to leave out the fact that she never knew from one minute to the next who she was, what else is there to say?"

"You mentioned sports," Hal put in helpfully.

"Oh, yes, well, sports, she was always good in sports, especially baseball and basketball, but then all three of us were. Dad liked to teach us pitching and catching and batting and dribbling and making baskets, and we were good at it, though both Alexandra and Cindy were much better than I was. That's—what else can I say? She liked china kittens and puppies, but one time we got a real puppy—I thought she would like it—and she killed it about two weeks later because it kept her awake at night."

. . . . .

"That sounds like quite an overreaction," I said. "How did she—"

"She bashed its head in with a rock!" Cindy said. "Just like somebody did to our mother. At least that's what Georgina said, but I—" She subsided, looking at Georgina.

I looked at Georgina too, and she nodded. "That's what happened. That's another reason why I think she saw our mother killed, because she killed the puppy the same way. She was only five when Mother died, but the rest of her life all you had to do was mention Mother in front of her and she'd curl up and start sucking her thumb."

"She'd curl up in fetal position," Hart confirmed.

A picture flashed into my mind, a case I'd worked years ago when I was in Homicide, an elderly woman hacked to death with a butcher knife, her twenty-three-year-old daughter who lived with her charged with the murder but later acquitted on the grounds of insanity—a verdict I agreed with. I had gone up to the jail and tried to talk with the daughter more than twenty-four hours later, and found her, still sticky with her mother's blood that she had deliberately scooped up by the handful and spread all over her body, curled in the fetal position in front of the cell door reciting Bible verses. The jailer told me they'd tried to get her to take a shower, but every time they got her near the shower she started kicking, shrieking, and fighting so frenziedly that they'd decided it wasn't worth the trouble. Slowly I asked, "Is there any possibility whatever Alexandra could have killed her mother herself?"

"Deb, she was only five years old!" Georgina exclaimed.

"Anyway she wouldn't," Cindy yelled. "My sister wouldn't do that! I'll bet she didn't kill the puppy either. I'll bet the puppy just fell off the bed or something."

"She killed the puppy," Hart said flatly. "She told me that herself." Pushing away the dishes and steepling his hands, a gesture several male psychiatrists I've known frequently make, he said, "But I have no reason whatever to assume—or even suspect—that she killed her mother or that she did, or would, kill or even harm any other human being. To get on into her personality otherwise—I would not say any of this to anyone except for the fact that Alexandra is dead and we're looking into the question of who killed her. But given the situation, I strongly feel the privacy issue must give way to the justice issue, which is why I agreed to accept Georgina's invitation to dinner. The cold fact is that there are many people with reasons to dislike Alexandra. But I am not aware of anybody who had a reason to kill her."

He paused a moment, as if expecting questions, and then went on. "Alexandra's personalities, though volatile, were stable. What I mean by that is that they didn't continue to multiply; rather, she moved quickly through her repertoire, apparently drawing out the personality which seemed most useful or applicable at the time. Her repertoire included herself as she had been before the splintering started, a frightened five-year-old listening to the grown-ups fight and trying to make sense of her universe."

Both Georgina and Cindy had stiffened at that, and he went on. "I'm sorry, but it's true. Elias and Miranda were not well suited to each other; they did not appreciate each other's value system, and they fought frequently. Georgina, you're old enough to remember."

"They did," Georgina said, in a small, thin voice, "but they didn't mean anything by it. They loved each other."

"But what does that mean?" Hart asked. "What does it mean to say they loved one another? True love, I should think, would cause people to respect each other's feelings and points of view, but what many people call love is a desire to remake the other in one's own image."

"Agency," Georgina said to the tablecloth.

"The Mormon concept of agency, yes," Hart agreed. "As I understand it from the outside, it means that each person has the right and indeed the duty to make his or her own decisions and then to be responsible for those decisions, and that no person is held responsible for the actions of another person. Is that correct?"

"Approximately," I said, seeing Hal nod. Georgina, Cindy, and Lori were all staring at Hart, and Cameron was apparently beginning to tire of his dinner. He dropped his spoon, which clattered into the dish, and yawned widely.

"But Elias and Miranda, though they both were apparently devout Mormons, constantly attempted to deny one another the right to choose. Elias wanted to remake Miranda in his image, that of a businessman and sports aficionado. He wanted her to learn bookkeeping so that she could work in his jewelry store when the children were older. He wanted her to learn to play basketball, and to enjoy watching television sports with him. He thought she should play on the women's softball and volleyball teams with her church. He truly felt those things would give her more reason for living than she presently had, given the fact that she did none of her own housework and precious little of the child care. Georgina, is this a correct picture? Obviously I'm building it from things Alexandra said and didn't say; although I lived in the neighborhood and knew them both by sight, I was a child then myself and I didn't really *know* them."

Georgina nodded. "It's accurate enough."

Hart went on, "Miranda wanted to remake Elias in her image, that of a free-spirited dancer. She wanted ballroom and modern dancing, ballet, the theater, the opera, the symphony orchestra. Of course all of these things are available in Salt Lake City and he did take her ballroom dancing, though not as often as she wanted to go. As to the rest of it, she could have gone by herself or with other women, and in fact he had no objection to her taking part in modern dance and ballet herself, but she wanted Elias to go with her. She was convinced if he watched enough operas, saw enough live theater, heard enough symphonies, he'd learn to love them as she did. Georgina?"

"That's right."

"So they argued quite a lot about values and choices. And the children had to watch, or at least listen to, all the quarreling. Isn't that right, Georgina?"

Still looking at the tablecloth, Georgina said, "They tried just to fight when we were asleep. But we'd wake up. Yes, we heard them. I heard them."

"So that was one Alexandra," Hart said. "Let's call her Sandy, the five-year-old lying under the covers listening to her parents scream at one another. And Miranda had quite a temper, and she didn't always consider the consequences; she'd sometimes throw things, and the children would hear breaking glass. Sandy heard a lot of screaming, shouting, breaking glass, and it terrified her. When she found her mother dead, or saw her mother killed—I was never able to determine which happened—the terror of that experience pushed her over the edge. She splintered, and there was Sandy, stuck forever as a frightened five-year-old. There was another Alexandra, we'll call her Alexandra, the one who continued to grow, an adult who graduated from high school and then from LDS Business College and worked as a secretary for a freelance geologist. She was adequate as long as he was in the office, but when he went out on field trips and she had to spend whole days alone in the office she tended to revert, and several times he would return to find small Sandy had taken over and crayoned flowers all over several sets of survey results. It was only the fact that he had the results on computer and could easily reprint them that kept him from firing her. He called me several times about the problem—"

I opened my mouth and then closed it again, but not before he noticed. "You were going to say?"

I shook my head. "Nothing." This wasn't the time to tell Georgina that Alexandra's boss finally had fired her.

. . . . .

"Then there was Sandy Lu." Hart looked apologetically at Georgina. "I know you don't like this to be discussed, but I'm afraid we're going to have to discuss it now. Of course Alexandra was raised LDS, and there was no coffee, tea, or alcohol used in the household. But Sandy Lu was an extreme extension of what Alexandra—the bits of Alexandra that were never integrated into one—must have imagined her mother's life as a dancer, before she married Elias, to be. Sandy Lu took off her CTR ring and left it in Alexandra's desk drawer, and went out drinking and dancing and sleeping around. She also, I'm afraid, did some minor blackmailing along the way."

"She what?" Georgina's voice shook. "Nobody ever told me that."

"I saw no reason for you to know. I took care of the problem. So I'm sorry, but it's got to be mentioned now because it could be relevant to her cause of death. She did some minor blackmailing along the way. Nothing serious, so far as I know, and I made her return the money to her victims and promise never to repeat the offense. So far as I know, she did not."

"But you don't know for sure," I heard myself say.

"No. I don't know for sure. But I don't think she did." Hart paused briefly, theatrically, and then went on. "Then there was another personality, this one a boy. I knew him—Ron Harkness. He was twelve when they met and she was ten, and he was rather violent, but he liked Alexandra and tried to protect her from bullying. When he was killed in a traffic accident at the age of seventeen, Alexandra, then fifteen, took over his personality also."

"So it's—it was—Ron who kept picking a fight with me?" Hal asked.

"It would be, yes, though of course it was Ron as filtered through Alexandra's mind, Ron not as he necessarily was but Ron as Alexandra perceived him to be. But her Ron personality often tried to fight men and older boys."

. . . . .

"Who did Ron protect Alexandra from?" I asked.

Hart hesitated. Both Georgina and Cindy glared at him, and he said, "I'm afraid I'm not at liberty to discuss that at present."

"Then those are all her personalities?" Harry asked.

"Almost," Hart said. "Very rarely she takes over—took over, I should say—Miranda's personality as she saw it to be, and once since his death I have seen her slide into the personality of Elias. Rather startling, really, because somehow for those few moments she actually *looked* like Elias. If I believed in spirit possession—but I don't, of course."

I don't either, and I considered the statement silly until I remembered an earlier discussion. "Did Alexandra?"

"Believe in spirit possession?" He hesitated. "I'm not sure. She believed in ghosts. Yes, I think she did believe in spirit possession."

"So did she believe she was possessed by the spirits of other people?" I persisted.

"Do you know, I never asked her? I should have. . . . Yes, indeed I should have. And probably I would have gotten to it eventually."

"And that's all you have to say?" I asked.

"That's all," Hart said. "And that's all the personalities. At least that's all I ever met. But I have been working with her for six years, and I think I would have known if there were any others."

"Then I suppose what's important," I said, "is first to figure out which Alexandra was murdered. I don't see how we can do anything at all about finding out who murdered her until we know that, and my guess is that as soon as we know that we'll know why and who."

"That may be true," Hart said, "but I fail completely to see how anyone can find out which Alexandra was murdered. You've been working on it all day and from what Georgina told me over the phone, I gather you haven't gotten far."

"We got far enough to get the tires slashed," I said.

"I don't understand the connection."

"If somebody slashed all four tires, and it had something to do with this case, which Detective Sosa seems convinced it does and I agree, then we were getting closer than we realized to something that mattered. As to time, it usually takes far more than a day to find out much about a complicated murder. Doesn't it usually take you more than one session to figure out much about a deep-rooted psychosis?"

Hart grinned, the first real smile I had seen on his face. "You're right," he said, "it does. All right, you have a point. That's all I have to say right now. Cindy, you wanted to speak earlier, do you want to add anything now?"

"No," she said. "You've said it all. You and Georgina. Maybe there were people mad at her. Maybe there were people who had reasons to dislike her. But nobody had any reason to kill her." Quite suddenly, she started to cry. "She was my sister and I loved her. Now it's just Georgina and me. My husband left me and Georgina's husband left her, so we're both all alone. Just us. I want somebody to find out who killed my sister." She stood up, still crying, and said, "I'm going home." She stumbled toward the front door.

"Drive carefully in this rain," Georgina called after her.

"I will. Quit worrying, Georgie, you know I'm always a careful driver."

After the door slammed, Georgina said, "Deb, just so you'll know, Ron—the real Ron—often had to protect Alexandra from Cindy, because when Cindy was a child she tended to take out her troubles on other people and Alexandra—Sandy we called her then—was there and vulnerable. Cindy never had MPD or anything like that, though she's been depressed a lot, but she deliberately took on some of our mother's personality, and to be perfectly honest, Mother was a pain."

"Oh?" I queried.

"She was bossy to everybody, even to Aunt LaRae, and she was very—emotional, I guess that's a good word. She had good qualities—she was more like a playmate than a mother a lot of the time, but you never knew when she was going to want to pick up her dollies and go home. Cindy's like that. Mother liked to garden, that's where Cindy got that from, so not all Mother's character traits were bad. But of course it was a long time ago that she, Cindy I mean, took out her frustrations on Sandy, and now that she's a reasonable adult she doesn't like to be reminded of it. So I'm telling you just so you won't go trying to find out who bullied Sandy when she was a kid and see if that was the person who killed her. It was her twin, and I think you see that it couldn't have been Cindy who killed her."

Frankly I didn't see that at all. I doubted that it was Cindy who killed her sister, but I couldn't positively rule her out yet, and mentally I questioned how reasonable an adult Cindy had grown up to be. But for now I accepted the statement. "Hart," I said, "there's one more thing I can't help wondering about."

"What's that?"

I gestured toward the vacant lot next door. "What kind of an effect did it have on Alexandra to have her bedroom window looking down on that family cemetery? Especially believing in ghosts as she did?"

His hesitation this time was much longer than just perceptible. "She never talked about it," he said finally. "And the fact that she didn't is probably meaningful. If it hadn't mattered to her, she would have mentioned it casually, in passing, at least once or twice, something like 'Well, yesterday we went and mowed around the graves.' But she never mentioned it at all. So I don't know. *In the midst of life we are in death*—it could have meant no more to her than that. Or it could have been a constant reminder to her of her mother's death, or it could in some way we don't understand have made her feel as if she herself were living in death. I don't know. I really don't. If she had committed suicide, this might be applicable, but since she was murdered, I don't see any connection between this and her own death."

I didn't either, and I didn't really know why I had asked. We said our good nights—it turned out Hart was escorting Georgina to the funeral home—and I took Cameron upstairs and washed him and put him to bed, where he was thoroughly ready to go. Then I went down and helped Lori and Hal finish clearing the table and washing the dishes because Georgina had had to dash off without doing it and we didn't want her to have to come home from the mortuary to a dirty kitchen.

Then I went up both flights of stairs, back into Alexandra's room, and looked out the window for a long time, down onto the rainwashed night-dark graves below and the rain-mist drifting above them, and wondered how they would have looked to a terrified five-year-old.

. . . . .

Seven

Tuesday morning the phone rang while we were still at breakfast. Georgina talked briefly, and then called me to the phone. "I don't know if you remember me," a rather businesslike female voice said, "but I'm Kate Rolley from the medical examiner's office. There are some things about the body that are puzzling me just a little. I asked Mrs. Grafton if I could come and talk with her, and after that, I wonder if you and your husband could spare time to go with me to Gilgal for a few minutes?"

I pointed out to her that Gilgal isn't open except on Sunday afternoon, and she said, "I've already made arrangements to get in. They lent me the key; I told them I might need to go back several times this week."

"Just a minute," I said, "let me check with my husband." As much as Harry had enjoyed playing Dirty Harry yesterday, I was well aware that he had already announced that *today* we were *really* going sight-seeing and leave the policing to the people whose job it was.

Fortunately, because I would have had to go no matter how he felt about it, Harry was agreeable to my going to Gilgal, as long as he went too. But he added, "I want some of our vacation to be *vacation*. After the medical examiner's office gets through with us, we're going to Wendover."

I wasn't totally enthralled by the idea of visiting Wendover, which Georgina had described to us as a town on the Utah-Nevada border that exists to support several huge gambling casinos, which are on the Nevada side but are normally frequented almost entirely by people from Utah. But on the way we would see the Tree, which Georgina had told us was an extremely bizarre sculpture, and we would see a small part of the Salt Flats, where so many of the world's speed records had been set.

After breakfast Hal, Lori, and Cameron set off in the van, promising to return by eleven, and I took Pat for another walk while Harry belatedly shaved, something he tends to be a little careless about while on vacation. The rain had finally stopped, and it was a glorious cool bright day. Even with a cane, I enjoyed being out, though I deliberately avoided the small cemetery by turning left after I reached the sidewalk, turning right at the end of the block and walking two blocks, turning right again and walking one block, and so on until I arrived back on the corner to the same end of Georgina's house I had left from. By the time I had returned and reattached Pat's collar to the chain on the tie-down stake, Kate Rolley was just getting out of her Buick. We went together into the house, and I called, "Georgina, Dr. Rolley's here."

"Okay," Georgina yelled from the kitchen, and came out wiping her hands on her apron. "You're the pathologist?" she asked.

"I'm a pathologist, yes," Kate said cautiously.

"But are you the one that—that did the autopsy on Alexandra?"

"Yes, I am." There was considerable pity in Kate's voice; she had not yet grown hardened to her work as some pathologists do.

"How long did she suffer? I need to know. . . ." Probably without realizing it, Georgina was twisting her hands around inside the apron, twisting the apron around her hands.

"Death was virtually instantaneous," Kate assured her. "She didn't live more than about three minutes after she was struck."

"She what?" I exclaimed. "But—"

Kate glanced at me, that we'll-talk-about-it-later glance I sometimes get from fellow officers, and I subsided. "Really there was just one thing I needed to ask you, Mrs. Grafton," Kate said. "I noticed that there was evidence—the tan line and so forth on her hand—that your sister frequently, but not always, wore a ring on the ring finger of her left hand, and I'm wondering whether whoever attacked her"—*Nice euphemism,* I thought—"could have taken it. If you could tell me what the ring looked like—"

"Nobody took it," Georgina said. "She left it in her desk drawer at work. She did that sometimes."

"Would it be possible for me to drop by where she worked and have a look at it?"

"Deb and Harry cleaned out her desk for me and brought me the ring. It's—on her now."

That meant we had to go to the mortuary before going to Gilgal. Actually I suppose nobody but Kate had to go in and look at Alexandra's left hand with the sterling silver CTR ring on it, but in fact we all did, and Harry and I signed the guest register on some sort of pretense that we were there only as friends.

Kate lifted the cold hand, which was far more than I wanted to do, though of course in the past, on my own cases, I had when necessary done just the same thing, and looked closely at it. She slid the ring up and down on the finger, looking at the not-quite-clear tan line, and said "Hmm," under her breath.

Practically all the pathologists I know do this "hmm" bit, and there's no use asking them what they mean by it because half the time they don't know they're doing it and the other half of the time they either don't know why they're doing it or refuse to explain. I asked anyway, going closer to the coffin in hopes that I could see whatever it was she was seeing.

Kate semi-explained. At least she said, "I wonder whether she had another ring she wore sometimes."

"I can find out," I said. Now I, too, could see what she was looking at: the tan line did not quite fit the CTR ring, even if Alexandra didn't wear it all the time.

"Please do," Kate said. "And let me know as soon as it's convenient. I've got photographs, but I really need to know before the funeral if possible." The funeral, I knew, had been scheduled for Saturday, a full six days after the death, which seemed a little late to me. I told Kate that, and she said, "Well, that's good, but still the sooner I know, the better."

Kate carefully put the hand back in the position it had been in, and we left. I for one was glad to leave. This was definitely a nice funeral home, but I do not like the way even the nicest funeral homes smell.

I was glad to get to Gilgal, because something was puzzling me. Actually a lot of things were puzzling me, and had been since Kate dropped her bombshell, but most of them were in my conscious mind. At least one thing was crawling around in my subconscious, however, and I couldn't figure out what it was.

As we went down the small walkway between the houses, the little dog at the house on the left began to bark wildly and I stopped short, so suddenly that Harry nearly fell over me. "That's it," I said.

"What's it?" Kate asked.

"That's what was puzzling me. Kate, you said she didn't live over three minutes after she was struck. Can you be absolutely certain of that?"

"I *am* absolutely certain of that."

"Okay, then how did the killer escape? I mean, that dog always barks when anybody goes past it and usually three to five minutes afterwards. We all know that. Well, when we parked here the dog was silent. All told, it probably took us two or three minutes to get everybody out of the car—"

"Why so long?" Kate interrupted.

"Because of getting Cameron out of the car seat," Harry said.

"We keep him strapped in pretty thoroughly, so he can't get out and wander around the car. I agree, it was at least three minutes."

"And the dog was silent all the time. But it started barking as soon as we started down this walk. So what that means is the killer escaped another way."

"Well, yes," Kate agreed. "But not necessarily, because he could have run out just before you got here and you might not have noticed."

"Yes, we would," I said, "and I'll show you why in a minute. Anyway, that would have put her death closer to seven minutes after she was struck, and even I can tell there wasn't enough blood for that." Indeed there wasn't; head wounds, even minor ones, bleed profusely.

"If he didn't go that way then he had to have gone another way," Kate said. "It's not as if there were no other way."

"All right, *what* way?" I demanded. "Because Charlie Sosa checked everything pretty thoroughly. He didn't go out that way"—I gestured to my left—"because of the bakery. It's impossible. He didn't go out that way"—I pointed straight ahead, to the back of the sculpture garden—"because he'd have had to go through the parking lot of that church, and there were people in the parking lot who would have seen anybody running. I saw them when we came in. He didn't go that way"—I pointed to my right—"because he'd have had to run through the backyard of that house, and they were having some kind of party or family reunion or something, and even with the rain there were a lot of kids running around outside. I *saw* Charlie stop and talk to them. So that leaves only the walk we're on—but watch." We walked on into the sculpture garden itself, and the dog continued to bark for two more minutes by my watch. "That's how long the dog continues to bark. And sometimes even longer; it was three minutes at least once Sunday. So if he went out this way, even if you're a couple of minutes off in your estimate, the dog would have still been barking when we arrived. So how did he get away? How did he escape?"

"I've talked with Charlie," Kate said, "and he did talk to the people in the church parking lot and the people in the adjoining houses. You're right about that. They're all certain they'd have seen somebody running out of Gilgal, and nobody did. And even if he was walking instead of running—in the yard they'd have noticed a stranger; in the church parking lot they'd have seen somebody going over the fence. I don't think he talked to anybody at the bakery, but—" She turned, gazing at the high wall. "I'm with you. I don't think anybody could have gotten out that way. So unless I'm wrong on the timing—But dammit, I'm *not* wrong. Maybe five minutes at the very most, but that'd still put him escaping at the same time you got here. This is impossible," she said, half under her breath. Then, more loudly, she said, "I don't believe in locked-room mysteries. If it did happen, then it could have happened. . . . All right, we all saw the body. It was right here. And we all saw that round white stone—I know Charlie already did this, but let's do it again, in the sunshine. Let's see if anywhere in this park there are any stones like the one she was struck with."

We walked a grid, first north-south then east-west, with the three of us side by side and spread out so that there were at least two people looking everywhere. At the end of that time we were in agreement: there were no round fist-sized whitewashed stones anywhere in Gilgal.

"This bothers me," Kate said. "Where did the weapon come from? And the other thing that bothers me is just *how* it happened."

That had been bothering me too, the angle and position of the wound, but I hadn't been able to articulate my reasons. Kate put them into words. "Either the stone was wielded by a very short person—and I mean the height of your average eight-year-old—or else it was slammed against her head from a rather odd angle when she was already facedown on the ground and somebody was crouched over her. But I don't know any murderous eight-year-olds, and if she was already facedown on the ground, why?"

"There were kids at one of those houses—"

Kate shook her head. "Charlie talked to all of them. And he's got a good feel for something like that. Anyway, there wouldn't have been any reason. Dammit, if what *obviously* happened *didn't* happen, then what *did* happen? Well, I'll tell Charlie what we've found, and then *he* gets to think about it some more."

She dropped us back by Georgina's, where I asked permission to have another look in Alexandra's room. "Look all you want," Georgina said. "Now, didn't you tell me you wouldn't be here for dinner tonight?"

"That's right," I said.

"Well, I think I'll go over to the funeral home. Be sure to lock up when you leave."

We promised, and while Harry took a brief nap preparatory to driving across the desert, I went up and looked in the jewelry box we'd found in Alexandra's room. She had four Avon rings, different sizes, different shapes. I called Kate and told her, and she said, "Thanks. That clears one question. Now if we could just clear the others . . ."

The kids arrived from wherever they had been—I didn't inquire—and we all loaded into the car. We left Pat, whom we would have normally taken, because I wasn't sure how long Harry would insist on staying in the casino, and I didn't want to have to leave the dog in the car in the sun. And off we went toward Wendover, driving into the sunshine as we headed generally southwest.

There were more interesting things to see than I had expected in a drive across what I've heard is about the bleakest part of the Great American Desert, beginning with a 1920s-style resort near the beaches of the Great Salt Lake. Although it was called Saltair, it reminded me of nothing so much as the pictures I had seen of the eighteenth-century prince regent's palace at Brighton. Vaguely I remembered an article I saw in a *National Geographic,* about ten years ago when the lake was flooding very badly, that showed the new owner of Saltair rowing about the grand ballroom in a motor-boat. But it appeared now that he was in a fair way to recoup his investment; although there weren't a lot of people at the beach, probably because people expected it still to be chilly from the rain, there was a water slide and several concession-type booths, and an entire marina full of sailboats with bright sails adjoined the edifice.

By now the day that had started off cool had turned hot and muggy; in the division between the westbound and eastbound lanes of the highway often were large puddles or whole ponds of water left over from the week of rain. To the left was a huge pile of blackish sand. Georgina had told me to watch for it; she said it was tailings from industrial mining, reduced only minimally from the tons that had been taken from it to build a flood wall to protect the highway from future rises of the water. A little bit farther on, a huge black rock stuck up from the depths of the lake on the right, as if some mechanical giant had ripped it out of a nearby mountainside and flung it into the water. I asked Harry whether it was volcanic.

"I haven't the slightest idea," he answered. "Where's that book I bought you at Golden Spike?"

That book he had bought me at Golden Spike was *The Roadside Geology of Utah.* And I had left it at Georgina's, where it was doing not a particle of good.

Then the road veered away from the lake, and I began to see, on the left and right of the road, frequent ordered piles of rock with an occasional bottle stuck open-side-down, spelling out words and names, drawing symbols ordinary and mystical. There were the inevitable *J.H. LOVES R.W.,* several peace signs, and a lot of other initials, signs, and symbols that meant nothing at all to me. In other places I could see that waters from the recent rain had disarranged or half buried such markings, leaving a clear sandy slate for somebody else to write on. This, I surmised, must be great fun for everybody, both artists and travelers.

All this time I couldn't help fretting about what was going on behind me, but I conscientiously reminded myself that I was on vacation, that this wasn't my case, and that Charlie Sosa and Kate Rolley had the murder investigation well in hand.

My self did not listen very well. I kept on worrying.

We did indeed see the Tree, and like just about everyone else—I say this with confidence; the tire marks had worn grassless ruts in the road shoulder—we totally ignored the NO STOPPING OR STANDING sign, parked the car, and got out and looked at and photographed it. It was a very tall pole with several huge multicolored balls arranged around the top of it; around it on the ground were several quadrants, which all together did not add up to another ball. Some of the balls were spotted, some were striped, some were spotted *and* striped, and some were solid colors. What it all was supposed to mean I had no idea. Why anybody had put it out here I had no idea. But it was certainly different.

We stopped at the Salt Flats, which were rather a disappointment because the salt—which, Georgina had told us, usually glittered like a fresh snowfall and squeaked when you walked on it like very dry snow—was almost entirely covered by a shallow layer of water where seagulls were wading. I could understand the presence of the seagulls; I had already been told that the Utah state bird is the California seagull, which had struck me as a little bit ludicrous until I heard the story about the seagulls and found out why there is a huge statue of a seagull in Temple Square.

When the first pioneers arrived in the Salt Lake Valley, there had been one tree in the entire valley. They looked down from Emigration Canyon to see a barren expanse of sagebrush and juniper weed, watered by a few streams, which did virtually nothing to encourage plant growth. They went down into the valley, dug gardens by hand out of the rock-hard soil, and dug wells or drew irrigation water from City Creek and the Jordan, which runs north from Utah Lake to the Great Salt Lake in imitation of Israel's Jordan, which runs south from the freshwater Sea of Galilee (which is almost the same size as Utah Lake) to the Dead Sea.

The soil was fertile once they dug past the hardpan and reached it, and the crops did well, until a swarm of locusts descended on them. Normally the locust is just an innocent little grasshopper, but under certain weather conditions the number multiplies by a factor of thousands and the little grasshoppers change color, grow larger, and gather in voracious swarms. The locusts could strip a field in five minutes before moving on to the next one. The pioneers, with starvation staring them in the face in the midst of what had looked to be plenty, prayed for help, and suddenly from nowhere whole clouds of seagulls arrived, landing in field after field. At first the pioneers feared that the seagulls also would devour the crops, but instead the seagulls devoured the locusts, and most of the crops were saved.

It was a normal migration pattern: the seagulls winter, and hatch, on the California coast, but in the spring they fly inland to spend the summer in the Salt Lake Valley, returning to California in the late fall. But to the pioneers that was the miracle of the seagulls, and an old song still speaks of the seagulls arriving on angel wings. And now no one in Utah sneers at or abuses the seagulls, even when they raid garbage dumps and brazenly snatch sandwiches out of picnickers' hands. They have earned their keep.

As we drove on I looked avidly at the scenery, seeing the occasional opening to caves or mines. At one point, high on a bluff to my right, there were two small cave openings side by side shaped exactly like eyes, and some wit had climbed up there with wood and paint to create eyeballs to fit in the openings.

Just past that we left the freeway to drive down into the town of Wendover.

Words fail me.

. . . . .

Virtually the entire town, such as it is, consists of casinos. Harry had decided we would have a large midday dinner there and just have a snack in the evening because, he pointed out, casinos are well known for having excellent food at low prices since they make their profits from gambling. So we picked out the Golden Frog Casino for no other reason than that it was easy to get into and out of.

Circus Circus in Las Vegas has chosen the circus as its motif. The Golden Frog has selected as its motif the small gold frog amulets found in such plenitude in Central America. To the right as we walked in was a brightly lit glass display case filled with hundreds of what I certainly hoped were replicas of the frogs, as that many real ones couldn't possibly have been either collected or exported to the United States legally—to say nothing of the danger in keeping that much gold bullion around. Frogs adorned the walls; frogs adorned the tables. Some of the slot machines had substituted golden frogs for cherries to show a win.

We had to walk through the gambling area to get to the restaurant. I have never in all my life seen so many people trying to get something for nothing and, in general, not succeeding. Old ladies who looked as if they ought to be at home in rocking chairs seemed glued to the handles of slot machines or were walking around—sometimes in walkers, in one case trailing a canister of oxygen attached to her walker (which frightened me in view of the number of smokers surrounding her)—with fanny packs full of nickels or quarters in front of them rather than behind.

Harry gave me four quarters and told me I could not go to Nevada for the first time without gambling. "Play till you lose it," he said.

With Hal and Lori watching *very* disapprovingly, I located a quarter machine, dropped in the quarter, and gingerly pulled the handle. Bells rang, things swirled around, and two golden frogs and an iguana lined up. *Good,* I thought, *at this rate it won't take me long to get rid of a dollar.* But the next time three iguanas lined up and six quarters fell out of the machine. Now I had nine quarters to get rid of.

Would you believe it took me half an hour to do it? Every time I was down to one quarter those three darn iguanas, or three turtles, or once three golden frogs, would line up and quarters would fall out. When the turtles lined up four quarters fell out. When the iguanas lined up six quarters fell out. When the frogs lined up twelve quarters fell out. Obviously here at least frogs were worth more than turtles or iguanas.

I am told that in most slot machines it is cherries, apples, and lemons. I'll take their word for it. The only term that came to my mind to describe this place was Temple of Mammon, filled with devout worshippers of whom I did not wish to be one.

I found it difficult to believe that anybody would spend all day dropping nickels or quarters into the machine to see if three cherries, apples, lemons, iguanas, turtles, or golden frogs lined up, but it was quite evident that people did. If my experience was anything to go by, most of them, in eight hours, would lose at least sixteen dollars, with only an occasional win to keep them suckered into continuing to play—if you call that playing. Harry says it is called gaming. I thought gaming was what Hal did with Dungeons & Dragons. Whatever it is called, I have better things to do with my time.

Now that I had officially gambled and could stop, we went and got in the restaurant line, which had grown quite a lot (I wasn't sure what time it was, as Utah is on Mountain time and Nevada is on Pacific time) while we were doing other things. Right ahead of us was a man wearing a clerical collar. He had his arm around the most absolutely beautiful young man, probably about Hal's age, that I had ever seen. I told myself he was an Episcopal priest or a clergyman from some other denomination that has married clergy and wears clerical collars, and that was his son. My self did not believe a word of it.

. . . . .

Dinner, I must say, was excellent, even considering how spoiled Georgina had us and how many times we were interrupted by keno runners. I had London broil, roasted potatoes, a vegetable medley, and an excellent salad bar. After dinner somebody brought around a dessert cart, and Lori, relaxing a little by now, laughingly insisted she wanted the whole cart, though she finally settled for chocolate pie. Hal really did get two desserts, which did not surprise me at all, and Cameron ate half of his pudding and went to sleep in his chair. I got what I thought was key lime pie, but after one bite I must have looked startled, because Harry said, "What's wrong?"

"It isn't key lime pie," I said.

"Well, what is it?"

"Peppermint pie."

"Is that all right?"

"I guess it is," I said, "but it wasn't the taste I was expecting."

By that time I had noticed a woman near us, and was staring at her. She was very thin and heavily tattooed, which was quite evident as she was wearing only shorts and halter and sandals. She had with her two children, presumably hers. The girl, about eight, was dressed like a princess: shining auburn hair in Shirley Temple curls, white patent leather shoes with clean white socks, and a dress that couldn't have cost under a hundred dollars. The boy, about six, was in dirty brown shorts, a torn striped shirt, and sneakers with holes in them. He appeared as if his face hadn't been washed in three days and his hair hadn't been cut, combed, or even washed in at least three months.

I didn't say anything. What was there to say? But I'll admit I thought a lot. And if I had to be one or the other of those children, I believe I would rather have been the boy. The girl was a little too obviously merchandise.

"I might just go play a few hands of blackjack," Harry said when we were through eating.

"What would you suggest the rest of us do while you're playing?" I asked, trying to sound reasonable, although the best I could figure out there was absolutely nothing else in town to do.

He looked at me. At Hal. At Lori. At Cameron. And then he shrugged and said, "I guess I don't really want to play blackjack anyway."

"Thank you," I said.

"But I will get in one hand while you're tending to Cameron."

I took Cameron to the rest room and washed him and saw to it that he attended to other needs. Then I removed Harry from the blackjack table, which wasn't hard to do as he had dropped twenty dollars in the time I was gone, and we left, though I could still smell the smoke in my hair and expected to continue to do so for several hours.

He insisted on stopping at one more casino just to walk through it, he said, though he wound up throwing away another ten dollars on the slot machines while I waited with steam coming out of my ears. It took him an hour. I took half an hour to lose only one dollar. But he was dropping in three quarters at a time, trying for bigger prizes.

Driving back to Salt Lake on a highway that by now was blazing hot, I was fascinated at seeing not only the usual mirages you see on any hot road, of water that always stays somewhere just a little ahead of you, but also to the left the mirages of mountains reflected in lakes that weren't really there at all. They seemed so real. The mountains were really there, and the reflections were definitely of the same mountains. But how could they reflect out of water that—when we got closer—we could tell did not even exist? One of them was shaped like a dinosaur, perhaps a brontosaurus, lying flat on the ground with its neck stretched out and the long diamond of its head like that of a python. Behind its neck was its huge bulky body, and then its tail rippling out behind it. The belly of the dinosaur lay on the belly of another dinosaur that lay faceup in the water that wasn't really there.

. . . . .

When we got back to where the lake really was, at first I thought I was looking at another mirage when I saw Antelope Island rising precipitously out of the water that reflected it. But then I realized that one was real, and a brief look at the map told me what it was.

It was after six by now, and I would have been quite ready to go get some rest. But we were actually sightseeing for the first time in days, and Harry had the bit in his teeth. We went up to the mouth of Emigration Canyon to look at the "This is the place" monument, which commemorates July 24, 1847, when Brigham Young, lying sick inside the covered wagon, crawled out leaning heavily on his cane, looked down at the valley ahead to see if it matched the place he had seen in his vision, and said, "This is the right place. Drive on," and the wagon train carrying a hundred and forty-three men, three women—Ellen Kimball, wife of Heber C. Kimball; Clarissa Young, wife of Brigham Young; and Harriet Young, wife of Lorenzo Young—and two children drove on down into the valley.

I have often wondered what those three women, who had come from the lush green bottomlands of Illinois and Missouri, thought as they looked down onto that barren valley with only one tree where they would spend the rest of their lives. I wonder if they cried. I think I would have. I wonder if they could envision even a village growing there, much less the city that is there now. They went there knowing that mountain man Jim Bridger, who knew the area as well as anybody, had offered a hundred dollars to anybody who could ever produce a single bushel of wheat in the Salt Lake Valley—and now they had to live there, and find a way to feed themselves and their children.

Digging and planting began that very first day, in ground that was so hard they broke two iron plows. That must have been heartbreaking. But despite the breakage they got gardens dug and planted. And although I was sure planting season is later in Utah than it is in Texas, July 24 is still very, very late to plant seeds and expect to reap a crop.

Also on that first day, Brigham Young picked out a spot, leaned so hard on his cane as to puncture a hole in the hardpan, and said, "Here we shall build our Temple." And there, when the time was right, the cornerstone was laid of the soaring granite Temple that stands today, although Brigham Young was not to live to see its completion.

Now you look down from the mouth of Emigration Canyon onto a city of houses, businesses, churches, trees, soft, richly mulched gardens, orchards of apples and plums and peaches and cherries, lawns, and fountains. It's hard to imagine what it must have looked like to those first settlers.

By the time Georgina's ancestor Elias Howe had arrived, in 1880, Salt Lake City was already a thriving community, with gardens and orchards and shops and a multitude of different religions represented. The Tabernacle had been built, and oddly enough the first Catholic mass ever presented in Utah had taken place in the Mormon Tabernacle. The Temple was steadily rising from its foundation. Since the first transcontinental railroad was completed in 1869, more than likely Elias and whatever wife or wives he had then—my guess is he had arrived single or with one wife and married the other two later—took the intercontinental railroad as far as Ogden, and then offloaded onto the Mormon-built railroad spur from Ogden to Salt Lake City, where their goods would have been picked up and delivered by oxcart to wherever they lived to start with. He must have brought the stock for his first jewelry store with him, along with household goods, clothing, and food.

I watched Cameron happily scramble around on the monument with Hal, who had temporarily taken charge of the camera, taking his picture, and I wondered what ages those first two children had been and how they had felt looking down onto the spot where their homes would be. What became of them? Did they live their entire lives in Salt Lake City, or did they migrate again and again as Brigham Young, in a planned settlement of the entire territory, sent whole families to go to new places to establish new villages and towns?

"You ready to leave?" Harry said in my ear, and I jumped. I had been lost in the historical past, studying the monument and the inscriptions on it, remembering the things I had read when Hal was studying church history, and I had virtually forgotten the twentieth century.

But here we were and heading with what seemed like interstellar speed on into the twenty-first. "I guess," I said, looking down once more into the valley now lit by streetlights and by the lights shining out the windows of thousands of homes.

Despite the size of the dinner we had had, everybody was hungry again by now. We dropped by an Arctic Circle for burgers and shakes, and then went back to Georgina's. By then it was close to ten P.M.

Georgina's was pitch-dark. At best the yard was always dark, because she had a huge tree with branches that filled the whole front yard and overhung the porch and the driveway, but now it was darker than I'd ever seen it. The streetlight was out; the porch light was out. I heard Harry swear and then mutter, "I left my flashlight inside. I didn't expect to need it. I can understand her going to bed early, with all she's had to cope with the last few days, but you'd think she'd have remembered to turn the porch light on."

"Maybe she did and it burned out," I suggested.

"Maybe. Well, let me see if I can find the key." He turned on the dome light of the car and sorted out keys. "You guys stay here until I get some lights on."

With an unfamiliar lock, an unfamiliar key, an unfamiliar front porch, and a dog curled up in a small ball shivering and whining urgently, it took fully two minutes for him to get the front door open and the living room light on. We all stumbled out of the car and raced one another for the two bathrooms in the house, and then I went out to check on and medicate the dog, who was still curled up in a ball whining and shivering, and check his supply of food and water. "What's the matter, boy?" I asked him, and he barked once and went on shivering.

I couldn't find his water dish. Apparently he had knocked it off the porch and into the front yard. Disgusted, I went back in and went up to Harry's and my room, to rummage through luggage until I found the flashlight. "Mom, you need some help?" asked Hal.

"No, I'm all right, the silly dog just lost his water dish." I went back out with the flashlight on, shining it around the front yard until I saw the glint of metal, and then I froze.

There was something near the metal that hadn't been there this morning. And now I knew why Pat was shivering and whining.

With a chill in the pit of my stomach, I walked closer and looked more carefully, and then backed away, slowly, and went in the house and picked up the phone and dialed 911. I gave the address and said, "It's Georgina Grafton. She's dead. You'd better call Detective Sosa, because it's tied up with a case he's working."

Then I sat down, hard, and Harry said, "Oh, shit."

· · · · ·

Eight

WE HAD TO lock Pat in the car. Even if he didn't dislike anybody in uniform, which he does, he strongly dislikes commotion; for a pit bull, he is a peace-loving animal, and he will cheerfully eat anybody whom he perceives as interfering with his peace and quiet. (Eating commotion-makers is a pit bull's definition of peace, which is why nobody who can't control such a dog should own one.) Four uniformed officers, one detective, one detective sergeant, two crime-scene technicians, and one assistant medical examiner, along with a lot of floodlights, added up to commotion in his book. In Cameron's book too, for that matter. He had napped a little in the car, but not as much as he should have, and it was way past his bedtime. Being on a cold front porch—without even the dog, who was presently prohibited from kissing him in case whatever he had was human-contagious (which meant we had to keep Cameron away from the dog because keeping the dog away from Cameron was impossible if they were within touching distance)—did not suit his likings at all.

Hal had had to carry Pat part of the way to the car. That was not amusing even for him, as the dog weighs forty-five pounds and wiggles a lot. I started out leading him with my hand in his collar. But he continued whining and trying to curl up in a ball, and when we passed by Georgina's body he started shivering even more, trying to get his cropped tail between his legs. That was when Hal picked him up. After locking him in the car, still shivering and whining, we returned to the porch where Harry was holding Cameron. Hal went to stand beside Harry, and Lori was just inside the door looking outside.

The dog started coughing again, so loudly I could hear him from the porch, and Harry said, "Why don't you give him a cough drop?"

"Harry, he's a dog," I objected. "He wouldn't know what to do with a cough drop."

"You give *me* a cough drop," Cameron observed. "Give Pat a cough drop."

The dog was still coughing, and Harry said, "Give him one anyway."

I shrugged and got out one of the cherry cough drops I always carry in my purse to give to people who start coughing in church or in a courtroom, unwrapped it, and opened the car door enough to lay the cough drop on the seat in front of Pat. To my astonishment, Pat forgot about shivering and whining long enough to pounce on the cough drop and consume it loudly with every sign of glee. He looked around for another but I'd only brought him one. I headed back to the porch as the coughing abruptly stopped. Whether or not that was coincidence I cannot say, but I will say that I would never have thought on my own of giving a cough drop to a dog.

"Pat's all better," Cameron said. "Let me in the car now. I can play with Pat."

"Negative," Harry said. "Pat is *not* all better. He's still sick, and we don't want you to get germs."

Cameron began sniffling, at first faking it and then really sobbing. Harry handed him to me. When he started crying inconsolably despite my efforts to rock him, I handed him back to Harry and went looking for Charlie Sosa, finding him in the back of the driveway with several other officers. "I can't keep the baby up all night," I said. "Why don't we go and find a motel and put him to bed, and leave Lori and Hal to watch him, and then just Harry and I can come back and answer your questions?"

Pete Young, a tall blond probably in his early fifties who had been introduced to me as Charlie's sergeant, said, "You might as well put the baby to bed wherever he's been sleeping. You paid to stay here. It won't hurt for you to stay one more night. Unless you're afraid of ghosts, that is."

I wasn't too crazy about his tone of voice *or* his suggestion, which violated all rules of crime-scene preservation, and, more important, risked the safety of my family. I wasn't the only one. Harry, who was right beside me with Cameron's wails now subsiding to sleepy hiccups, said in a rather acerbic tone, "Ghosts are one thing. Keeping your family in a place where a murderer is still at large is another thing altogether. Would you do it?"

"She was running around in the dark by herself," Young said, glancing at Georgina's body and pointedly ignoring Harry's question. "You wouldn't be, would you?"

"No, we would not," Harry said in a rather emphatic voice that I knew perfectly well was aimed at me.

"Certainly not," I said meekly. "Not after this." But I felt it necessary to add, "But was she really alone, or was she with her murderer? That's the problem, you see. We don't know who the murderer was. It could have been somebody she felt safe with. It could be somebody we could feel safe with. In fact it probably was, because either he didn't get close enough for Pat to reach him, or it was somebody Pat trusted."

"Who's Pat?"

"The dog. And I've seen him pull the screw base of a tie-down post completely straight by pulling it out of the ground when he thought somebody was threatening a member of the family. And he likes—liked—Georgina. He'd have gone after anybody who hurt her."

"Anybody'd own a pit bull is crazy," Young said under his

breath, and then, more loudly, he said, "Then maybe your family had better stay together. If none of you go wandering off alone or with somebody else, then you ought to be safe. Charlie, you got it covered here?"

"Yeah," Charlie said, continuing to look at the body rather than at his sergeant.

"Then I'm going home."

After his taillights went out of sight, Charlie said, "He's not always very reasonable. But this time I agree with him. It's the middle of the night, for cryin' out loud, and whatever happened happened outside." I wished I were as sure of that as he was. He continued, "With a sick dog and a tired baby, why go hunt for a place to stay now? Nothing's happened inside the house."

Nothing that we know of yet, I thought as Harry nodded, walked back up on the front porch, unwrapped Cameron from around himself and handed him, now sound asleep, over to Hal to take inside. Cameron stirred, whimpered a little, and then cuddled up to Hal as he had to Harry. Harry and I stayed on the front porch where we'd be out of the way of the crime-scene work as Kate Rolley arrived to pronounce the victim dead. She talked quietly with Charlie Sosa for a minute, and left with little more fanfare. Lori stayed with us a while, and then she went indoors and sat down in the living room. I think she was crying, but she didn't want me to notice, so I carefully did not notice.

There wasn't really a whole lot for the crime-scene people to do, though I supposed they would be back in the morning to look again by daylight. All there was was Georgina's body, lying facedown on the hard-packed, grassless earth under the perfume-sweet Russian olive tree, atop the pale green blossoms the rain had washed out of the tree, with the nearly round whitewashed stone that had crushed the base of her skull lying near her. A crime-scene tech took one more photograph and then carefully maneuvered the rock into a cardboard box, and then two EMTs removed the body.

. . . . .

I found myself wondering if there would be a double funeral on Saturday or if Cully, who had the right to decide unless he was the killer, would be against that.

I found myself with a ghost of an idea, one so frail I couldn't yet figure out where it was leading. And never mind Pete Young's sarcasm, that was the only kind of ghost I really believed in. "Charlie," I called, leaning over the balustrade of the porch, "can you find something about a murder twenty-one years ago?"

"Probably," he said without turning toward me. "It'll take a while. Why?"

"Well, several times when I've been talking with Georgina, she's started to say something about her mother's murder and veered away. I'm just wondering how her mother was murdered."

"Twenty-one years ago? I don't see how that could be relevant."

"It could if the MO is the same."

This time he did turn toward me. "Why should the MO be the same?"

I walked down off the front porch with my hands wrapped around my upper arms; even with the sweatshirt, the night had turned uncomfortably cold. "I know that the mother—her name was Miranda Howe—was murdered about twenty-one years ago, in this yard. Cynthia was in the house watching TV or something and apparently didn't know anything about it until her father told her. The father had gone somewhere, and Georgina was with him. They got home to find Miranda dead in the front yard with Alexandra curled up on the ground beside her crying. They think Alexandra probably saw the murder, and that was what triggered her splitting, but every time somebody asked her about it she'd start screaming. I know Georgina said something about her mother being hit in the head with a rock. So, if it's the same MO—"

"Then it's a copycat or it's the same person," Charlie said slowly. "Yeah. I see your point. But why now? Why so long after the first one?"

. . . . .

"Maybe," I said, "because Elias Howe died just six weeks ago. Maybe Elias knew who did it. Maybe Elias was somehow holding the person in check. But now that he's dead—"

"Yeah," Charlie said, even more slowly, pivoting on his heel and looking around at the scene. "Yeah. I see what you're getting at." I was glad he did, because I really wasn't at all sure what I was getting at; I just felt it was something I would check out if the case were mine. His voice sped up now and got slightly louder. "Yeah, I'll check tomorrow. Look, you people might as well go get some rest. You've told me about all you can, and I'm going to pack it in too—we'll leave somebody to sit on it overnight and then get Crime Scene after it again tomorrow. One more thing, you said she was divorced?"

"Separated," I said. "Not divorced."

"You know where I could reach the husband? It's that Grafton fellow I already talked to once, isn't it? But I left the info about him in the office."

"I've got it inside." I told him. He followed Harry and me in, where I gave him the name, address, and phone number of Cully Grafton and, for good measure, of Cynthia Harvey. As for "packing it in," I knew he would go and notify those two tonight before he rested, no matter how little sleep that let him get. It wasn't a task he could leave to a uniform officer because, just as I would, he would want to see their reactions on being notified.

But that wasn't my concern. I got Pat out of the car and returned him to the porch, after warning the patrol officer who would sit on the scene not to get anywhere near the dog. Harry retrieved Pat's water bowl, which an ident tech had fingerprinted just in case, took it and washed and refilled it while I got Pat's last antibiotic of the night down him. We then went inside and locked up, and Harry headed upstairs to our room. I went to chase Lori upstairs also, and found she was still crying, entirely silently, sitting in a faded red brocade Louis Quinze chair with her knees drawn up to hide her face. I sat down beside her, in a similar chair we all usually avoided sitting in because the gold-plated brass hobnail-looking thingies that secure the upholstery were working loose. "What is it, Lori?"

"What if I killed somebody one day?" she asked, her voice muffled by her position.

"What makes you think you would do that?"

"My mom did."

That was, unfortunately, true; Lori's mother had been responsible for the most spectacular series of ax—well, hatchet—murders I had ever seen, and probably the most spectacular the entire city of Fort Worth had ever seen. "It's not hereditary," I said.

"How do you know?"

"It just isn't," I said. "In the so-called crime families what happens is learned behavior, not innate instinct."

"But some people are more likely to lose their temper than other people. That's innate."

"Perhaps it is, but in some cases that also is learned behavior," I said. "Anyway, you don't have that kind of a temper."

"Neither did Mom. Not until—not until she did."

What can anybody say at a time like this? I didn't know, and I felt completely helpless, especially since this was the first time since her mother's suicide that Lori had brought up this topic. "Why are you thinking about that now?"

"It's like—like this is inherited murder."

"The mother was killed twenty-one years ago. Two of her daughters have been killed this week. If the mother killed somebody twenty-one years ago and two of her daughters killed somebody this week, I'd say it was an inherited disposition to murder, but even then it might be learned rather than innate. But this—it's not three people committing murder, it's three people being murdered. I'm absolutely certain the same person, whoever it was, killed Alexandra and Georgina. I'm at least entertaining the possibility it might be the same person who killed the mother. So—I just don't see what it has to do with you."

"Why did my mother start killing people? Other people get hit by cars and their mothers don't go kill the people that were driving."

I sighed, not audibly but internally, and said, "There is—or there was, I think he's dead now—a doctor named Selye who studied the effects of stress. You could call him the first stress medicine specialist. He had a theory that every organism is born with the capability of coping with a finite amount of stress throughout its lifetime, and this finite amount varies from being to being, from person to person. Different people are capable of coping with more, or less, stress than other people. And once that lifetime amount is reached, the organism begins to deteriorate. There are different ways it might deteriorate. If it's a guinea pig, it'll probably just turn up its little toes and die. If it's a person, he or she might suddenly get very sick, or might develop some kind of nervous problem, or might suddenly drastically change his or her behavior. My guess is that's what happened to your mom: she had coped with a whole lifetime of stress in only half a lifetime, and she snapped under the strain. But Lori, I think you're made differently than your mom was. I think you're able to cope with a lot more stress than she was."

"If I had just looked before I stepped off the curb—"

It was Lori's being struck by a hit-and-run driver that had triggered her mother's killing spree. I answered, "Lori, as fast as that car was going, it wouldn't have mattered whether you looked or not. It probably was a block away when you stepped off the curb. And in fact I expect you *did* look."

"But you don't know that."

"No, I don't. But I know you usually do. And you don't know you didn't."

I knew she didn't know. She still could not remember anything at all about being knocked a hundred and twenty feet by a speeding Lincoln and lying like a broken rag doll on the side of the street behind the downtown library. She remembered leaving the library, and she remembered waking up in a hospital room with our dog—who was there by permission—trying to get in bed with her. She never saw her mother again, alive or dead, because her mother was dead by the time Lori had been awake five minutes, and Lori couldn't leave the hospital to see her buried.

After a long silence, Lori put her feet back on the floor and looked up. "Am I being morbid?"

"Probably," I said, "but I can certainly see why you'd feel that way."

"Deb, why did these people live next door to the graveyard? Especially if Alexandra was afraid of ghosts?"

"Because it's their family home, and maybe they couldn't afford to go live somewhere else."

"Okay, I guess I understand that, but why put the graveyard right under everybody's noses?"

"I don't know," I said, "and I've wondered too. The most obvious answer is that it was easiest—there can't have been much left of the woman and children who burned to death, and maybe they just used the cellar or something like that as the funeral vault without ever trying to sort out the remains."

"That's awful."

"I agree. And that might not have been the reason at all. Maybe Elias—the first Elias—felt that he was keeping them closer to him by burying them next door."

"That doesn't make sense. My mom, wherever she is, she isn't where the cemetery is. All that's there is her empty shell she's not in anymore. And my dad too. I don't even *know* where the cemetery is. But I know my parents aren't there."

"That's true," I agreed, "and I'm sure Elias knew that. But he probably wasn't thinking straight. Remember he lost ten people he loved within two weeks of each other. And that's pretty horrible."

"Yeah, but how could he love three wives at once?"

"I don't know. But I'm told the polygamist men did, and I'll take their word for it."

"If Hal wanted to marry somebody else besides me I bet I *would* kill him."

"Then you're very fortunate both the Church and the state have outlawed polygamy," I said.

"Do you s'pose somebody *set* the fire?" she asked.

"I don't know any reason why anybody would have," I answered. "And from what Sister White said, the women got along very well."

"But Sister White wasn't there to know. What does she have to go on?"

"Probably the first Elias's journals."

"Which would have whitewashed everything," Lori said, contemptuously and possibly correctly.

"And the journals of the surviving wife."

"Well—maybe. But if she did it they would have whitewashed everything too."

"Maybe so," I agreed.

"And if that's the case, then maybe murder does run in the family."

"Whether or not it runs in this family, it doesn't run in your family," I said. "Your father was a wonderful police officer, you know that, and your mother was a good mother and a perfectly adequate police officer until she snapped."

"I don't want to be a cop," Lori said.

"Then don't," I told her. "Nobody ever expected you to."

"But you're a cop, and Mom was a cop, and Dad was a cop."

For the moment she sounded much younger than her actual age of eighteen. We'd gone through this repeatedly—sometimes she seemed eighteen, sometimes she seemed fourteen, sometimes she seemed twelve or younger. The shrinks—mine, as well as my friend Susan Braun, who operates a private psychiatric hospital—had assured me that this was a result of the accident, of the bereavement, and of the readjustment as she accustomed herself to living in a new family, and that she would get over it eventually. I was sure they were right.

What I was not sure of was where she had ever gotten any idea that she was expected to become a police officer.

Responding to her last sentence, I said, "That's true. But that doesn't mean you ought to be one. Harry's a pilot. I don't know yet what Hal's going to do with his life, but I very much doubt he'll be a cop. Vicky's a secretary. Becky's probably never going to take up any career but mother." Which was keeping her plenty busy enough: besides her husband's half brother whom she had adopted, she had produced two babies between Vicky's first and second, and was well advanced on baby number three. Fortunately Olead could afford that many; most people can't. And most people, seeing Becky, her brood, and her midsection in the grocery store, automatically assume that she is Catholic, Mormon, or irresponsible. She is none of the three. Both my daughters have remained Baptists and look on my Mormonism the same way my mother does, as a temporary aberration I will undoubtedly recover from one day.

"But they're not your birth children," Lori argued, drawing her knees back up and wrapping her arms around them with her chin resting on her knees. "So genetic things don't apply. Just environment things."

She had been studying the effects of genetics and environment in school at the end of the semester, so I knew what brought that up. "So what?" I said. "I am quite sure there is no police gene, just like there's no murder gene. I certainly don't think you ought to be a police officer because I am, or because your parents were. All I want you to be is the best Lori you possibly can be, and you're managing that just fine. Beyond that, it's your decision. What do you think you might like to do?"

"I don't know. I used to think I knew, but I don't know right now. Something. I would want to go on a mission, but I'd have to be twenty-one and Hal wouldn't want to wait that long. And really neither would I. I don't know. I don't want to be a doctor and I don't want to be a nurse and I don't want to be a lawyer and I don't want to be a truck driver and I don't want to work in a store and I don't want to be a milkman"—by then her face was dimpling into a smile, and she continued—"and I don't want to be a pilot and I don't want to be a shrink and I don't want to be a circus clown and I don't want to be a professional cardsharp—" She dissolved into giggles, and I was happy to laugh with her.

"Keep going," I advised her, "you'll eventually have to narrow it down to one thing you *do* want to do."

We went upstairs together, with Lori chanting, "And I don't want to be a veterinarian and I don't want to be a poodle-groomer and I don't want to be a taxi driver and I don't want to be a—"

I hugged her good night, left her at the door to her room, and went back to Harry's and my room, where Harry had, without nagging mind you, crawled into the red-striped pajamas he had bought as a nod to decency in a bed-and-breakfast. "What was that all about?" he asked.

"She mainly doesn't want to be a murderer," I answered. "She's been thinking about her mom. I think she's feeling better now."

"I sure as hell hope so," Harry said, and changed the subject. "What are we going to do about breakfast in the morning? You want to make it here, or shall we go out?"

"Ask me that in the morning," I said, halfway into my nightgown. "I'm busy worrying about what we're going to do with Pat when we go to a motel."

. . . . .

"I'd hate to have to leave him in the car," Harry agreed unhappily. "It's cool enough, but still . . ."

"Yeah," I said. In the first place Pat does not like confined places; in the second place I wouldn't care to have to answer for the condition of Olead's van after we had locked a dog with tonsillitis in it for several days; and in the third place we really wanted to leave Pat behind when we did our sight-seeing around Salt Lake City, of which we were doing little enough anyway.

"I was thinking," I said as I began to make my way under the covers beside Harry. "We're supposed to take Hal to Provo Friday morning, so we're kind of stuck in the area until then, but we could get a place for Wednesday and Thursday night and maybe it wouldn't hurt to leave Pat in the car just those two nights if we take him with us during the day."

"Maybe." Harry sounded unconvinced.

"I mean, his cough seems better," I said. "But of course we'll have to keep Charlie advised of where we are, in case he needs to ask us something else."

"We'd have to do that anyway," Harry agreed. "Anyhow, I figure as soon as we leave Hal we'll head for home by the fastest route. I'm about burned-out on sight-seeing. It'll take what, about two days? You were looking at the maps yesterday."

"Two or three, depending on how tired we get." I yawned widely.

"I think you're pretty tired already."

"Got it in one," I said, and he didn't say anything else, so I went on to sleep.

At eight-thirty the next morning, with the dog already medicated, fed, and back in the car for the protection of the crime-scene crew, and us all dressed and starting to pack our suitcases and figure out what to do with the door keys, the front door opened. We weren't expecting anyone, at least not anyone who wouldn't have to knock. Harry tore downstairs to see who it was, and I of course was right behind him with Hal bringing up the rear only because he couldn't figure out how to get past me without knocking me down the stairs.

"Good morning," Cully Grafton said. He looked very tired and worn, which is how I would expect a man to look after finding out his estranged wife whom he still wanted back was dead. "Sorry, I didn't mean to startle you. I guess I wasn't thinking."

"That's okay," Harry said. "We just—didn't know what to think, when the door opened."

"The cops let me through," Cully said, and I thought, *Of course, I remembered that half an hour ago, when I put Pat in the car. I should have remembered now that Charlie left uniformed officers here all night; we should have realized they wouldn't let the killer through—at least not if they suspected that person of being the killer.*

"I guess you're trying to decide where to go now," Cully continued.

"We thought we'd go on to a motel," Harry began.

"You don't have to do that," Cully interrupted. "Georgina and me, we owned the place jointly, so it's mine now. I'm not going to try to run it as a bed-and-breakfast—I'm no cook; I even buy my sandwiches ready-made—and it's too damn big for me to live in by myself, so I'll be putting it up for sale as soon as it's decent to think about business, but you might as well stay here till you were scheduled to leave. Use up what food's in the refrigerator if you want to; I know you paid Georgina in advance and so the food's yours too."

"You sure?" Harry asked. "Because we'd hate to intrude on your grief—" It sounded stilted, the way he said it, but I realized his main problem was he didn't know quite how to react to what seemed like hospitality from a man he'd threatened to punch out.

"I'm sure. I won't be in your way. I'll just be staying in Elias's old room for the next few weeks—there's too much junk in Georgina's for me to get my stuff in there—while I decide what to do about the furniture and all, and right now I'd just as soon not be alone, if you know what I mean." He grinned tiredly. "And I don't get drunk every night. The other day was—was unusual. It was just that Alexandra, she drove me batty, she was so jealous of me, and I thought sure that with her gone I'd be able to get Georgina back. . . ." His voice tightened, and he turned his face away and mumbled, "Sorry. Anyhow, you're welcome to stay."

"We'll stay," Harry said abruptly, making the decision for all of us.

I'm still not quite sure how it all came about, but the next thing I knew, I was in the kitchen making breakfast for all of us, including Cully, with Lori helping me, and Cully was bringing in his possessions from his snack truck with Harry and Hal assisting him. Cameron was helping too, but he wasn't much help.

Need I say that breakfast was not as elaborate as those Georgina had been making? I scrambled eggs, microwaved bacon, and made toast, while Lori set the table with plates, silverware, paper towels for napkins, glasses, salt, pepper, the milk bottle, strawberry and chocolate Quik, and some of Georgina's homemade jam. Of course I didn't even think of coffee, but Cully went and made some himself, and Harry drank some of it too.

After breakfast Cully went to Elias's room, which was the only bedroom on the ground floor, and came back in a suit and tie. He looked very uncomfortable in what was clearly not usual garb for him, but he must have been headed for the funeral home, which is not a place one goes in khaki work clothes with your name embroidered above the left pocket in bright red thread.

While Lori and I were putting the dishes into the dishwasher Charlie Sosa called. "I followed up on your suggestion," he told me. "Miranda Howe was found lying facedown in her front yard. I had a look at the pictures, and I'd say she was in virtually identically the same place and position you found Georgina in last night. She'd been struck in the base of the skull by a fist-sized round white-washed rock that came from her own yard, where she had borders

. . . . .

of whitewashed stones around the flower bed. Are they still there? I think I'd have noticed if they were, but—"

"I think I'd have noticed too," I said, "but let me check." I put down the phone, went out the front door, walked all the way around the house, and returned to the phone. "No," I said.

"So where in the hell did they come from this time?" he asked, more to himself than to me. Then, to me, he said, "Nobody ever got even the ghost of a lead on who did it. Nobody saw anything. Deb, twenty-one years, and this case hasn't been in the papers since right after it happened. None of the local papers have done crime retrospectives, and to the best of my knowledge it hasn't been written up in any of those detective magazines. That's too long an interval for a copycat killing."

He sounded about as unhappy as I felt. We both had reached the same conclusion. A woman was murdered twenty-one years ago, two women were murdered this week, and the same person did it all. "Have you warned Cynthia?" I asked.

"I'm way ahead of you," he said. "I found the paperwork at eight o'clock this morning and called her at eight-fifteen. I told her to get out of her house, move into a motel, sign a phony name to the register, and not tell anybody but me where she went. I'll let Pete know, and that's as far as it goes. Well—I just thought I'd let you know the situation. You got any ideas?"

"I'm trying," I said. "All I can think of is, Elias knew who did it and could keep that person in check, but now that he's dead nobody else can. I think I said that yesterday."

"But *why?*" Charlie demanded. "Why murder Alexandra? The woman was a nutcase. Why murder Georgina? The woman was harmless."

"She must not have been harmless to somebody," I answered. "As for Alexandra, she learned things. She was always sitting in corners listening; she heard things, she saw things before anybody noticed she was there. And remember, she was probably the only witness to her mother's murder. Georgina said she never told anybody what she saw—but what if she did? Or what if somebody thought she did?"

"Okay, I know you've been prowling around asking questions," Charlie said. "I'm not going to yell at you about it again. All I want to know is, have you talked to anybody who knew them back then?"

"Just Sister White."

"Who's that?"

"LaRae White. She's Georgina's grandaunt. She's eighty-two and Georgina told me she has a bad heart, so take it easy when you talk to her."

"What do you think I am, some kind of grizzly bear?" He sounded hurt.

"No, I just think you're a cop on the scent," I answered, and gave him Sister White's address and telephone number. "Come to think of it, there were others," I added.

"Who?"

"Anybody they know now who's the same age as Georgina or older could be old enough to remember something," I said. "Charlie, twenty-one years isn't really that long ago. There are probably a lot of people they knew then and still know now. I couldn't possibly know all of them. The ones I do know are Cully Grafton—he's moved back in here, by the way—and Hart Bivins."

"The psychiatrist."

"The psychiatrist," I agreed.

"Well, I know Hart Bivins," Charlie said.

"From trials?" I asked.

"Yeah. He always proves the defendant was insane unless we want the defendant to be insane and then he proves the defendant was sane. I don't like him much, but I know him and I don't have any reason to believe he's likely to be a killer. Cully Grafton—I don't know about Cully Grafton."

. . . . .

"I don't either," I said. "But this morning he wasn't sounding like a killer."

"I checked his record," Charlie said.

"He's got one?"

"Yeah. One DWI, several public intoxes, and some fights in bars. Nothing real serious, but enough to show he's got the capacity for violence. Where is he now?"

"He left. He had on a suit and tie, so I figured he was probably going to the funeral home."

"I'll try to catch him there," Charlie said. "Kate isn't finished with the body yet, but he asked me to have it released to Russon Brothers. Deb . . ."

"Yes?"

"Don't be alone with Cully Grafton. And don't leave any of your kids alone with him."

"I won't," I assured him.

Then, leaving everybody else unpacking clothes that had just been packed, I told Harry my intentions and then I went to get Pat out of the car and take him for his morning walk. I felt perfectly safe: there was a police car blocking the front driveway and another blocking the back driveway, and anybody would have to be crazy to attack me in broad daylight on a public street when I had a pit bull escort. They couldn't even sneak up behind me without Pat warning me. I knew that from long experience of walking Pat.

I turned left after I went out the front door, walked past the house that had once been the twin of Georgina's house before both had been slightly remodeled in different ways, went to the end of the block and the end of the next block, turned left again, and circumnavigated a two-block area, remembering somewhere in the middle of the trip that I had come out without my cane again and my feet wished I hadn't. But I was thinking furiously all the while.

We'd concluded at one time that we had to figure out which Alexandra had been killed before we could begin to find out who did it. But now, I felt, we knew. Or at least we could narrow it down sharply. It was Alexandra-today who was killed, or it was five-year-old Alexandra who was killed. Because the party girl, the incompetent secretary, and the boy who loved to fight wouldn't have anything to do with a murder twenty-one years ago. And Georgina had to have been killed as herself, because she had no other selves, which meant it was virtually certain that Alexandra also had been killed as herself . . . whatever and whoever herself was.

Harry was probably champing at the bit to get out and go sightseeing. Well, he'd just have to wait, because I wasn't through thinking yet. I sat down on one of the two black wrought-iron benches in the private cemetery and stared unseeing at the mass grave of a woman and eight children who had burned to death on a cold, windy night more than a hundred years ago and thought about what Lori had said, about the possibility that those deaths had been murder. No, she couldn't be right about that. The sister who later died of milk leg wouldn't have gone next door, or two houses over, on a blizzardy night when she was in bed with a newborn baby. And the sister who was staying with her wouldn't have set a fire that would have killed her own children. That was an accident, pure and simple. So nobody had inherited the propensity to murder from some ancestress a hundred years ago. That was out. I went on thinking. Why would Cully . . . why would Hart . . . ?

And then something caught my eye.

The burial lot, as I have mentioned before, was bordered with trees and with a vast, overgrown iris bed. And each iris bed was bordered with round, fist-sized, whitewashed stones.

Or rather, almost bordered. There were gaps in the border here and there. Gaps that to my eye added up to about fifteen stones.

I stood up. "Come on, Pat," I said. "I've got to call Charlie Sosa."

Nine

I GOT BACK to the house I continued to think of as Georgina's despite Georgina's death, convinced that Harry would be ready to kill me for taking so long to walk the dog when he wanted to go sight-seeing. But instead the van was gone and Harry was in bed, shaven and fully dressed except for his shoes. When I went in to check on him he opened his eyes and said, "I had Hal take me to the service station to get Alexandra's car so we could go on using it. Then I told the kids they could go to the zoo or something. Deb, I'm pooped. We were up too late last night and I think I'm still not caught up from camping. And with another drive across the country coming up—you mind if we just rest today?"

Actually I was delighted with the idea, and said so. "But I've got to call Charlie Sosa first," I added.

Harry had closed his eyes; now he opened them again and asked, "Why?"

"Something I thought of. I won't be long. And I'll try not to disturb you."

I still didn't know all the places there were phones in this house. I knew there was one downstairs in the living room and another one downstairs in the kitchen, one in each of the guest bedrooms, and one in Georgina's room on the third floor. As I didn't know when Cully was likely to return, I had no idea which I was least likely to be overheard on. Finally I decided on the kitchen; Cully had made it plain he wasn't a kitcheny sort of person.

"Charlie, I'm just thinking," I said five minutes later. "So don't feel like I'm trying to tell you how to run an investigation. I'm just—I want to bounce some ideas off you."

"Okay," he said, sounding tired. I suspected he looked tired, but of course I couldn't tell that for sure.

"I don't know how much you know about the Howe family."

"Some. Probably not as much as you do."

"Well, from what Georgina and Sister White told me, Elias lost his jewelry store just about the same time his wife died. Sister White didn't seem to know why he lost the jewelry store."

"But—"

"I'm sure she really did," I interrupted quickly. "But she didn't want to tell me. Georgina said she couldn't remember the details—there was something expensive that was lost and wasn't insured. Actually I was sure she did remember, but just didn't want to tell me. So something a little strange was going on. And I was just thinking, if you could talk to Sister White—"

"I was about to go out the door when you called, to do just that," Charlie said, not sounding as patient as he probably thought he was sounding.

"Well, she wouldn't tell me. But she'll have to tell you. If you'll let me know—"

"I'll do that, if it looks at all relevant." I started to object, and he said, "All right, I'll tell you anyway. What else?"

"Is it okay with you if I search Alexandra's room again? And maybe Georgina's, since nobody ever did search it?"

"It's okay with me," he said, "but you've got to get permission from Cully Grafton, if he owns the house now. I don't know what you expect to find."

"He says he does. I'll have to wait till he gets back from the funeral home. And as to what I expect to find—I don't know, Charlie. It's just—all I can think of is that somebody killed Alexandra for something she knew or something they thought she knew, and somebody killed Georgina because Alexandra might have told her whatever it was."

"And you figure you're going to find whatever it is, all nice and written down."

"Maybe," I said. "Or maybe I'll find something that will give me a good idea of what it was."

"Well, have fun searching," Charlie said, and added, "At least when you're doing that you're not in my hair."

I put down the phone gently, which was not what I felt like doing, and went into the living room, just as the front door burst open and Cully and Cynthia burst in, arguing at the top of their lungs.

Cully was in midsentence. ". . . *knew* I bought your share, for crying out loud, you and I and Georgina sat right there in that lawyer's office and signed papers up the gumpstump, and—"

"I know that!" Cynthia screamed. "I'm not stupid, I know you bought my share of the house! But Georgina told me she'd make up for it by leaving me her share! And now, with Alexandra dead, I should own—"

"You don't own anything! Look, I know this is your family home, you want to buy the whole thing back I'll sell it to you for what I paid for your half of it and what I put up for Georgina's business—that's only thirty thousand dollars, for cryin' out loud, and the land alone is probably worth half of that and the house is worth another fifty or sixty thousand at the very least."

"I haven't got thirty thousand dollars!" Cynthia screamed. "I haven't got twenty thousand dollars, or ten thousand dollars, or five thousand dollars, or one thousand dollars. And you can't take my family's house away from me because—"

"I can't help what you don't have," Cully retorted, "and the fact remains Georgina didn't leave—"

"She said she was going to, and—"

"I can't help what she told you, she—"

They both saw me about that time, and shut up, both of them staring at me glumly. "I gather there's a problem," I said as pleasantly as I could, since I obviously couldn't pretend not to have heard.

"You're damn right there's a problem," Cully said. "Tell this nitwit than when a husband and wife jointly own a house it belongs to the husband if the wife dies."

"But . . ." Cynthia began. She stopped and then began again. "My father owned the house. He had put in his will that Georgina and I inherited it jointly provided whichever of us lived here continued throughout her life to provide a home for Alexandra."

"And you sold your share of it to me before he died," Cully said patiently. "So when he died and the will was probated the house came to Georgina and me."

"Has the will been probated yet?" I asked. "It seems to me if he's only been dead six weeks . . ."

Both of them looked at me, startled. "Well, Georgina . . ." Cully began, and stopped.

At almost the same second, Cynthia began, "Georgina was going to . . ." She stopped too. Both of them were staring at me.

"I'm not a lawyer," I said. "I know Texas criminal law pretty well, but not Utah civil law. And this case sounds complicated. I don't even know whether you *can* legally sell your inheritance before you inherit it"—and as I said that I couldn't help thinking of Esau, who sold his birthright for a mess of pottage, which my primary Sunday school teacher at Shiloh Baptist Church had told me meant a pan of cooked beans—"and my guess is the will's not through probate, if it ever even has reached probate. It sounds to me as if you need to find an attorney."

"I'll do that right now," Cully said. He reached for the phone book and the phone, engaged in a muttered colloquy, and then said, "Come on, Cindy. Reisner says he can see us right now."

"Before you go," I said quickly, "would either of you mind if I go and straighten Alexandra's and Georgina's bedrooms and just see if I notice anything that might help the police while I'm doing it?"

"I don't care," Cully said. "Do anything you want in there."

"Yeah, go ahead," Cynthia said. "Just—don't put any of their stuff in a DI bag yet, because I'll want to go through it myself and see if there's anything I want to keep."

"I wouldn't dream of making that kind of decision for anybody else," I assured her. "Anything that might relate to either of the murders I'll have to turn over to the police, but other than that I'll just finish washing the clothes—I started that the other day—and I'll put everything away neatly. That'll put you that much ahead on your sorting."

And that put an end to my idea of lying down and taking a nice nap; like Harry, I had had too many late nights recently. But like it or not, murder takes precedence.

To maintain the fiction that I was trying to help Cynthia more than I was trying to help the police, the first thing I did was locate Georgina's laundry baskets, take them up to the third floor, and sort Alexandra's dirty clothes into them. That took care of at least half the room cleaning; although Charlie and I, in our earlier search, had moved the clothes from the floor to the bed, the only ones I had washed then were the ones that were already wet. I went into Georgina's room, which was far tidier than Alexandra's but still obviously a highly multipurpose room, and grabbed her clothes. Then I went back down to the second-floor laundry room and started a load of whites.

On second thought, I checked Lori's room, the room Hal and Cameron were sharing, and the room Harry and I were sharing and added our laundry to the baskets. No sense in doing laundry in Utah and still returning home with a whole trip's worth of dirty clothes.

"You coming to bed?" Harry asked rather somnolently.

"After a while. Not right now."

· · · · ·

He didn't ask for an explanation—I think he was half asleep—and I didn't offer one. I had just started up the stairs again when the phone rang. I went on up to Georgina's room to answer it. "Me," Charlie's voice said succinctly. "What went missing was five hundred thousand dollars' worth of jewelry—already paid for by the customer, and uninsured. Half a million dollars down the tube."

"How in the world can anybody lose five hundred thousand dollars' worth of jewelry?" I demanded. "Was it a robbery, or burglary, or what? You'd think a jewelry store would be well insured."

"You'd think," Charlie agreed, "and Sister White says the store was. But the bracelet wasn't. And that's what it was. One bracelet. Umpteen diamonds and sapphires set in platinum, ordered for the wife of a mining mogul, paid for by said mining mogul. Elias had it made in Amsterdam. He paid for it and paid the duty on it and then used his profit to pay off some loans he had on the store. The bracelet was brought to him by a bonded courier, and he didn't expect to have custody of it more than two days. But what the insurance company wanted to insure that little bauble for a week was enough to eat up his entire profit. He hadn't planned very well, you see, and he had underbid. So while he was waiting for said mogul to pick the bracelet up he never let it out of his sight while he was awake. He carried it around in his pocket and slept with it by his bed. And then, the day said mogul's messenger arrived to pick up the bracelet, behold, Elias reached in his pocket and the bracelet was not there."

"Ye gods," I said involuntarily.

"I think ye gods," Charlie answered. "Nobody ever did figure out what happened to it. Well, Elias didn't want to declare bankruptcy, which would have been his only way out at that point. So he sold his store and everything in it to repay the mogul, and still had to take out loans that he was paying on for the next twenty years. Then he went to work for another jewelry store. Which, by the way, never trusted him to carry around half a million dollars' worth of jewelry."

"If he'd declared bankruptcy he'd have lost the store anyway," I pointed out. "But—"

"But what?"

"I don't know what I was going to say. It just—honestly, I don't see how anybody could lose anything like that."

"You know what Sister White told me?"

"Obviously not."

"She said in her opinion he did it subconsciously on purpose. He didn't want the responsibility of owning, or even managing, a store. He wanted a boss to tell him what to do, and he wanted to be able to go home in the evening and forget about work. When you're the owner you can't ever do that."

"She could very well be right," I said, "but what a way to go about it!"

"Okay, that's what I have for you. Now what have you got for me?"

"Not much, yet," I said. "It seems to be somewhat up in the air who owns the house now."

"How so?"

I explained, and then added, "So I've got permission from both of them to search the rooms. But I've just gotten started."

"You're not going to find anything."

"Probably not," I agreed, "but I'm still going to look."

It is, I have noticed before, always easier to clean up somebody else's house than your own, because you don't have to worry about finding things again, or putting them in the most convenient place. You just put them somewhere that seems to make sense and looks decent, and then you forget about it. But if you are careful, you can learn quite a lot about somebody by cleaning up their house, especially their bedroom or den or wherever they keep their private possessions.

Because we'd already searched Alexandra's room once, I started in Georgina's room.

The guest quarters, and the downstairs rooms, were spotless. Georgina more than made up for that in her own room, which apparently hadn't been vacuumed in a month. Mine can get that bad in a week, but then I have a long-haired cat and a four-year-old, so I thought a month because Georgina seemed normally tidy.

I don't care how messy a room is, it always looks better if the floor is clean. So I started by vacuuming. Then I stripped her bed and turned the mattress, in order to look under it. I put the bedspread back over the bare mattress and hauled the sheets downstairs into the laundry room, and then went on down to the main floor to get a broom, which I used to poke the miscellaneous possessions out from under the bed.

Said possessions consisted of two winter house slippers she'd probably forgotten the location of, a plyboard box that looked like the top tray out of a footlocker filled with Harlequin romances, several pair of panty hose, and a lot of dust bunnies. I threw the slippers into the closet floor and the panty hose and dust bunnies into the trash, picked up one of the Harlequins to read later in the day, and slid the box back under the bed.

Next stop, dresser. I pulled out the bottom drawer and looked behind it and under the bureau, as things sometimes migrate out of the bottom drawer of a dresser. Nothing there. I dug through the drawer, finding only a conglomeration of outdated and dried-up makeup, a small sewing kit, and a lot of rubber bands, bobby pins, and hair curlers of various sizes and ages. Nothing was taped to the bottom of the drawer, not that I have ever found anything in such a location anyway. I think that's a hiding place used only in fiction.

Next drawer. Again, I pulled it out and looked behind and under it. Nothing, except the top of the bottom drawer. These drawers were not separated by a piece of wood; rather, each drawer rode on runners directly above the drawer below.

This drawer contained one swimsuit, three girdles (I didn't know anybody still wore those), two slips and a half-slip, and four bras. They were semisorted, so that at least one got a vague idea what belonged where. There was nothing else in the drawer and nothing attached to the bottom of the drawer.

The third drawer up contained white cotton panties, long-legged and trimmed with lace, and undershirts also trimmed with lace. Again, they were roughly sorted.

The top drawer contained socks and stockings.

There was nothing there at all to show why she was killed, not that I expected anything.

Next stop was the closet, which—depressingly—had nothing out of the ordinary either. An assortment of skirts, blouses, sweaters, and slacks and three dresses hung on plastic hangers. Several pair of shoes and boots littered the floor. The shelf, which I climbed on a chair to check thoroughly, held nothing but more shoes and several handbags, all neatly arranged and put in plastic bags to protect them from dust.

She had no dressing table in the room. Like many women, most likely she did her hair and face in the bathroom.

Finally, and with considerable trepidation, I turned my attention to the desk and computer table. That was where most of the mess was—the desktop itself was totally invisible under the piles of paper, and it was a double-pedestal desk.

The washer had stopped. I went down to the second floor, threw a fabric-softener sheet and the whites into the dryer, and started a load of light-colored clothes in the washer before returning to Georgina's room. I started taking papers, one at a time, off the desk, checking them and stacking them, somewhat more neatly than they had been stacked, on the bed. When I finally finished the desktop, I started on the drawers.

. . . . .

Two hours later, with the last load of clothes in the wash and the first two loads sorted and put into the appropriate owners' bedrooms, I was ready to admit defeat, at least for Georgina's room. The only thing left was the computer, and I'd have to get Harry to tackle that. I can use a computer—you have to be able to, in any modern large-town police department—but that was about it. I did not feel up to trying to locate unknown files in an unfamiliar computer. And anyway, I wasn't sure my permission extended that far. Snooping around in someone's computer certainly didn't fall under the heading of cleaning rooms.

The front door banged open, almost directly under my feet, and I went downstairs. Either I was going to hear more of Cully and Cynthia's argument, or I was going to discover that one of them had won it.

It turned out to be the latter. At least so I assumed; Cully entered alone with a tired but rather triumphant look on his face. "What happened?" I ventured to ask.

He sat down. "What happened is, I was right, but it took Reisner to get it across to Cynthia. Jeff Reisner is—was—I don't know what I ought to say. Anyway, he was Georgina's attorney, and he's the one who helped us when I was buying out Cynthia. Seems the next week Elias went to Reisner and signed the house over to Georgina. See, I knew he was going to and Georgina knew he was going to. That was what the whole thing was all about, me buying out Cindy's share. I didn't know he had remade his will at the same time, but he did. He said in it that because his daughter Alexandra was not responsible for her actions, and his daughter Cynthia had sold her birthright, all his possessions were left to his daughter Georgina—not that I know what he had to leave, with the house already in Georgina's name. And Georgina's will was just as simple. It left everything to me on condition that I provide a home for Alexandra as long as she wanted one. Since Alexandra's dead, that clause no longer matters. The whole kit and caboodle is mine. He said it wasn't into probate yet, and he didn't know how complicated it was going to be with Elias and Georgina dying less than seven weeks apart, but that's the way it is. And look," he added hastily, though I hoped I wasn't looking disapproving, "I'm no monster. No matter what the deeds and the wills said, I told Cynthia she could have all the family stuff she wanted, and whatever I sell the house for, anything above the twenty thousand dollars I put in and Georgina's ten thousand that we'll have to pay, I'll split with her." This, I noticed, was not quite as generous an offer as he'd made in my hearing, but it was still quite generous. "But I've got to get the twenty thousand dollars back because I had to borrow it. I guess this doesn't make sense to you, does it?"

"It's not really any of my business," I began.

But he wanted to talk, and he'd found a listener. "Thing is, Georgina had to do some repairs before she could run the place as a bed-and-breakfast. She had to put in a sprinkler system, you know, in case of fire, and she had to redo the kitchen to bring it up to some kind of health code. Even with the ten thousand I borrowed for her she didn't have enough. And the SBA wouldn't do anything about helping her to get a loan unless the house was in her name. And Elias said he wouldn't mind putting the house in hers and Cindy's names but he couldn't put it just in her name. Georgina asked him how it would be if she and I bought Cindy out, and he said he didn't think we could do that but if we could, more power to us. So I borrowed the second ten thousand, and let me tell you that wasn't an easy loan to get, and I went and offered it to Cindy. Didn't really think she'd take it, because her half of the house was worth a lot more than that, but that was absolutely all I could raise. But she said for all she knew the old man might live forever, and she needed the money. So we went to Reisner's office and she signed her future share of the house over to me, and then we took that paperwork to Elias, and then Elias went to Reisner's office. So I have to pay back the twenty thousand I borrowed. And I have to pay back another ten thousand Georgina borrowed from the SBA. That's thirty thousand dollars. I'll get more than that for the house and land, and I *told* Cindy I'd split it with her. That's fair, isn't it?"

It sounded fair to me.

But he was still talking compulsively. "Thing is, Cindy keeps insisting I cheated her. And I didn't, damn it, I stuck my neck out so far I looked like an ostrich. That's part of why I was so mad at Georgina for making me move out because that little witch Sandy didn't want me here. What business was it of hers? Georgina was my wife. I was her husband. And I did a lot of the work myself, getting things ready. She'd been running it as a guest house for two years. We were just now to the point—I mean, when Elias died, we were just to the point where she was starting to show a profit. It was tough for her. She's never been a businesswoman—just stayed home and kept house for Daddy. And then when Elias retired and went on Social Security it was damned hard for her. I mean, the house was clear, good Lord, I guess it had been clear for a hundred years, but taxes, and insurance, and maintenance, and upkeep—and Sandy didn't see why she should pay for anything. Elias told her she had to give Georgina a hundred dollars a month out of her salary and she had to make her own car payments and buy her own gasoline and car insurance and clothes, but for that Georgina was cooking and cleaning for her and buying groceries. When I came along with a halfway decent income I must have looked like manna from heaven. They were glad enough to take my money then, but soon as Elias died there it was, Sandy wanted me gone and Georgina said I had to go. *Why,* dammit? If I'd been living here Georgina might not have—have—"

He stopped, then. "You don't want to hear all this, do you? Sorry for dumping on you, but . . ." He got up, started pacing around the room.

Harry, who had come downstairs sometime in the midst of the tirade, said, "Why don't you sit down and rest?"

"I don't want to rest," Cully said. "Damn it—with no money coming in, and two funerals to pay for, and those three damned loans—I don't know what I'm going to do. You like computers? I need to sell Georgina's. I don't know what I'll get for it, but it'll help some, whatever it is. I tried to give it to Cindy and she said she doesn't like computers."

"I have a computer," Harry said. "But maybe I can give you some ideas how much you might get for it."

"Would you? That'll help. Damn it—"He got up and went into the bedroom he was presently using, leaving Harry and me behind and somewhat more in sympathy with Cully than I had ever been before.

But not so much in sympathy that I didn't think to ask Harry, while he was looking at the computer, to look for any kind of file like a diary or personal notes that might let us know what kind of secret Alexandra might have told Georgina.

Then I returned to the third floor, stopping on the second to unload the dryer and move the last load of clothes from the washer into the dryer, and start the dryer again.

The load I'd taken out of the dryer this time was almost entirely Alexandra's. She seemed to have quite a preference for red clothes, which I always wash separately because I never can tell what red things will bleed onto other things and which won't. I hung the clothes in her closet and only then noticed something Charlie and I had missed before.

Stacks and stacks of sketch pads on a shelf.

Come to think of it, Charlie had searched the closet. He might not have thought the sketch pads were worth looking at. I did.

I took them out and sat down on the bed and started leafing through them. The oldest were so old the paper was yellowed and brittle; the newest, on the top of the stack, was only half-full. It was a fascinating excursion through Alexandra's mind, because by looking at the pictures I could tell which persona had drawn which one.

The naked women with overemphasized genitalia, obviously, had been drawn by "Ron," and I began to wonder exactly what his relationship to Alexandra had been and whether it had been as innocent as Georgina had obviously assumed it to be.

There were careful, detailed studies of leaves and flowers which might have been drawn by the adult Alexandra; there were Degas-like sketches of ballerinas that might have been drawn by Alexandra's impression of her mother.

But the most important series of drawings, to my mind, were those obviously drawn by Sandy, the persona who had stayed five years old.

In some of them, a little girl was sitting behind a door sucking her thumb, while indoors stood grotesque, giant-like figures. But in most of them there were three little girls all the same size—Alexandra's subconscious seemed to be denying her knowledge that Georgina was older than she and Cynthia were and had, as a child, certainly been much larger—and a man, all drawn stick-figure style. It didn't seem, from that, that Alexandra saw herself as having much of a relationship with her mother. It was always three little girls and a man, presumably Elias.

Three little girls and Elias having a picnic. Three little girls and Elias flying a kite. But most often, three little girls and Elias throwing a ball.

But Elias had worked with kids other than his own daughters. There were sketches of that, too: the man and the three little girls and other little girls and little boys, all of them throwing balls. Sometimes there were as many as ten children in a single sketch, every one of them throwing balls.

In later sketch pads, often there was just one little girl throwing a ball. Sometimes she was on a softball field; other times she seemed to be standing under a tree throwing a ball. Could they have had pitching practice in their own front yard, under the Russian olive tree? If they did, I wondered how many windows they broke before the girls learned to control their pitches.

I could tell from the position of the hands that they were throwing overhand rather than the easier, but less controlled, underhand pitch most women use. No wonder all three girls had been outstanding in athletics; I've been told, though I don't know whether it's true or not, that the reason very few women ever learn to throw overhand is because a woman's skeletal structure is so different from a man's as to make the highly controlled overhand throw virtually impossible. But Elias must have been a born athlete, to have worked so patiently with his daughters as to teach them something that is nearly unteachable. And the daughters must have been born athletes, to be able to learn something most women apparently can't learn.

What a waste, I thought, *to keep Elias stuck in a jewelry store because his great-great-grandfather had owned a jewelry store, when his own abilities were so different. And what a waste, to keep three women who had so much athletic potential stuck in "proper" women's roles. Admittedly, there still aren't as many openings for women athletes as for men, but tennis and golf have been available for generations, and anybody who could learn what these women had learned could play tennis, could play golf, probably on a professional level.*

But Alexandra never knew who she was going to be when she woke up in the morning. Would that problem have gone away if she had been taken away from this gloomy old house next door to a graveyard and told that henceforth she could make her living on the tennis or golf circuit?

Maybe it would. And maybe it wouldn't. Nobody would ever know.

I returned to the pictures, to the one set of pictures that recurred over and over again from the oldest of the sketch pads to the newest.

The sketch of three little girls and a man standing around a woman who lay on the ground. Very often that picture was preceded by one of a woman standing under a tree while something unidentifiably round and white sailed through the air toward her from behind. In some of the pictures the woman was alone; in others there was one little girl with her.

Oh, yes, Alexandra knew how her mother died. Alexandra saw it happen. But did she ever know who? That I questioned as I looked back to the very earliest of the yellowed sketch pads.

I found the sketch that must have been made very soon after Elias and Georgina discovered Miranda's body in the front yard, with Alexandra curled up beside her, crying, the sketch of the woman lying on the ground, a little girl lying beside her, a round white unidentifiable—something—lying nearby.

I needed to discuss this with Charlie Sosa; I needed to show the sketch pads to him. Until I could do that, none of this speculation was getting me anywhere. I put the sketch pads back on the shelf and went into Georgina's room. Harry was sitting at the computer. Totally ignoring my request, he had signed onto Prodigy and was reading a bulletin board. "You want a computer?" he asked me.

"Harry, we've *got* a computer," I pointed out.

"You mean *I* have a computer. I never let you get a chance at it. Honey, this one's damn good. It's a Tandy Sensation, two-fifty-five-meg hard drive, Multimedia CD, send-fax—"

"Wait a minute," I said. "You mean it'll play CDs?"

"It'll play CDs, and it'll also read information CDs. Look what all it's got built in. . . ." He signed off Prodigy, inserted a small silvery disk into a slide-in drawer, pushed a couple of buttons, and said, *"Voilà!"* I was looking at what announced itself as a bookshelf: it had two books of quotations, an almanac, an encyclopedia, and two or three other things I forgot as soon as I looked away. "Great for Lori's homework," he said craftily. "And Cameron's when he's a little older."

I happened to know that a CD ROM was the one thing Harry's computer lacked that he wanted, and I knew he'd spent a lot of time lately looking at catalogs trying to decide what external CD ROM unit to get to plug into his. "How much chance would Lori and Cameron and I get to use it?" I demanded.

"I'll go on using my own," he said, sounding very hurt. "I'll still get my own CD ROM. But until I did, we could both use this one when we need CD. And you could start checking out CDs from the library. . . ."

He knew perfectly well that I wanted a CD player, and we had decided not to get one because we couldn't think of a place to put it.

"And that grocery store that delivers, I could just move the grocery list from my computer to yours and then when you wanted to order something . . ."

He was finding all my hot buttons. Now that he was in management, he was bringing a lot of work home, something that he never had to think about when he was a test pilot. And it was true that there were times I found myself going out to the grocery store when I would really have preferred to have the groceries delivered, just because I couldn't seem to get my turn at the computer.

"I'll offer him eight hundred dollars for it," Harry said, "and I'll bet he'll take it."

"What's it worth?"

"I don't know, I haven't been in Radio Shack lately. Brand-new—I really don't know. But used, and I'll have to delete all her files—I think eight hundred dollars is fair."

"Harry, please don't delete the files until you've read them," I said, and Harry grinned. He knew he'd won.

We went downstairs together. Harry offered eight hundred dollars, which Cully immediately accepted, and Harry immediately signed over eight hundred dollars' worth of traveler's checks. Now the computer was ours. Now Harry could play with it as much as he wanted to.

He went back upstairs to do exactly that, and I, not feeling like cooking, located Alexandra's car keys and said, "I'm going to Arctic Circle. Anybody want anything?"

That brought Cully back out of his room and Harry back down the stairs.

Armed with orders and money, I went out the front door. It was finally feeling like June, and Pat was no longer on the porch. He was stretched full length under the Russian olive. Just as I leaned over to scratch his ears he began to bark, and I felt, or maybe heard, something whiz through the air. Something hit the right side of my head, hard, and I felt myself falling forward into darkness.

My last conscious thought was, *So that's how it was done!*

. . . . .

Ten

. . . .

I CAN'T HAVE *been unconscious long,* I thought, rolling over from my left side onto my back. *Pat started barking wildly just before I was hit. He was still barking just now, and then he stopped. But I must have been unconscious a little while, because Harry is beside me, holding my hand. No, I was out even longer than that. What is Charlie Sosa doing here? And those EMTs? I'm not hurt that badly!*

Maybe not, but I was thoroughly surrounded: Cynthia, who was supposed to be in a hotel room hiding but was here crying; and Cully, whom I had last seen headed for his own bedroom but who was here looking very serious; and Harry, who was supposed to be upstairs playing with a computer but was here looking like he was about to start crying too; and Charlie—and two EMTs. What was this, a convention in Georgina's front yard?

I started to sit up, and Harry said, "Oh no you don't," and firmly pressed me back against the ground. My head got a little swimmy again from no more motion than that.

"I know how they did it," I said. Then I realized I must have passed out for a minute or two, because nobody was in the same place they'd been when I last looked. An EMT was washing my face and another was taking my blood pressure on my right arm while Harry was holding my left hand. I couldn't see Charlie at all; Cynthia, in the intervals between feeding dog biscuits to Pat (so that was why he stopped barking), was continuing to cry, saying, "He meant it for me, whoever it was, he meant it for me!"

Which actually was entirely possible. She was wearing black slacks and a blue sweatshirt. I was wearing black slacks and a blue sweatshirt. She was a little taller than I, but proportionally her weight was about the same and somebody in a hurry and bent on murder might not notice the height difference. We were about the same coloring: premature gray hair must run in her family, because both Cynthia and Alexandra were—or had been, in the case of Alexandra—as gray as I was despite being only twenty-six. Our hair was different lengths, but that wouldn't be all that noticeable in the heavy shade cast by a Russian olive that was almost totally leafed out.

Despite the sunshine, the ground was still damp and a little too cool. *It must be windy today,* I thought, because the light green sweet-scented blossoms had fallen on me and were lying on my head and on my clothes.

Harry, ignoring what Cynthia had said and replying to me, said, "Tell me later. Right now you've got to go to the hospital."

"Oh, that's nonsense," I tried to protest vigorously, but my voice sounded weak even to me.

"Oh, no, that isn't nonsense," one of the EMTs told me. "You've had a nasty crack on the head and we're going to get you to X-ray."

That reminded me that I'd been trying to talk to Charlie, and I said again, "I know how they did it."

"You know how who did what?" Harry asked.

"Where did Charlie go? He was right here."

"He left. He'll talk to you later, after you get back home."

"But this is important," I tried to protest.

"So is getting your skull X-rayed," Harry said firmly. "Deb, Cynthia found you lying outside twenty minutes ago. We called nine-one-one and waited fifteen minutes for the ambulance, and it had been here a couple of minutes before you woke up. You've blacked out twice more since then, whether you know it or not.

. . . . .

That tells me at the very least you've got one hell of a concussion, and we're not going to talk about anything else until you've seen a doctor and the doctor has seen the X rays. If you're worrying about the rock, don't. Charlie took it with him."

"Cynthia?" I asked.

"Right here," she said. "But every time I leave the dog he starts barking."

"I didn't know you were here until I saw you."

"I was just thinking about what Cully said. I guess I was being pretty unreasonable. So I came over here to talk with him. But when I stopped the car I didn't want to go in yet, I felt so sad about the house going out of the family after so long, so I was just walking around looking at the house—went over to look at the graves, I guess the city'll make us move them now—and I was thinking about what I wanted to get. I don't have room for much, but—there's so much history here. And then I heard the dog start barking. He sounded—I know dogs pretty well. And he sounded like one mad dog, well, I don't mean mad like rabies, you know, angry. So I came over to see what he was angry about, and—I saw you. Lying on the ground like that. So I ran and knocked on the door and Cully opened it and I told him to call an ambulance."

While she was speaking the EMTs had been loading me onto a stretcher, with a backboard behind my head to keep me from moving any more than I already had. And that was that. I didn't have time to continue the conversation because the ambulance took me to LDS Hospital, with Harry following in Alexandra's car so that he could take me home—such as it was at present—if they let me leave, and so that he could get home himself if they didn't let me leave.

I spent a long time lying in half a room partitioned off from the other half with a yellow curtain of some sort that rode on a metal track attached to the ceiling. Then somebody took me off to X-ray, where they X-rayed the front, back, and right side of my head, taking about three shots each and carefully covering my abdomen with a lead curtain each time, even though I could have told them I wasn't pregnant if they had asked me. But nobody asked me anything. They must have assumed I wasn't up to answering, or else I was too groggy to be believed, because they asked Harry everything.

Then they took me back to the half a room and left me there for a long time longer. Harry was in and out the whole time, except in X-ray, where they made him wait in the hall. He kept having to go fill out papers about insurance and so forth. Not that that was a problem; between his insurance through Bell Helicopter and mine through the Fort Worth Police Department, we are, if anything, overinsured.

The doctor came in, finally, and said, "I'm Dr. Vainuku, and I'm sure you'll be pleased to know you do not have a skull fracture."

"Good," I said feebly, looking for his name tag, which my eyes were too blurry to read. "Dr. who?"

"No, not Dr. Who. He's fictional."

"I know. My son reads them. I meant what is your name. I don't think I heard it right."

"Vainuku," he repeated patiently, as if this happened all the time, which it probably did. "It's a Tongan name."

"What's a Tongan doing in Utah?" I demanded. "I mean, I'm not trying to sound rude, but it doesn't sound like a place where a Tongan would be very happy."

"I'm not a Tongan," he answered. "I was born and raised in Utah. My mom and dad are Tongan, and you're right, they don't like the weather here. Every winter they say they're going home, but they never do. I don't know, there are a lot of Tongan Mormons, and a few of them came to Utah, and then a few more came because the first ones were here, and then some other Tongans came because they had relatives here even if they weren't Mormons, and all of a sudden it was like a mass exodus from Tonga to

Utah. Finally somebody looked around and there were a whole lot of Tongans here. Some Mormons, some Methodists. There's a big Tongan contingent in the Pioneer Day Parade. We march right behind the Salt Lake Scots. Now hold still, I want to look at your eyes."

Which he did, carefully examining both eyes with that little light thingy the doctors use. He proceeded after that to turn out the overhead light and see if my eyes could follow a small light spot on the wall. Then he turned the lights back on and checked to see if my eyes could track moving fingers, and see if I could tell how many fingers he had stuck in front of me. I thought it was all very silly, which shows just how normal my thought processes were not.

Finally he told me I had quite a concussion and would probably have at least one shiner, probably two. I knew that; I'm familiar with the way the brain bounces around inside the skull when the head is struck violently, so that a person hit very hard in the back or side of the head frequently winds up with black eyes. He said I could go home in a couple of hours, but he wanted to keep me in the hospital under observation a little bit longer. Under observation, I figured out, seemed to mean that every ten minutes or so somebody would come in and ask me two or three questions just to see whether I could answer them. The questions weren't important; it was my ability, or inability, to answer them that was.

Charlie Sosa showed up again, looking outraged. To Harry, he said, "Thanks for letting me know she's awake. But I wish you'd keep your wife out of trouble."

"Anybody who could do that," Harry fervently assured him, "could chew bubble gum, climb Mount Everest, and fly a Jet Ranger simultaneously."

"Okay, what have you got?" Charlie asked me.

"What do you mean, what have I got? I've got a knot on my head, that's what I've got."

"You told your husband you knew how it was done."

. . . . .

"Oh, that. Simple, once you think of it. The rock was thrown. At me, and probably at Georgina and Alexandra. And for that matter, probably at their mother."

"Thrown?" Charlie repeated incredulously. "With enough accuracy to kill?"

"Yes. If you can throw a ball with control you can throw a ball-shaped rock with control. Elias taught a lot of people to throw with control, and one of those people killed his wife and later two of his daughters and tried to kill me—or his other daughter, because I really don't know who the target was. And Alexandra saw her mother killed. Everybody was right about that. If anybody had ever looked at her sketch pads they'd have realized it, because she kept drawing pictures of the murder. But I don't think she saw the person who did it."

Charlie was stuck on a previous sentence. "Her sketch pads?" he demanded.

"Yes. We missed them the first time we searched the room. They were on a closet shelf. Oh, and it's definite Cully owns the house. He's probably there, and he'll give you permission to get them."

"Good—I want them." Charlie left at a fast walk, looking as if he'd rather be running.

A while after that Dr. Vainuku came in and went through the same series of tests all over again: the eyes, the lights, asking me questions. Then he told Harry he could take me home, but I had to stay in bed the rest of the day. He handed a prescription to Harry and said, "This one's for pain. Get her in bed first and then go fill it." He went on to inform me that I'd probably be very sleepy, but Harry had to wake me every hour all day and all night long. Each time I had to be at least alert enough to tell him my name, where I was, and who the president was. Not wanting to stay in the hospital, I said, "I'm Deb Ralston and I'm in Salt Lake City and the President is Hillary—I mean, Bill Clinton."

Dr. Vainuku chuckled at my deliberate mistake, but he said, "Right. And if you can't remember that at two A.M., or three A.M., or four A.M., you get to come right back to the hospital."

I did not want to come back to the hospital, so I wobbled back to the car, reminding myself that I was in Salt Lake City and the President was Bill Clinton.

Harry asked me if I wanted any lunch.

He had to stop the car for me to barf.

No, I did not want any lunch. Furthermore, I did not want the smell of lunch anywhere near me. He could go back out while I was in bed and get himself some lunch. He could get lunch while somebody was filling my prescription. He could take Cully with him and get Cully some lunch, only if he did he had to leave Pat with me even if he did barf in the house unless the kids were home, because I did not want to be left alone when I had no strength at all to defend myself just in case whoever it was really was aiming at me rather than at Cynthia. But he was not to mention lunch to me again.

But before I went to bed I wanted to make a few phone calls.

"You *always* want to make a few phone calls," Harry said resignedly. "You're like Columbo and his 'Oh, one more thing.' "

"So? I'm a detective."

"You're also a human being. A very damaged one, at present. The calls can wait till later."

He helped me out of the car, and I wobbled up the stairs to the front porch with Harry assisting me. But I did manage to get the house door open by myself, after Harry unlocked it while I leaned on the wall.

Charlie was sitting in the front room talking with Cully. He turned when I came in. "Deb," he said, "I've got news for you. There aren't any sketchbooks."

"Oh, nonsense, of course there are. You must have looked in the wrong place."

"Then suppose you take me and show me the right place," Charlie suggested.

I looked dismally at the staircase. "You want me to walk up to the third floor?"

"Unless you'd rather I carry you."

With Charlie and Harry both assisting, I managed to get up to the third floor.

Charlie was right. There were no sketchbooks.

"But I left them right here," I protested.

"You sure you didn't dream them while you were unconscious?"

"Charlie, I do not dream sketchbooks," I retorted indignantly. "They were right here, there were about thirty of them, and now they're gone."

"Well, I've just been downstairs talking with Cully," Charlie said, "after I came up here and looked and didn't find them. He says nobody's been in the house. He was replacing washers on all the faucets in the house and says the only time anybody could have got past him to go up the stairs without him hearing was when he was in the kitchen, but the front and back doors were both locked and the dog never started barking."

"The doors being locked doesn't mean jack," I pointed out, "because the killer got away with Alexandra's purse and keys. As to the dog not barking . . ." I paused. Pat is a pretty barky dog. But if it was somebody he knew, somebody who had already been to the house several times—

Who could that be?

Hart Bivins. Cynthia Harvey. Cully himself, of course. LaRae

White, but I could not even force myself to conjure up a picture of LaRae White committing murder.

That narrowed the field considerably.

The three of us went down the stairs together, not stopping on the second floor for me to lie down. Harry deposited me on the couch, with a couple of throw cushions under my head, and said, "All right, who did you want to call?"

"I'll wait on that," I answered. "Cully, is it okay if I ask you some questions?"

"Ask away," Cully said.

"Why were you replacing all the washers today? I hadn't noticed any of the faucets leaking."

"I hadn't either," he answered, "but I don't want one to suddenly decide to start leaking while I'm showing the house to a prospective buyer. Anyway, it's something to do."

"If you want something to do, you could fix that damned electrical outlet in the second-floor bathroom," Harry said.

"The one under the towel rack? I keep meaning to do that," Cully said, "but I always forget about it because nobody needs to use it most of the time and really I'm not much good at wiring. But I'll get the parts next time I'm at a hardware store and tend to it soon. Maybe tomorrow."

"You sure you know how?" Harry asked. "We'll be here a couple more days. I'll be glad to help you. I've done a lot of wiring."

"Well, tell you what—I'll take the switch plate off this afternoon or tomorrow and have a look at it. It may be something simple, like a wire that's worked in two, but if it's not I'll ask you to have a look at it."

"Can we stop talking about electrical outlets?" I asked. "Cully, when is Georgina's funeral?"

The look on his face told me that was a gauche question. He was trying not to think about Georgina's funeral. But he answered,

"Saturday. The medical examiner's office said they'd release the body this afternoon. I figured—I didn't like Alexandra, but Georgina loved her. They might as well be buried at the same time. And there's room in Elias's plot for them. Cynthia and me too, for that matter."

"It's kind of funny, your calling your father-in-law by his first name. How long had you known him?"

Cully stretched, walked over to the liquor cabinet and opened it, and poured himself a glass of Canadian Club. A somewhat smaller glass than last time, I was pleased to note, but still a lot more than I would ever have wanted on an empty stomach. "All my life," he said over his shoulder. "Almost, anyway. I grew up just a couple of blocks over from here. He used to coach every kids' athletic team in the neighborhood. I mean, one team for each time of the year. He coached Little League and he coached church softball—I wasn't a member, but they always let me play—and he coached church basketball and he coached neighborhood soccer even before it got to be fashionable, and he coached some kind of neighborhood touch football he dreamed up himself. Elias was wonderful with kids. And my dad was a drunk, he never was at home. Elias was the closest thing to a dad I ever had."

"Was that why you married his daughter?" I was appalled to hear myself asking.

Luckily Cully wasn't offended. "Uh-uh," he said. "I've been married before. I was a jock—I was on the high school football team, and you know that old storybook romance, jock marries cheerleader. Well, I don't know how those things usually work out, but ours was a disaster. Claire was a real good cheerleader. She was gregarious, that's the word—she got along with people. She knew how to do her hair and how to do her makeup and she always dressed real well. But when it came to cooking and sewing and housecleaning—no way. Well, if she'd been able to hold a job so we could have two incomes we could have eaten out and maybe had somebody come in once a week to do the housecleaning, but she couldn't do that either. And I found out dressing real well when you can't sew gets real, real expensive. We've got two little girls. I'd have brought them to live with me, after I married Georgina, but they were scared of Sandy, and to tell the truth I don't blame them for that. But anyhow, Claire couldn't be a housewife and couldn't hold a job. Finally she went back to live with her mother. I didn't try to get her back. I didn't *want* her back. So I went on and let her divorce me and I took to hanging around over here. Sandy never did like me and I don't know why, but Elias, he liked me, and the more I hung around over here the better Georgina looked to me, and I started wondering why I hadn't noticed her while we were in high school. But I never did then, except as sort of—sort of part of Elias. You're where Elias is, Georgina's usually there too. But she didn't dress like Claire, and she couldn't do her hair and makeup like Claire, and those are the things you notice when you're sixteen. It wasn't till I was thirty that I noticed she could do the things Claire couldn't. Like cook a decent meal on a budget, and keep the house looking decent, and make a man feel comfortable. I just—I wish I'd married her ten years earlier. And I wish I'd been able to figure out a way to get Sandy to go somewhere else. Look, I didn't want Sandy dead, I'm sorry somebody killed her, but she should have been in an institution. Georgina always insisted Sandy wasn't dangerous, but damn it, she was. Came after me with a butcher knife one time. . . . You didn't want the story of my life, did you? I'm sorry. But damn it, I loved Georgina—I'm sorry. I'm talking too much."

"It's been very informative," I said. "Did Elias teach you to pitch?"

"Oh, yeah, he taught just about every kid in the neighborhood to pitch."

"Who besides you, that's still around here?"

"Oh, Hart Bivins, you know, that shrink. Uh—Ted Mullins.

He's a geologist now, gave Sandy a job to please Elias. I respect him for that, but I never did like him much, him and his prissy ways. You ask me, I think that was why Elias wanted her working there; she could turn into Sandy Lu and throw herself at him all she wanted, but he wasn't going to give a shit." Reading between the lines, I took it that Cully meant Ted Mullins was gay. "Let me see—Jeff Reisner, his dad was Elias's attorney, and Jeff's Georgin—my—attorney now. Who else? If I could just think straight. Damn, I guess just about everybody else's moved away—who else—Laura, what's her last name now, she married some guy from out of town and he wound up a bishop, I'm sorry, I can't think. LaRae'll know who I mean. I'm sorry, I can't think of anybody else."

I was looking at Charlie, to see if he understood what I was getting at with these questions. Clearly, he did. He stood now and said, "I'm going back to work. If any of you think of anything else, please let me know."

"You want a ham sandwich before you leave?" Cully offered. "I had one a while ago."

So he hadn't been drinking on an empty stomach. Idiotically, because Cully's habits were no problem of mine except as they impacted on me, I was relieved to know that.

"No, thanks," Charlie said. "I've got too much on my plate already."

"Huh?" Cully said. But I knew exactly what he meant.

"I'll take one," Harry said. "No, don't," he said, as Cully moved toward the kitchen. "I can make it myself, soon as I've got Deb settled down."

"You sure?" Cully said. "It just seems to me you're not getting what you paid for. I'd refund your money, except Georgina already spent it and I sure as hell haven't got it. I mean, even that eight hundred you paid me for the computer, that's got to go to Georgina's funeral."

"We don't want our money back," Harry said, and I assured Cully I agreed.

"Though if she had a personal cookbook, I'd sure appreciate a copy of it," I added, and then blushed at my own crassness. No matter what I thought, I'd never have said that if I hadn't been bashed on the head.

"She did," Cully said, "and you can have it."

"I didn't mean—"

"That's okay," Cully said. "If you don't take it I'll give it to DI. So you might as well have it."

Cully and Harry helped me back up the stairs; I was so wobbly it took both of them. Then Cully left, and Harry helped me out of my dirty, damp slacks and shirt and into a cotton nightgown. Then he said, "I'll just run out and get this prescription filled. Then I'll get on back to that computer. I don't think there's going to be anything in it, but—"

"I don't either, honestly," I said, "but I still want you to try."

"I'm going to make printouts of all her stuff that has to do with the bed-and-breakfast," Harry added, "because Cully'll need them later for income tax. You know, he's turned out to be a pretty decent guy. I never would have thought it, after that performance he put on the first night we met him."

"But I can understand how he felt, now," I said sleepily. "He really loved Elias, and then Elias died. He really loved Georgina, and then Georgina threw him out because Alexandra wanted her to. I wonder—I really wonder why she did that?"

"So do I," Harry said. "You get some rest now. Want me to put a glass of water beside the bed?"

"Yes, please."

I don't know how long I had been asleep when the lawn mower started up outside. Harry had awakened me at least twice; I had vague memories of muzzily assuring him I knew who I was and

. . . . .

where I was and could I please go back to sleep now? I rolled over with my head throbbing far worse than it had earlier, cursed Cully's need for activity and wished he'd at least find something quiet to do, drank half a glass of water and swallowed one of the pills in the prescription bottle Harry had left right next to the water, and went back to sleep.

The next time Harry woke me I said, "Do we really have to keep discussing the President? I want the phone book and the phone."

"You're awake," Harry said, and brought me the items requested.

Thinking for sure I was on the right track, which I will admit now I definitely was not, I called Hart Bivins.

I knew perfectly well he was a shrink. It was, according to my watch, four o'clock and still Wednesday, which made it four o'clock Wednesday afternoon. I should have expected him to be playing golf, which doctors often are on Wednesday afternoon but which he was not, or busy, which he was. His nurse told me she'd give him the message and he'd call back later.

Sitting cross-legged in bed leaning back on the headboard—we don't have a headboard at home, only the wall behind the bed, and when I lean back too hard the mattress sort of slithers forward, so I found the headboard a luxury—I asked Harry, "Did you get anything on the computer?"

"No," he said. "I've been making printouts, like I told you I was going to, and her printer's slower than the seven-year-itch. Deb, I'm not taking that thing home, it's prehistoric and I wish I knew why she put it on a good computer."

"Probably because she couldn't afford a good printer," I pointed out. "And maybe she didn't expect to need to do that much printing. Maybe she figured she could just look on the screen for most things."

Since Harry's own printer is an HP LaserJet IIIP, he is likely to consider any printer that prints fewer than three pages a minute, does tractor feed instead of sheet feed, or makes enough noise to be heard four feet away to be a dinosaur. But I would scream bloody murder if he tried to put out the money to buy a second LaserJet. Maybe he could just put in some sort of cabling so that my computer could print on his printer.

Come to think of it, I was sure that was what he'd do. Anybody as mechanically gifted as Harry could do something like that easily. I would ask him to. That would give him the excuse to have several of his buddies over, all of them crawling around in the attic fishing the walls, emerging dirty and sweaty and as proud of themselves as the caveman who brought home the biggest mastodon in town for Mrs. Caveman to cook.

Normally Hal would help him. This time Hal wouldn't, because we were going to be leaving Hal at the MTC and we wouldn't see him again for two years. For the first time since his formal missionary farewell, I found myself tearing up. He was only nineteen now. When he came home he'd be twenty-one. I'd never have my little boy back again.

I tried to remind myself of all the scatterbrained things he had done in the past: the time he waxed the floor with Karo syrup because, as he virtuously pointed out when I started screaming, the floor wax and the syrup came in identical-sized cans, and it wasn't his fault the label was off the syrup. (The label was not off the floor-wax can, but he hadn't looked that far.)

The time he called me at work thinking he was disgraced for life because he had fallen off a horse at Sammy's father's dairy farm. "Then go get back on," I advised hard-heartedly.

"Mom, you don't understand," he wailed. "The horse didn't buck me off. I *fell off a horse!*"

"So did Prince Charles, in a polo match last week. Go get back on the horse. Everybody falls off when they're learning, and most people fall off every now and then for as long as they ride."

A little mollified, he went and got back on the horse and fell off again, but by the time he was fourteen he was riding as well as I had done when I was five.

The time he and Lori took off for New Mexico, hitchhiking with the driver of an eighteen-wheeler, so they could look at Los Alamos during spring break. They wound up tangled up with one of the nastiest murders I had come across in a long time. Harry was in the hospital, so I had to fly out there—nine months pregnant—to bring them home, which was how Cameron happened to be born in Las Vegas, New Mexico, instead of Fort Worth, Texas.

The time he had an abscessed tooth and absentmindedly took his codeine twice and his penicillin not at all, which left him sliding rubber-legged down the side of the car at the doctor's office and mumbling, "Mom, do people really do this on purpose?"

"Indeed they do," I assured him, trying to catch him, which was rather a lost cause as I am five feet two and he even then, at fourteen, was over six feet tall and quite husky.

"Mom, they're *carraaazy!*"

The dentist had to help me carry him into the office.

All right, at times he was a nightmare to raise. But damn it, he was always such a sweet kid, and he was always so interesting to be around, and now he was going to be gone two years and when he came back he would belong to Lori, not to Harry and me, and I was sitting cross-legged on the bed crying with Harry patiently handing me Kleenex without asking me why I was crying. The only time he ever asks is when he's pretty sure he's done something to make me mad, but on those occasions I'm too upset to explain until I get through crying and he knows that perfectly well.

But this time he knew, rightly, that whatever I was crying about, it wasn't anything he had done.

The phone rang, and I sniffed a couple of times and grabbed it. As I had hoped, it was Hart Bivins. "I've only got five minutes," he warned at once, "but the nurse said you had a couple of questions. Let's make them fast."

"Okay. Did Elias teach you any kind of athletics?"

"He taught me everything I ever learned about athletics."

"Including how to pitch?"

"Yep. He taught every kid in the neighborhood how to pitch."

"How fussy was he about making sure people learned to control the ball?"

"I am convinced," Hart said carefully, "that any kid Elias worked with who wasn't all thumbs could go to any big-league park you want to name and strike out any five big-league ballplayers in succession. If Elias worked with you, you knew how to make the ball go where you wanted it to go. The carnie people used to hate us when the fair was in town, because those baseballs they give you to pitch at the milk bottles are always weighted a little wrong, so you can't throw them straight even if you think you know how to throw, but the kids Elias taught would go out there and win all the pink elephants and blue seals they wanted."

"Were you treating Georgina and Cynthia, or just Alexandra?"

He hesitated and then said carefully, "Alexandra was the only one with MPD. I thought I made that clear."

"That wasn't my question."

"All right, yes, I was treating Georgina for depression. I had her on Prozac, and it was helping a lot. And in case you're wondering, I don't know whether it was genetic depression or situational. I can tell you that if I had to live with Alexandra I'd be pretty depressed myself."

"What about Cynthia?"

Dead silence. Then, finally, he said, "Cynthia is alive. The doctor-patient relationship forbids me to discuss her without her permission."

"Georgina told me Cynthia was depressed."

"Did she? I can't comment on what Georgina told you."

"If you were asked in court whether Cynthia was in any way a danger to anybody, what would you answer?"

"Ask me in court or get a court order and I'll tell you. Otherwise, I simply cannot. I'm sorry."

Well, what had I expected? I knew perfectly well that Susan Braun, a good friend of mine who runs a private psychiatric hospital in Fort Worth, would have told me exactly the same thing.

"What about Alexandra?"

"She made a lot of noise. But I honestly don't think she'd ever have harmed anybody."

"Did you know Alexandra did a lot of drawing?"

"I was aware of that. But she had not progressed far enough into treatment to allow me to look at the drawings. I asked about them twice, and each time the Alexandra persona instantly withdrew and left behind the Sandy persona, sitting in a chair crying and sucking her thumb. I decided not to ask again, but to wait until she was willing to offer them."

"Which of her personas do you think was doing the drawing?"

"The word is *personae.* To the best of my knowledge they all were. That, by the way, should be expected if she had been drawing before the splitting began. Is there anything else you need to know? Because my next patient is here, and I hate to keep him waiting."

"No, that's all, thanks," I said, and hung up. I blew my nose again and tried to lean over to drop the tissue into the trash can beside the bed, which proved to be a very bad mistake. That was farther than I could lean, as dizzy as I was right then.

Luckily Harry caught me before I totally fell out of bed, and put me back where I belonged. "You want me to stay with you, or should I get back to the computer?" he asked.

"You might as well go on back to the computer. Is it time for me to take another one of those pills?"

. . . . .

"When did you take the first one?"

"I don't know," I admitted. "I can't see the clock from bed, and I didn't think to look at my watch."

"Then I don't know, either," Harry said.

"It was when Cully or whoever it was started mowing the lawn."

"Then that was only about two hours ago. You'd better wait another couple of hours."

"Harry," I said, "when we get home, would you make us a headboard for the bed?"

. . . . .

Eleven

. . . .

People always lie to the police, and to people who are—as Harry and I had been the last few days—in any way representing the police. The problem always is to figure out not who is lying, because you can pretty safely assume everybody is, but rather what the lies are and why they are being told.

As I saw it, I had three possible suspects: Hart Bivins, Cully Grafton, and Cynthia Harvey. I really didn't think Alexandra's ex-boss, even if Elias had taught him to pitch, was in the picture, and I figured it was fairly safe to assume that Laura whoever-she-was who had married a man who later became a bishop was out of the picture. I couldn't see any motive for Hart Bivins, but that didn't put him out of the picture because there could be a motive I didn't know about. I could see reasons for Cully to kill Alexandra but not Georgina, unless Georgina figured out he killed Alexandra. I couldn't see any reason at all for Cynthia to kill her two sisters.

And without knowing more than I knew, I had no earthly reason for any of them to kill Miranda Howe, especially in view of the fact that so far as I could tell, every one of the possible suspects was still a preschooler when Miranda died.

Maybe I was wrong. Maybe it was none of them. Maybe I should look farther afield.

I remembered Kate saying to me on Monday, "I don't believe in locked-room mysteries. If it did happen, it could have happened."

I'd worked one locked-room mystery. Literally. All the possible suspects were locked inside a very small motion-picture theater, and it seemed impossible for the victim to have been stabbed in the back of the neck by anybody either from outside or from inside. But when I found out the answer it was ridiculously easy. I was certain this one would be, too.

Alexandra's murder had been a locked-room mystery, as long as we thought somebody had to be standing right behind the victims. But it wasn't anymore. Somebody just had to be within the range of accurate throwing.

Yeah. That's all . . . which meant somebody had to throw the rock from a church parking lot full of people, or from a backyard full of kids without either the people going home from church, or the kids playing whatever they were playing, noticing anything amiss.

I still had a locked-room mystery. And I didn't like it.

To be perfectly honest, Charlie Sosa had a locked-room mystery. The fact that my son found the body and I immediately turned and looked at it did not make it my case. But I've got this damned relentless sense of responsibility.

I thought I knew now who had committed the murders (as I have said, I was quite wrong), except for two small problems. I couldn't figure out why, and more important, I couldn't figure out how. You can get by without a why, if you have to. But you can't do anything at all without a how.

The phone rang. I did not try to answer it; it was just out of reach, and I had already learned that it was not possible for me to lean that far without getting so dizzy I was in immediate danger of falling out of the bed on my head. About five minutes later Harry came in, looking very hassled. "That was Hal," he said. "They're in Park City; they went up there to ride a ski lift."

"In June?" I asked involuntarily.

"In June. I asked that too. Hal said they run them all summer long because you get a glorious view of the mountains from them. Anyway, when they got back to the parking lot the van wouldn't start. Hal called a mechanic to come look at it, and the mechanic says the starter's gone out and it's so late in the day he can't get another starter till tomorrow. We've got a choice: I can go get the kids and bring them back now and then take at least Hal back to Park City in the morning to drive the van back, or we can let them stay overnight. Hal's got that credit card we gave him and he says he already checked to be sure there were two motel rooms available. What do you think?"

I hesitated. Common sense would say to leave them there overnight, and I was sure they wouldn't do anything they wouldn't do if we were there. But Mormon missionaries, like Caesar's wife, must be above suspicion. "You'd better go get them," I said.

"That's what I thought, too. But I figured I'd see what you thought. You want me to help you to the bathroom before I go? I don't think you can get there on your own."

"Yes, please. And how far is it to Park City?"

"I asked Hal. He said it was about an hour's drive, and told me the way."

Obviously he would have to tell Harry the way. The maps were in the van, not in Alexandra's car, which Harry was driving.

"By the way," I said after he deposited me in bed, "you'd better get you guys some supper while you're out, or bring some home—I may be able to eat by then. It's a sure thing I won't be up to cooking anytime today, and I really don't want Lori to have to do it."

"I don't either. Okay, hamburgers okay?"

Since we arrived in Utah, I had developed a distinct liking for Arctic Circle's Ranchburger. I suggested it, and Harry said he'd see what he could do. He would, he added, ask Cully to check on me at least once while he was gone. There was no possible doubt that I had a concussion; he could see for himself that my pupils were of somewhat different sizes. I couldn't see much of anything except pretty fuzzily, unless I closed my right eye and squinted through my left one. Of course, my left eye felt somewhat swollen by now, too. Which it probably was. I was developing those shiners Dr. Vainuku had warned me about.

It wasn't until after Harry left that it dawned upon me that he had left me alone in the house with one of my three possible suspects. The fact that he hadn't been worried about going, and I hadn't been worried about being left, assured me that although my conscious mind still considered Cully a possible, both Harry's and my subconscious had dropped him from the list.

That left me with two suspects: Hart Bivins and Cynthia Harvey. And for the life of me I couldn't figure out why either of them would commit these crimes or how, and even less could I figure out how, or why, either of them would have murdered Miranda Howe. Maybe I was on the wrong track altogether. Maybe it was somebody I had never met, somebody I had never even heard of, who killed Miranda, and maybe the others were copycats. Except if they were copycats they were copycatting something that happened twenty-one years ago and had not been publicized since, which put me right back where I had been.

What was it Lori said the other day about inherited murder? Maybe that was what this was, an inherited murder. Maybe somebody's father or mother or older brother had killed Miranda and now he or she was killing Miranda's daughters. But that sounded like something from a James Bond movie. It made no sense whatever.

My mind was going in circles and getting nowhere, and I was relieved when LaRae White tapped at my bedroom door and then stuck her head in. "Hello, dear," she said. "Brother Grafton called and told me what happened—my goodness, that left eye looks awful, do you want me to get you some beefsteak to put on it?"

"No, that's okay, the doctor told me it'd do this," I said.

. . . . .

"But why?" she demanded. "That wasn't where the stone hit you, was it?"

"No, it hit the right side of my head," I said, "but it's pretty common to get shiners from a head wound anywhere."

"Now, I wonder why that would be?"

I explained, and she said, "Oh, of course, that makes perfect sense, I should have realized it for myself. Anyway, Brother Grafton, Cully I suppose I should call him, told me that your husband had to go to Park City. I thought if you didn't mind, I'd come by and keep you company for a while before I go over to the funeral home."

"I'm so glad you came," I said. "Please come in and sit down. Sister White, I've been trying and trying and trying, and I just can't think of anything that makes sense."

"In what way, dear?"

I explained, and she shook her head. "I can't think of anything either. When it was just Miranda—well, you know what they say about speaking ill of the dead. But she was really a terrible wife and mother. She was just such a flibbertigibbet; if they hadn't had the money to hire people to come in and take care of the cleaning and cooking and child care I just don't know what would have happened to those poor children. Of course Miranda spoiled them terribly, she was always giving them things to make up for the care she couldn't give them, pretty clothes that were really very unsuitable for them; poor Georgina had her first pair of high heels when she was in the fifth grade and she tried to wear them to school and of course the other children mocked her terribly and she came home crying, I had to take her and get her penny loafers, and Miranda always gave them too much candy and that sort of thing, she really loved them but she just didn't know how to care for them any more than she knew how to care for Elias herself. You know, I always thought it was fortunate Elias didn't lose his money until after she was dead, because I don't know what she'd have done, but on the other hand I might be wrong, once it became necessary she might have taken hold in a way she never had to before. I'd have done more but of course I had my little ones still at home then. As it was, after Miranda died and then after Elias lost the store I had the two younger girls over at my house during the day, and Georgina came by after school. I sent them home to Elias after they had their supper; he'd usually eat downtown."

"Tell me about your children," I urged. "Maybe one of them would know something or think of something I haven't thought of—if they could come talk to me—"

"I'm afraid that's not going to be possible," Sister White said. "My oldest girl, Lacey, is in Oregon now with her husband, and my second girl, LaDonna, is in Japan with her husband, he's in the Navy, and my first boy—I named him Elias but I'm afraid he never did like the name, so now he calls himself Elton—is in New York, he thinks he's going to be able someday to make a living as a singer, but oh, dear, I don't think he'll ever manage, the poor boy can't carry a tune, though of course he says that doesn't matter anymore, he tries to sing that awful heavy metal music, you know, and those drums and things just cover up the lyrics, though with what the lyrics are like we all ought to be grateful for that, and my other boy, Jason, my baby, moved to San Diego. He started out working for the zoo here, he always did love animals so much, but he says the San Diego zoo is much nicer, he takes care of tigers can you imagine, I'd be glad to give you all their telephone numbers, of course—" She reached for her purse as if prepared to pull out an address book at once.

"That's all right," I said hastily. "I was just hoping they were somewhere local—but if they've all moved away, well, they wouldn't have been keeping up with things here."

"Oh, dear, no, not at all. In fact I think that's part of the reason why they left. They were all so embarrassed by poor Alexandra's carryings-on, and she spent so much time at our house, but of course when she was still a child I didn't have the *heart* to send her home, especially when Elias was at work and Georgina had after-school activities—Alexandra was so frightened of the graveyard, you know, very silly but there you are. The poor child was so frightened of anything to do with death—"

"Did you ever see any of her drawings?" I asked.

"Oh, dear, yes, when she didn't remember to bring her sketch pad over to our house she'd draw on everything, I remember I always used to keep all the junk mail that wasn't printed on both sides so I could give it to her to draw on. Dreadfully *gloomy* pictures she always drew—Miranda in her coffin, I remember she drew simply dozens of pictures of that but when she finally got tired of that image and went on to another, it was pictures of her mother actually being killed, poor child, any five-year-old seeing a white ball flying through the air on a snowy day would think it was a snowball. And she never did understand the funeral, or the showing before it. She used to ask me why her mom didn't get out of that bed, she thought the coffin was a kind of bed, I remember when we took her to the funeral home you know how they close part of the lid but not all, and she thought somebody had cut off her mother's legs, she screamed and screamed and we had to open the lid and show her her mother's legs were still there, but she still kept asking why she didn't wake up, and why she didn't get up in the front yard when she heard everybody crying. I tried to explain to her that when people are dead they don't get up, but she always used to watch all these television shows, you know, the cartoon shows where the coyote gets blown up with dynamite and run over by a train and then after the commercial he's right back chasing the roadrunner, and she kept saying it was just a rock, it was just a little rock, why didn't Mommy get up? And then she went from that to thinking her mother was alive in the grave, and then thinking that the people in the graveyard next door might come out and chase her—and she kept reading *totally unsuitable* books when she was old enough to read, she was always reading ghost stories and Stephen King and that kind of thing, and they might be all right for other people to read but they were not all right for her. I tried to get Elias to watch her reading more carefully but he was totally incapable of being at all strict."

"Obviously," I murmured, wondering what I was agreeing to; this woman could cover more topics, in less time, than anybody else I had ever met in my life. "Sister White, I'm still confused about the sequence. You said Elias didn't lose his money until after Miranda was dead—and I understand what happened was he lost a very expensive bracelet—but *when* did he lose it?"

She stared at me. "Why, I thought you knew that," she said. "I told that nice-looking policeman, the Navajo, I'll bet he has no trouble getting dates, I can't imagine why he hasn't remarried but he told me he just never got around to it, you know if I were forty years younger I'd be chasing that one myself, and I thought he was going to tell you. He lost it that same day, the very day Miranda died. I always wondered if he absentmindedly took it out of his pocket at the hospital—she was still breathing, you know, when the ambulance came, although of course she couldn't possibly have survived but as long as she was still breathing they had to treat her as if she were alive—and the ambulance rushed her off to the hospital, and Elias called me to come get the girls so he could leave, because the servants had left by then, and I rushed right over. And if he took it out of his pocket, or it fell out, at the hospital, why, anybody could have picked it up, either knowing what it was or more likely not knowing, thinking it was junk jewelry—an awful gaudy thing it was, Elias showed it to me, and I wouldn't be seen wearing it if I *could* afford it."

"What time of year was that?"

"It was the spring equinox, but spring came late that year, I remember, and after it was warm Elias couldn't stand to see those white stones in the front yard where they'd been lining the flower bed, and he carried all of them next door to the graveyard and put them there, around the iris beds. But it was the spring equinox when Miranda died. March twenty-first, and snow still all over the ground, in fact we'd had a very heavy lake-effect storm the night before, so it was fresh snow, the big wet flakes you get with a lot of moisture in them—when Elias came home, he and Georgina had been out to the grocery store because poor Miranda had forgotten to order milk, she was always forgetting things like that, and there she was lying on her back in the snow with poor little Alexandra curled up beside her and her tears melting holes in the snow, and of course their body warmth had melted more holes—somebody, I forget now who, told me by the time she got to the hospital her body temperature was down to seventy-eight, so even if her brain hadn't been about destroyed she'd probably have died of hypothermia, she didn't have a coat on, you know, just a dancing dress, because Elias had promised to take her dancing later that evening and they were expecting the baby-sitter soon, in fact she came before I got over there and Elias didn't think, he could have left her with the children and gone on and let me pay her and take her home, but instead he sent her home and went on waiting for me, and he didn't even think to get the children inside, except that Alexandra did run in to use the bathroom, but she didn't change clothes, she just came right back out just the way she was. And of course poor Alexandra was about frozen, she did have a coat on, I thought she might have been outdoors playing with snowballs because she had on her mittens, but even so she was wet clean through and I never have seen a child shivering so much, I took her home and *rushed* her into a hot bath—Cynthia didn't have a coat on, she'd rushed out from watching television when she heard Georgina scream, but at least she was fairly *dry,* and Georgina had a coat on and was dry, so physically she wasn't bad though all the children were just in shock, of course, and who can blame them, seeing their mother like that."

"She was lying on her *back?*" I repeated. "Miranda, I mean?"

"Why, yes. Georgina and Elias both told me that. Of course Cynthia was indoors watching television and never knew a thing about it until Georgina and Elias got home and Georgina got out of the car, it was after dark of course but the porch light was on, and she saw Miranda and started screaming and that was when Elias came around the car and saw her for himself and then he ran in the house to call an ambulance—that was before nine-one-one of course, so he called the operator and the operator called the ambulance—and then that was when Cynthia rushed outside to look, but I never could get her to talk about it to me, though Elias said she would talk about it to him, and nobody could ever get Alexandra to talk about it at all, until the day she died, she'd just curl up and start crying and sucking her thumb and curling that lock of her hair—but of course when she drew it she always drew Miranda lying on her back."

That was true. I had seen the pictures myself, but it hadn't registered that Miranda was lying on her back, or else if it did I must have just assumed that was Alexandra's impression of the way things looked rather than the way things actually looked.

"Where was the wound on Miranda's head?" I asked, wondering if I had misunderstood something.

"Why, right here." Sister White turned and pointed to the back of her head, about two hand spans above her neck. "Right here. I saw her before the body was prepared for burial, and poor thing, her skull was just fragmented and her brain—I had to come over the next day, in the daylight, and clean the front yard before I let those poor children go home, because there were fragments of her brain just lying around in the yard like dark oatmeal on the snow. I felt—Sister Ralston—I felt like a murderer myself, using a shovel to dump parts of Miranda's brain into the garbage can, but I didn't know what else to do and I couldn't let those poor children go home and see their mother's brain lying in the yard."

The picture was sufficiently vivid to make me shudder. But the fact remains that a person struck that hard and violently on the back of the head falls forward, not backward.

Somebody had moved the body between the time it became a

body and the time the ambulance arrived, apparently with the police there first or at the same time as the ambulance, because Charlie Sosa distinctly told me he had seen photographs of the body in place.

Alexandra saw the killing—Alexandra saw something flying through the air, a white ball that she might very well have thought to start with was a snowball, only it wasn't, it was a round whitewashed stone from the border around the flower bed, and she saw her mother fall and she couldn't understand why her mother didn't get up again, because probably to her mind it was only a snowball—but she also saw somebody come and turn over her mother's body. Who?

Was Cynthia *really* in the house watching television the whole time? But Cynthia, like Alexandra, was only five years old, not big enough to turn over the dead weight of an adult woman.

Was Elias *really* at the grocery store with Georgina? But if he wasn't, Georgina would have remembered, and she never did—or at least she said she never did.

Georgina and Alexandra lived in this house all their lives. So did Elias. Cynthia moved out. Why?

Cynthia thought she was going to own the house, or at least half of the house, when Georgina died. Would she have killed her sisters to get a half share in a house?

Even if she did, why would she have gone after me? Because if whoever attacked me hadn't mistaken me for Cynthia because we were dressed alike, then there was no possible doubt that whoever it was had gone after me as me.

Why? Did someone think I knew something I didn't know? Did someone think I was closer to finding out something than I was?

And why would she have killed her mother? That had me totally baffled. Of course as a cop I, like most cops, have seen cases of teenagers killing their parents for nothing but trying to impose a little discipline and order onto their lives, but in the first place it was obvious from everything everybody told me that Miranda was no disciplinarian, and furthermore Alexandra had been a five-year-old, not a teenager.

And why, while I was thinking of whys, why had Miranda gone outdoors in a dancing dress and the thin dancing shoes she'd probably have been wearing with a dancing dress, without even throwing on a coat or sweater?

I could hardly wait for Sister White to leave so I could call Charlie Sosa. Of course he wouldn't still be at the police department, he'd undoubtedly have gone home by now, but I had his home telephone number. My purse was downstairs where I'd dropped it, but the card with the phone number on it was on the dresser Harry and I were using in this room. As she went down the stairs, taking the same ghoulish delight in funerals that so many of the women I had known as a child in Texas took, I thought, *What was she lying about? And why? This time, nothing, I think. She was lying earlier, all those things she told me she didn't know, but she'd come tonight not to keep me company, as she said, but to tell me the truth. Why? What was there in all of this that she wanted me, and through me the Salt Lake City Police Department, to know?*

The little yappy dog wasn't barking when we parked at Gilgal. . . . Cynthia had said, "Dogs always like me."

Maybe this wasn't a locked-room killing after all. I couldn't get past that yappity little dog without him barking. Charlie couldn't; Kate couldn't; certainly Alexandra couldn't. But if anybody could it was Cynthia.

I reached for the telephone.

It sounded like a teenage boy who picked up the receiver and said, "Yeah?" Meekly I said, "Could I speak to Charlie, please?"

"Yeah, just a minute."

Charlie came to the phone and I told him, all in a rush, sounding probably more like Sister White than like myself, what I knew and what I had surmised.

. . . . .

After I was through, Charlie said, "Deb, I knew the body had been moved. It was in the report. I knew the bracelet disappeared the same day Miranda was killed. Sister White told me, and then I looked up the police report on the bracelet. I've been thinking about Cynthia too. And I'll go on thinking until I've got some answers. I don't want to sound rude, but I wish you'd take care of your own business, which is being a tourist, and let me take care of my business, which is investigating these murders."

"But you said you didn't mind if I—"

"I didn't," he interrupted, "as long as you were safe. But you're not safe now. Hasn't it crossed your mind that if you hadn't leaned over to pet the dog when you did you'd be dead right now? Look, from everything I've heard I know you're a damn good cop. But you're out of your jurisdiction, you don't know the area, you don't have any armament with you, you don't have a radio with you, and you don't have any backups except your husband, and yes I know he's an ex-Marine, but he's unarmed too and he's limping like that guy on 'Gunsmoke.' Let me speak to him."

"He went to Park City," I said very quietly.

"He what?"

"He went to Park City," I repeated. "There's something wrong with the van and it won't be fixed till tomorrow. He went to Park City to get the kids."

Charlie's voice was rising incredulously. "Leaving you there alone with Cully Grafton, when he's as likely as anybody else to be the killer? Deb, are you and Harry both out of your minds? You want me to come over there and stay with you till he gets back?"

"Cully didn't do it," I said.

"How do you know?"

"I get these feelings. And I'm telling you, Cully didn't do it. No. You don't have to come over." My voice was wavering, and I was afraid Charlie was going to notice that.

. . . . .

Which he did. "Look, I'm sorry, I didn't mean to hurt your feelings or make you cry," he said.

"I'm not crying."

"I'm not deaf. You're crying. You've been really helpful and I appreciate what you've done. I'm just—look, one woman died last week because she trusted the cops to protect her and didn't know the cops didn't know they needed to protect her. I found her body. I dragged her body out of the river, and the feds think I'm the one that should have been protecting her. Now, I don't think I'm to blame on that one, but I feel bad about it anyway. And I feel bad about you having been injured doing my job. I don't want another dead woman on my conscience. And if you keep trying to work this case you're going to wind up dead. Capeesh?"

"Yeah," I said.

"And—you're assuming, if I hear you right, that Cynthia could have been the murderer, right?"

"It's on my mind as a possibility."

"So you're accusing a five-year-old girl of being capable of murder?"

"If it was murder."

"You think it was an accident?"

"I don't know what I think, Charlie, all right? I just wanted to call and give you the information, that's all, and I'm sorry if you think I'm poaching in your game preserve."

"It's not that," he said. "I told you it's not that and I mean it. I just don't want you to get hurt again. So stay in bed and keep your bedroom door locked until your husband and kids get back, okay?"

"Okay."

And I would have, I swear I would have, except I got up to go to the bathroom. I managed to get there by myself this time, with some wobbling. As I left the bathroom, Cully was coming up the stairs with a toolbox. "Hi," he said, "you feeling better?"

Of course I promptly burst into tears. A sympathetic voice can do that to me, when I'm feeling like shit. "I'm sorry," I sobbed, "I just feel perfectly awful. Don't pay me any attention, I'm going to go back to bed and take another pain pill and then I'll probably go back to sleep, I don't mean to be crying at you, you're the one with a right to cry—"

"Hey, that's all right," he said, "you've been hurt. I was just going to have a look at that electrical outlet in the bathroom, will it bother you if I do that?"

"No, it might if you were going to use a hammer or something, but just a screwdriver, no, that won't bother me."

"Well, if it does, or if you need back in the bathroom, you let me know. Promise?"

"Okay. Sure. Thanks, Cully."

I escaped back to the bedroom, obediently locked the door, and took another pain pill with the last of the glass of water Harry had left for me. *I should have thought to get some more water while I was in the bathroom,* I thought in annoyance, and picked up the glass and wobbled back to the bathroom where Cully was just laying down his tool kit on the seat of the toilet. "Will you get me a glass of water?" I asked.

"Sure thing," he said. "Why don't you go back to bed? I'll bring it in there to you."

I had no dignity left to preserve. I went back to bed and Cully brought the glass of water in and set it down beside me. So of course I didn't think to relock the door. Why should I? There wasn't anybody in the house but Cully and me. And Charlie was being silly about that. Cully was not the murderer. I was sure of that.

And I was right about that.

A few minutes later, as the pain pill began to take hold, I heard Cully saying, "Great jumping Jehosaphat! Now, who'd have ever thought—I don't believe—how in the world did that get in here?"

The electrical outlet must have been in worse shape than he and Harry had guessed while discussing it, I thought drowsily.

. . . . .

I heard Cully walk out into the hall. And then, with no warning whatever, there was an incredible cacophony of noise—shouting, banging, crashing, an indistinguishable assortment of voices and other sounds.

At any other time I would have jumped up and run to see what was wrong. This time I couldn't. I managed to get out of bed, but my head was swimming so badly I wasn't sure I was going to be able to stand. I got my cane, which was leaning in the corner—my foot doctor was probably going to be mad at me, because I hadn't used it much in the last few days and my feet were probably going to show new damage next time the doctor checked me—and staggered woozily to the door and opened it.

From my doorway I could see the staircase. And I could see Cully Grafton lying facedown, his feet on the second floor and his head on the stairs halfway down to the first floor, with the back of his skull a mass of red and gray. I didn't have to check his pulse to know that he was dead, and I didn't have to see the rock—which I couldn't see, probably because it had fallen on down the stairs—to know the cause of death.

And then she turned to look at me. She began to move toward me, with the inexorable slowness-turning-into-speed of a plane landing and seeming to speed up as its wheels touch the ground.

I retreated backward into the bedroom and threw the bolt, wishing I had something stronger than a simple privacy bolt, and grabbed the phone, hoping she hadn't thought yet to take it off the hook in another room.

She hadn't, yet. I dialed 911, but while I was dialing I could hear her turning the doorknob, beating on the door with her fists. "Hurry," I said into the phone, "there's been a murder and she's after me now." I gave the address and then laid the phone down and watched the door.

. . . . .

Twelve

. . . .

THE DOOR BANGING stopped abruptly; I wondered whether she'd changed her mind about trying to get in, or just thought of another way of reaching me. But then I heard a puzzled "Huh? What's going on?" There was a small silence, which was followed by a small, rhythmic, repeated thud on the floor, and the jangling of small pieces of metal on wood. For a moment I was baffled, then I recognized the sound I probably hadn't heard in forty years. Jacks. She was playing jacks.

Playing jacks, and singing.

"Jack and Jill went up the hill
To fetch a pail of water.
Jack fell down and broke his crown,
And Jill came tumbling after."

The childlike voice went on, speaking now. "You fell down. Now you can't play. It was mine. You tried to keep it, but it was mine. Now you fell down. Humpty Dumpty had a great fall. Mommy tried to get it back, but it was mine. Mommy fell down. Mommy isn't really dead. She's just playing a game. It was only a little rock. She'll come back pretty soon and she'll tell you it's mine. My sisters tried to get it, but it was mine. My sisters fell down. Now they can't play. One, two, three, we all fall down. You knew it was in the house so you made Georgina give the house to you so you could get it. But it was mine. I found it in Daddy's chair, and it was mine. Pretty soon my sisters will get up, just like Mommy. I'll let them play. But I won't let you play. You're bad. You and Georgina made bad noises at night. I won't let you play anymore."

I picked up the phone again. As I expected, the dispatcher was still there; normally in something like this the dispatcher will stay on the line, letting the tape recorders run, until the police are actually in the house. "How near are those cars?" I asked.

"They're close. What's going on?" she asked. "We've got a car en route from downtown and another one from the closest beat over."

"I'm trapped in a second-floor bedroom. There's a dead man on the only staircase, and an insane murderer on the landing playing jacks."

"Doing *what?*"

"Playing jacks and singing. But she's already tried to break this door down once, and sooner or later she'll remember me and try again. I've got it bolted, but it's not a very good bolt or a very good door. The front door to the house is probably locked. You're going to have to tell the officers to break it in. Tell them to watch out for the pit bull; he doesn't like people in uniform. He's never bitten anybody yet, but I can't promise he won't. But where he's chained he can't reach the door."

I heard faint sounds as the dispatcher relayed the message. Then she came back to me. "Okay, the officers are almost to the house. Two of them, with two more en route from farther away. But they'll come on in as soon as the first two are there. Can you tell me what she's doing now?"

"I think she's still playing jacks. Just a minute, let me see if I can find out without her seeing me." I eased open the door and peered out cautiously.

On the landing at the top of the stairs, the gawky, grotesque,

. . . . .

gray-haired woman in the black slacks and red sweatshirt was sitting on the floor, her knees crossed in front of her, playing jacks, with the fanny pack full of dog biscuits open and three more fist-sized white stones on the floor behind her. I watched her. She was up to twelvesies now. Triumphantly, she scooped up all twelve jacks while the ball was in the air, and then she started on pigs in a pen, with her left hand, its wrist surrounded by a gaudy, glittering, platinum, diamond, and sapphire bracelet, cupped over on the floor to make a hut that her right hand scooped the jacks into while the faded once-red rubber ball was in the air. Onsies. No trouble; she caught the ball each time. Twosies. Then she got confused and tried to do slow pigs, which takes more coordination but not, of course, as much as eggs in a basket, crack the eggs, and round the world, which I never could do right. But she must be less coordinated than I was last time I tried to play jacks, because on slow pigs she missed the ball. It rolled toward me, with the result that she looked around, saw me, and forgot she was playing jacks.

With an incoherent yowl of rage, she was up from the floor, dropping the jacks to scatter on the floor and catching up a stone to hurl at me as I slammed the door and threw the bolt. The first stone struck the door and then, apparently, ricocheted back toward her. She dodged well enough; I heard it skitter across the floor, and heard the slide of her feet as she dashed toward the other two stones. Then she began hammering on the door near the bolt not with both fists, which the wood might have withstood, but with the other two stones, one in each hand, fist-sized chunks of whitewashed granite.

I stood in terror, looking around for something, anything, that I could use as a weapon, knowing that my cane, which was all I could think of, was nothing against the stones she could throw with such deadly accuracy, knowing I was concussed and had taken a strong pain pill, knowing I could hardly even stand upright and certainly couldn't fight.

. . . . .

I didn't even have my pepper spray. I'd dropped my purse and keys in the living room, and it was on my key chain.

The door splintered, and her hand still with the sparkling bracelet on the bony wrist reached through to open the bolt. I struck with my cane at her fingers, and she yanked her hand back, but she pulled the bolt at the same time, shoved the door open, and came in toward me roaring with rage. It took only moments for her to wrestle the cane away from me and fling it aside.

Downstairs someone was yelling, "Police, open up!" and Pat, of course, was barking his lungs out. I wished, fervently, that I had told Harry to leave Pat up here with me, but he hadn't thought of it and neither had I, and the police were still yelling as if they expected this woman to leave off trying to murder me long enough to go downstairs and open the door. Damn it, I told them they'd have to break in the door, when were they going to do it?

"Hurry up," I wanted to scream, but I had no breath left to scream with. Now I had nothing but my hands to fight her with, to try to hold both her hands away as she sat on top of me trying to bang the stones into my face. But it is easier to push down than to push up; my arms were already shaking with exhaustion, and there was a triumphant snarl on her face as the stone moved inexorably toward my face. I couldn't even kick; she was sitting on my hips, and there was no way I could get my feet or knees into position to reach her. I tried to turn to my left side and realized that would leave the right side of my head, where the earlier stone had hit, exposed, and anyway I found I could not turn that way. So I tried to turn to my right, trying to buck her off while still holding her hands away from my face.

Downstairs Pat continued barking, and as I frantically tried to fend her off I heard the sharp crack of a pistol fired at a lock, and then I heard the front door burst open. There, they'd done it. But would they know to come upstairs?

She was still roaring. I tried to scream for help. I might have screamed. I don't know; my breath was nearly gone. But there was enough noise to lead them to trouble. Two uniformed officers scrambled up the stairs, making their way over and around Cully Grafton's body, and unceremoniously yanked her off me, tore the stones out of her hands, and threw her to the floor, where one sat on her while the other put handcuffs on her. "You have the right to remain silent," one began, but she went on screaming.

"Transport her," the other snapped. "We'll ask questions later. Just get her out of here."

But even with her handcuffed it took both of them to wrestle her down to the car, with her screaming every inch of the way, while a uniformed sergeant came up the stairs, looked at the body, and looked in on me. Before the first two got back Charlie Sosa was in the bedroom, after stepping on three jacks and a jack ball, sliding ten feet, and nearly falling down the stairs on top of Cully. "Get somebody out here to control the scene," he told the sergeant. "Otherwise we're going to have reporters walking in the door and over the body."

"Backups are en route," the sergeant said, "and I'll sit on it myself till they get here."

"Dispatch recognized the address and called me," Charlie told me. "Luckily I'd gone back downtown, so I was closer than coming from home. If that son-of-a-bitch Bivins had let us know he was treating two sisters for something like this—"

"He didn't tell us that because he wasn't," I said tiredly, and sat back down on the bed. I was shaking and cold, and it was all right to tell myself it was just shock, but the problem was that I needed treatment for shock and I wasn't getting it.

"You're telling me a sane woman did that? And then sat down on the floor and started playing jacks?"

"No, I'm not telling you that. Get LaRae White over here," I said to him. "She's at Russon Brothers Mortuary. Get her over here. She's the only one who knows the truth about this."

. . . . .

"I'll go get her," Charlie said, his rage abruptly vanishing. "But you better be right. While you're waiting, you go back to bed. You look like hell."

That was no surprise to me. I also felt like hell.

Harry got back while Charlie was gone. I could hear him arguing with patrolmen on the porch: "My wife is in there, I've got to know what happened—"

Then Charlie was back from the mortuary, and I wondered whether I had been blacking out again, because it didn't seem to me he'd been gone long enough to be back, and come to think of it neither had Harry from Park City. "Let him in," I heard Charlie order. "Ms. White, you too. Hal, Lori, Cameron, stay in your car. And I mean it. Hal, come get this dog and put him in the car too."

There wasn't much use trying to preserve the crime scene, after two officers by themselves, then two officers wrestling with a madwoman, then the sergeant, and then Charlie Sosa, had trampled right through the blood and brain tissue around the body. I was still in bed, and still feeling shocky, when Charlie came back in with Harry and with LaRae White, her face chalky from the shock of having to step over Cully's body.

Harry came to me and took my hands. He'd been outside, but his hands were warm. Mine felt like ice cubes, and he started rubbing them gently to warm them. Sister White just stood and looked at me with an expression like that of a woman who has lost her soul.

"Sister White," I asked her, "how long have you known that Alexandra was the murderer?"

If I had been seeking sensation, I would have been delighted with the results of the moment. Both LaRae White and Charlie Sosa, as well as my husband, stared at me, eyes wide, mouths open.

"Are you out of your mind?" Charlie demanded then.

"No. I'm just waiting for an answer to my question."

Sister White sat down, slowly, in a slipper chair by the bed, and took a long breath. "I promised Elias I would never tell," she quavered. "He was sure it wasn't her fault; he was sure she'd never hurt anybody else. And at first—I thought—she hadn't. At first I thought it really was Alexandra who was dead, and I was so sorry for Georgina, but I couldn't help thinking what a blessing it was that Alexandra was gone. But then Georgina died, and that was when I knew. And I tried to—to tell you without telling you. Because I had promised Elias."

"You succeeded," I said, "once I figured out why you came over. I was almost to the truth anyway. But I wasn't quite all the way to it until I saw her tonight."

Charlie sat down on the edge of the bed opposite the one Harry was sitting on. "I know you're shocky," he said carefully. "I know you're upset. But think through what you're saying. You didn't see Alexandra tonight. You couldn't have. Alexandra's dead. You saw her twin sister. Cynthia. You saw Cynthia."

"No. I saw Alexandra."

Harry had to comment too. "If she says she saw Alexandra, she saw Alexandra."

"That's right, dear," Sister White said to Charlie, her voice growing a little stronger. "Cynthia's dead. It was Alexandra she saw."

"Then somebody better tell me what's going on," Charlie said heavily. "Because I feel like I'm in the fun house of a carnival with the speed set on high."

"We had the first lead the day of Cynthia's death," I said. "In fact, we had several leads that day. But neither of us spotted them."

"Then tell me what leads we had that we didn't spot."

I began counting them off on my fingers. "Her purse, keys, and coat were gone," I said. "A killer might have a reason to take her purse, maybe even her keys. But a coat somebody had bought for seven dollars at DI? No way. Not unless this was an impersonal kill, but we knew it wasn't that because she was killed the same way her mother was. Second, she was wearing that lavender dress."

"Right," Charlie said. "She was wearing the lavender dress you saw her wearing in church."

"No. She was wearing an identical lavender dress. The lavender dress I saw in church was lying on the floor in her bedroom, with a wet jacket tossed on top of it. You and I both saw it, but all we thought was that she must have two identical lavender dresses. I should have spotted it even if you didn't. Because identical twins, when they're kids, often dress alike. Most of them outgrow it in their teens, but some go on doing it all their life. I should have realized when I saw the dress, but I didn't. That was before—" I came to a halt. "How much do you know about MPD?"

"Not much," he said, "but I suspect you're about to enlighten me." Funny thing, he had just about the same expression Captain Millner has when I'm trying to explain something.

"Georgina invited Hart Bivins and her sister to dinner. I think, then at least, she still thought it was Alexandra who was dead and Cynthia who came to dinner. Even Hart couldn't tell the difference. Both her sister and her psychiatrist failed to recognize her, so there was certainly no reason I should, especially since I had never even seen her before. I saw that she looked like Alexandra, but Alexandra's almost-identical twin would. And I noticed her hairstyle was distinctively different. But Hart made an interesting observation. He said that Alexandra took on the personalities of the people she loved who died. He said that at one point he saw her take on the personality of Elias, and it was eerie because for that moment she actually *looked* like Elias. Well, I've read a lot about MPD. It's weird because it's like each persona has a different brain and even a different body. There are documented cases in which some personae—Hart told me that's the correct plural, not personas—are right-handed and some are left-handed. There are documented cases where one persona is allergic to things the others aren't. There are even a few cases of different personae needing different eyeglass prescriptions. Well, who did Alexandra know best in all the world? Her twin sister. So when she became Cynthia, she *became* Cynthia, right down to wearing Cynthia's wedding and engagement rings and Cynthia's hairstyle and driving Cynthia's car and digging in Cynthia's garden even if she never wanted to garden when she was Alexandra.

"My guess—and this is only a guess—is that she called Cynthia over to the park with the intent of murdering her. Why? Or why now? I don't know for sure, but my guess is that Elias had been keeping her in check, and now that Elias was dead she was running rampant. Georgina knew it; that was why Georgina made Cully move out. She knew if Cully stayed there long enough, Alexandra would kill him. She was trying to protect him. But Alexandra had a secret. She'd hidden her treasure and then she was never able to get it back again, because if she did her sisters would know what happened to their mother—she didn't know that Georgina, at least, already knew. To her, though, at least to one part of her, it was all a game. She had already put her mother out of the game, and now she had to put her sisters out of the game. Cynthia came first, because Cynthia was harmless to her and she wasn't quite sure Georgina was. Cynthia, in Alexandra's mind, was another kid because Alexandra was still a kid so her twin had to be also, but Georgina had become a grown-up, and it's harder to deal with grown-ups unless they're like Miranda, grown-up kids. So she arranged to meet Cynthia at the park, knowing we were going there later and we would find the body. But after killing Cynthia she became Cynthia. And at that point, to all intents and purposes she *was* Cynthia. So there she was in Gilgal with no knowledge of what she was doing there. Her sister had asked her to come over, and now her sister was lying at her feet dead. She took Cynthia's wedding rings because she was Cynthia, and what right did Alexandra have to be wearing Cynthia's rings? But there was enough of Alexandra left in her that she wanted to keep her purse and keys and that coat she loved so much, so she took them, too. All this happened fast, probably in the time we were getting out of the car. Then she simply scrambled over the fence where the yappity dog was—remember, she was Cynthia now, and dogs love Cynthia. She probably tossed the dog a bikky or two, and kept on going. The dog never raised a sound. So she escaped the way we never looked, through the yard we never thought of because of the dog."

"So how'd her sister happen to be wearing an identical dress?" Charlie asked.

"That was simple, too," I said. "When Hart Bivins was having dinner with us, Alexandra—only she was Cynthia then—mentioned that she and her twin always checked with each other every morning to be sure they would be dressed alike. So Alexandra *knew* Cynthia would be wearing that lavender dress. LaRae dropped her off by her house after church, she ran up to her room to change clothes and threw the jacket she'd worn Saturday over the lavender dress so that it would look like it had been there longer, and then rushed back out. She walked over to Gilgal—it's not that far a walk—or maybe, even, she had Cynthia pick her up at home and drive her to Gilgal."

I looked at Sister White. "You gave me the last thing I should have needed to put it together," I told her, "when you came over this evening. You told me two contradictory things. You told me that any five-year-old child, seeing a white ball flying through the air on a snowy day, would think it was a snowball, and of course you're right. But you also told me that Alexandra kept saying it was only a little stone and asking why her mother didn't get up. So Alexandra knew it was a stone. How did she know? She didn't see it afterwards. A stone thrown with that force would have done its damage, bounced off Miranda's head, and buried itself in the snow. My guess is even the police didn't find it until the next day."

"You're quite right," Sister White said. "I thought they would take away the rest of her brain then, too. I was surprised they didn't."

. . . . .

"They should have," Charlie said.

"So Alexandra, as I said, never saw the stone afterwards. Was it openly discussed in front of Alexandra? No, because every time the topic was mentioned, she began screaming, then curled into a ball and started sucking her thumb. So how did she know it was a stone? She knew because she herself was the one who threw it."

"You're right, dear," Sister White said. "And Elias was quite wrong to forbid me to tell anybody."

"And that's why no psychiatrist, including Hart Bivins, was able to cure Alexandra. That's one of the things she said just now, while she was playing jacks in the hall. Humpty Dumpty had a great fall. Alexandra had a great fall that shattered her into dozens of pieces. Alexandra didn't *want* to be cured. All the parts of her were convinced that if she ever integrated her personalities back into one, she would have to admit she murdered her mother—and that's exactly what she didn't do, as she would have learned for herself if she had allowed herself to be cured."

"But she did murder—" Sister White began.

Simultaneously Charlie Sosa began, "But you said—"

"No. I didn't say she murdered her mother. You're hearing what you think I mean, not what I'm saying. I said she killed her mother. There's a difference. She was five years old. She had no reason whatever to know that throwing that stone at Miranda would kill Miranda. She was angry, she was probably throwing a tantrum, but she didn't know she was killing her mother."

"She found the bracelet," Sister White said. "I put it together, from what she told me, from what Elias told me, from what poor Alexandra said in her nightmares, and the child had so many nightmares afterwards. Elias was sitting in his recliner chair, and the bracelet slid out of his pocket. He didn't notice, when he left to get the milk, that the bracelet wasn't there. Alexandra had been out playing in the snow, and when Elias went out to get in the car he saw her and told her to go in because it was getting late. She went in, at once saw the bracelet in the chair, and picked it up. Miranda saw her playing with it and tried to take it away from her. Poor Alexandra was always such a spoiled, willful child; she refused to give it back. She said, 'It's mine and you can't have it,' and, bracelet in hand, she ran out the front door. Miranda ran after her—"

"That's why Miranda was outdoors in a dancing dress, without even a sweater or a coat," I said. "She had at least some idea what would happen if she didn't get that bracelet back."

"That's right. But by the time Miranda was out the door Alexandra was out of sight; she had run clockwise around the house, and Miranda was standing under the Russian olive looking for her, thinking she might have run over toward the graveyard, and Alexandra, now behind her, picked up the stone and hurled it. She was so angry—and Miranda fell down, and didn't say anything else, and her head was bleeding, and Alexandra didn't understand what had happened but she knew she had done something terrible. She wasn't angry anymore; she wanted her mother to get up and talk to her. And when her mother didn't she lay down in the snow beside her mother and began to cry."

"And that was when the splitting began," I agreed. "And after that, she was like Humpty Dumpty. She shattered into different personalities, and all the king's horses and all the king's men couldn't put Alexandra together again."

"So where's the bracelet?" Charlie asked. "If she took it—did she leave it somewhere? Did she lose it, or throw it away? Where is it?"

Only then did I realize that he hadn't arrived until after the patrol car left. So of course he hadn't seen the bracelet or mentioned it to Sister White, who now said, "Nobody ever was able to find out. She wouldn't tell. Even in her dreams she wouldn't talk about it, except to say it was hidden."

"It's probably in her property at the jail," I told them both, and Harry too of course. "She was wearing it when she was taken away just now in handcuffs. As to where she put it—I have a pretty good guess. Cully went to fix that bad electrical outlet in the bathroom, and I heard him being startled about something. Let's go look."

"Are you up to it?" Charlie asked dubiously.

"I'll manage," I said. And I did, leaning on the cane and wobbling a good bit, with Harry supporting me on the other side.

Cully's toolbox was still sitting on the toilet seat. On top of the toolbox was the white plastic cover of an electrical outlet, still screwed to a metal receptacle. Tied to the back of the receptacle with twine was a faded orange mesh sack with a label on it for California oranges. Inside the sack were different colors of stones, Cracker Jack prizes, a myriad of childish treasures. On top of it was the faded blue box with a white satin lining, with *Howe's Fine Jewelry* written across the box in elaborate gold script.

"Alexandra went to the bathroom before she left with her Aunt LaRae," I said, with Charlie Sosa and LaRae White trailing after me as I went back to bed. "Sister White, you told me that. She went to the bathroom, and then she came back down in the same cold, wet clothes. No telling how long she'd been using this as her secret hidey-hole, probably a year or so. My guess is she was maybe four when she discovered this electrical outlet came out of the wall and didn't have any wires on it. Then she got the bright idea—this was where she could hide her treasures and her sisters wouldn't ever know about them. She took the old orange sack and tied it to the back of the receptacle. The treasures were innocent, to start with: jacks, a rock collection, that sort of thing. But then, after Miranda's death, she put the bracelet in here. And she never dared open her safe again as long as her father was alive, as long as her sisters were alive, because if they knew she had the bracelet they'd know the rest of it. So I guessed right. Elias was keeping her in check. She was afraid of her father. After he died she became dangerous. Georgina realized that, but she thought that Alexandra was dangerous only to members of her family. She sent Cully away, because he was a member of the family and one that Alexandra had always seemed to resent—but she made a big mistake. She didn't tell Cully why she was sending him away, because she knew Cully would tell, Cully would insist—rightly—on having Alexandra locked up. And she was probably right. My guess is Elias made Georgina promise to take care of Alexandra, just as he made Sister White promise never to tell.

"But bed-and-breakfast guests weren't family, so Georgina thought at first they'd be safe. That was why she went on with the bed-and-breakfast business—but by the time we arrived she'd begun to realize that wouldn't work. I'm sorry for Georgina. She was given too heavy a load to carry. Now, here's how I put together the rest of the story:

"Alexandra either arranged to meet Cynthia at Gilgal, or she got Cynthia to drive her to Gilgal. Once at Gilgal, she killed Cynthia and then immediately turned into Cynthia and left, as I said, through the yard with the dog in it. She wasn't trying to create a locked-room mystery; that just seemed to her to be the best way to leave. Because she was now Cynthia, she went and got into Cynthia's car and drove to Cynthia's house. She remained in the Cynthia persona for several days, and she was still Cynthia when she came over that night for dinner. Obviously she didn't know everything Cynthia knew, because she hadn't lived with Cynthia for many years, but at the same time whatever part of her mind coordinated her selves saw to it she didn't know anything Cynthia didn't know.

"But some time after that she turned back into Alexandra. As Alexandra, she wanted her bracelet—it was hers; you should have heard her talking to herself after killing Cully. She tried to come and get it. I don't know what happened then; I don't know whether Georgina recognized her and threatened to have her locked up, or whether she just panicked. But she killed Georgina—and as soon as she had done that, probably as soon as the stone left her hand, she turned back into Cynthia. Cynthia didn't want the bracelet. Cynthia didn't even know where the bracelet was. All Cynthia knew was that for the second time in less than a week, she had the body of one of her sisters lying at her feet. In what must have been a horrible panic, she took off again.

"She tried again to come get the bracelet, and there I was. She didn't know who I was, but I was dressed just like she was, in black slacks and a blue sweatshirt. So she thought I must be her twin, and she knew she had to kill all her sisters to get the bracelet—but in one part of her mind she was still five years old. She thought it was like a game, we all fall down but then we get up and play some more. She actually said that, while she was playing jacks after killing Cully. She hurled the rock at me, and I was lucky enough to lean over to tend to the dog at the same moment. And the minute the rock left her hand she quit being Alexandra. Alexandra ducked out again, leaving Cynthia to face the consequences—and Cynthia saw me lying on the ground bleeding but alive, and she ran for help.

"Alexandra made yet another try for the bracelet. This time she thought there was nobody but her and Cully in the house and my own guess is she came over here intending to kill Cully because to her mind Cully had stolen her house. She came inside, probably with her own key, and Cully *had found her bracelet!* In her distorted mind, that meant he had known all along it was here; he had coerced Georgina into giving the house to him so he could get the bracelet, although in fact the entire arrangement about the house had been for Georgina's benefit, and Cully hadn't the slightest idea of the bracelet's existence.

"She killed Cully, she snatched the bracelet up and put it on, but this time she thought she was safe, and she didn't switch to being somebody else. She remained the persona her psychiatrist calls 'small Sandy'—and then she saw me. She flew into a hideous rage; when I locked the door in her face she tried to break down the door, but then 'small Sandy' withdrew. I don't know who she turned into for a moment, but that moment was enough for her to forget about me. 'Small Sandy' came back and sat down on the floor and began playing jacks and singing to herself. Then she dropped the jacks, looked around, and saw me again. This time she did succeed in battering the door in, and she was trying to kill me when the officers came in."

"So you're saying a five-year-old murdered her mother over a bracelet," Charlie said. "Just a minute." He got up, walked out into the hall, and said, "Photographs. That's probably about all. This one isn't going to court." He came back in, resumed the chair he had been sitting in. "I'm not sure a five-year-old is capable of murder, but you're saying she was."

"I just got through telling you that is exactly what I am *not* saying," I pointed out. "How many times have I got to say the same thing? To a five-year-old death isn't permanent. It's something that happens on television. As Sister White says, the coyote is blown up with dynamite and run over by a train and after the commercial he's back chasing the roadrunner again. The bad guy gets shot on Channel Two and two hours later he's back alive, as another bad guy on Channel Five. Alexandra found the bracelet and thought that made it hers. Her mother was trying to take it away from her. She was angry. She knew how to throw hard and accurately; her father had taught her that. She might very well have had it in her mind to make a snowball and throw it at her mother, and she reached down for the snow and her hand hit one of the rocks that bordered the flower bed. She was a spoiled child; she didn't have any brakes on her conduct. She picked up the rock and threw it. She must have been . . . awfully surprised . . . when her mother fell down and didn't get up again. That's not the way things happen. She was so surprised she spent the next twenty-one years drawing pictures of the scene. It's no wonder she started splitting into different people; it's no wonder her mother was one of her personae, because that was the only way she could bring her mother back . . . by being her mother . . . but she still wanted the bracelet too, because one part of her never stopped being the five-year-old who thought the bracelet was hers because she had found it. I hope you can feel sorry for her. I can. And even more for her sisters and her father, because at least Elias and Georgina knew all along what had happened. I'm not sure Cynthia did."

"Oh, dear, no," Sister White said. "Cynthia never did know. She might have suspected, might even have guessed, but she didn't really know. Just Elias and me, for a long time, and then Elias told Georgina when he had his first heart attack and thought he was going to die. Up until that time Georgina had been sure Alexandra saw the killing, but she had no idea Alexandra did it herself."

Throughout this entire discussion, I had been able to hear Crime Scene people coming and going on the stairs. Now Kate came in and asked, "Charlie, are you through with the body?"

"I'm through if Crime Scene is," he said.

"Okay, I'm going to have them take it away—Deb, you look awful. Could I go make you some tea or hot chocolate or something?"

"Hot chocolate would be wonderful," I said.

She withdrew, and the sounds went on outside, now of the body being zipped into a body bag, loaded onto a stretcher, and removed. The window above the bed, despite being well above ground, was alight with red and blue lights from police cars, strobes from print newspeople, floodlights from television news. *The big story is over,* I thought, *they can go home now, and I wish they would.*

"Did they take his brain away?" Sister White asked, her old voice shaking. "Because I was young enough to clean up Miranda's brain, but I don't think I'm young enough to clean up poor Cully's brain."

. . . . .

Epilogue

THE EMTs DID take away the brain, though that did little more for the condition of the hall than did the evidence techs' taking away the jacks and jackball and the orange sack and its contents. A lot of blood had accompanied the brain tissue, and because of the position Cully had fallen in, it had flowed on down the stairs to puddle on the living room floor. From there the myriad people who had swarmed up and down the stairs for the last hour had tracked it all over the house. Charlie and Harry, after one of those unspoken conversations people sometimes have with their eyes, went and got a mop and bucket and a lot of Pine Sol out of the kitchen and scrubbed that up before letting the kids come in. And all three kids came to check on me, to be sure I was *really* okay, and then went quietly, subdued, into Hal's room and shut the door.

But before that, while Charlie and Harry were hunting mops and buckets, Kate Rolley went downstairs to the kitchen and made hot chocolate for everybody; she even took some out to the car for Hal, Lori, and Cameron, and let them know what was going on—a relief to all, as it hadn't crossed Harry's mind to let them know I was all right. All they knew was that they'd been ordered to the van, while police and ambulances and other official vehicles came and went. The best I could figure out later, Lori cried the whole time, while Hal worried stoically and tried to console Lori. Cameron was mostly out of it; it was past his bedtime, this time he *had* had supper, and he slept in the middle seat.

I started to say Kate wasn't acting like a doctor when she made the hot chocolate, but on second thought maybe she was. Just not a pathologist, because most of their patients are dead. I think LaRae White was as shocky as I was, and with good reason. Not only was she eighty-two, which is not an age at which one should have to withstand major shocks, but she was also having to face the consequences of her nephew's poor judgment, and of her acquiescence in his decisions. I know Kate borrowed equipment from one of the EMTs, before they left with the body, and checked both Sister White's blood pressure and mine. Then she watched us both, carefully, as we drank our hot chocolate and afterwards.

"Poor Cully called me and told me you had bought Georgina's computer, and he was using that money to pay for Georgina's funeral," Sister White commented after she put down the Limoges cup carefully. "Don't go all delicate and go off and leave it now. I don't know what you paid him for it, and I don't know what you paid Georgina for staying here, but whatever it was you paid too much, considering the ordeal all of you have been through. I can't repay you—but my children and I are the only living descendants of the Elias Howe who built this house, other than poor Alexandra of course. I guess after all the wills are straightened out I'll donate the house to the Church. And I wish you'd pick out something nice to take with you, after all this trouble."

"I'm afraid it's not going to work that way," I said as gently as I could. "We'll take the computer, of course, because we bought it, but we wouldn't feel right about taking anything even if we could. Anyway, we can't. Georgina and Cully owned the house in joint tenancy, so when she died it became his. It will belong to his children now."

"Oh, dear, I hadn't thought of that," Sister White said, looking ready to cry all over again. "That's true. So I can't tell you to take anything except the computer, because that really is yours. None of it will come to me; it'll all go to those little girls."

. . . . .

"But the bracelet won't," Charlie said abruptly. "The lawyers will have to sort it out, but my guess is the bracelet's yours."

"Do you think I should donate it to the Church, or sell it and donate the money?"

Charlie shrugged. "If it were my choice, I'd say donate it, if you're going to do anything with it. That damned bauble has cost five lives counting Alexandra's, because for all practical purposes she hasn't been really living since the moment she laid eyes on the thing. I can tell you I wouldn't take it if you gave it to me. If somebody forced it on me I'd throw it into the river. Maybe the Church can make it clean. I don't know."

"I don't mind the little girls having the house and all," Sister White said then. "I mean—in effect, our family took their father from them. There's no way to make that up. They ought to have something in recompense. I'd mind, I think, if the house burned or was torn down, but there, it's probably a white elephant and past time to be torn down. And I always thought I'd mind if great-grandfather's things went out of the family. But I don't mind. Not anymore. Are you going to go on and stay here tonight and tomorrow night? I don't know if I would—I mean, the death and all—but people have died in most old houses. It's just that this is such a recent death. But you're ill—I think you should stay in bed. At least till tomorrow. Maybe tomorrow night too. Isn't it Friday you take that nice big boy to Provo?"

"Yes, it is," I said. "But staying here—I don't know. I'm not scared anymore. There aren't any ghosts haunting the house, and Alexandra's gone. But I'm not sure how the kids will feel." Mainly I wasn't sure how Lori would feel, because her mother's death was still so recent in her mind.

"I'll go ask them," Harry said, and strode out into the hall. He returned looking bemused. "Cameron's asleep in Hal's bed. Hal gave Lori a blessing, whatever that means, and Lori went on to bed in her room. Hal's still up, but he looks like he's on his last legs. At this time of night, I don't want to pack up and go anywhere."

So in the end we stayed there, in the house that had been Georgina's, finishing up the last of the food Georgina had bought for our visit, feeding the dog antibiotics and cough drops. The kids went out sight-seeing again Thursday, but I don't know where; I stayed in bed because I was still too woozy even to walk down the stairs, and Harry went on waking me every hour, which was about as exhausting to me as it was to him. I don't like concussions.

Friday when I came downstairs Hal took one look at me and started yelling. "Mom, you can't go to BYU that way," he screamed. "You look like Tammy Faye Bakker! Why did you put all that glop on your face?"

"Do you really think," I retorted, "that I want to walk into the MTC with two visible black eyes?"

But in the end we didn't go into the MTC at all. Hal didn't want us to, and it wasn't because of my makeup, it was because of his dignity. He hauled that monster suitcase in by himself—well, he'd have had to do that anyway, come to think of it—and waved goodbye to us and went on in. I think he was crying. I know I was. And Lori. And Harry, too, I think.

Maybe we'll come back to Salt Lake City in two years, when Hal is through with his mission and ready to come home. But if we do, we're leaving the dog at home, and we're staying in motels. No more bed-and-breakfasts for me, thank you.

. . . . .